OTHERS AVAILABLE BY DK HOLMBERG

The Cloud Warrior Saga

Chased by Fire
Bound by Fire
Changed by Fire
Fortress of Fire
Forged in Fire
Serpent of Fire
Servant of Fire

The Painter Mage

Shifted Agony
Arcane Mark
Painter for Hire

The Lost Garden

Keeper of the Forest
The Desolate Bond
Keeper of Light

Assassin's Sight:

The Painted Girl
The Forgotten

FORTRESS OF FIRE

THE CLOUD WARRIOR SAGA
BOOK 4

ASH Publishing
dkholmberg.com

Fortress of Fire

Published by ASH Publishing

ISBN-13: 978-1516829392
ISBN-10: 1516829395

ASH Publishing
dkholmberg.com

FORTRESS OF FIRE

THE CLOUD WARRIOR SAGA
BOOK 4

CHAPTER 1

The Shaping of Spirit

TANNEN MINDEN SAT with his legs crossed in front of him, the cold stone floor of the cell beneath him and the stink of damp air filling the air around him. The shaping he performed came more easily than it once did, though still was not as effortless as what he knew was possible. For him to do what he knew necessary, for him to understand *why* he'd been given the gifts the Great Mother had given him, he would need to master not only speaking to the elementals but also shaping.

The First Mother stared at him, exasperation plain on her face. "You lose focus so easily. If you think to save this creature, then you will need focus."

"I think my focus is fine," Tan snapped. After spending the last two hours sitting across from this woman—the one who had nearly handed the kingdoms to a man determined to simply shape it to his whims—he was tired. His mind ached from the constant repetition of binding the air, water, earth, and fire together. Worse, there was the distant amusement he felt from Asboel. The draasin thought all of this quite a game. From Amia, he sensed only annoyance.

"Fine? If you're to understand your gifts, you will need to be able to hold your focus regardless of what comes. You might never know you're being shaped otherwise. And you know how they transformed. They stole from the People. This is not some simple shaper you plan to face."

He shot her a look and then shook his head. She deserved his anger, but her punishment was severe enough as it was. No longer able to serve the Aeta, she was instead confined to this windowless room, held with chains wrapped to her ankles that kept her from going more than a dozen steps, and stuck teaching him what she knew of the ancient runes and of spirit shaping. She was one of the wandering people, now trapped for her crimes. What warmth could be found in the weak lanterns flickering in the room gave only enough light to see the bare, rock walls. Somehow, she still managed to carry herself as if she led.

Tan pulled on a shaping of fire and mixed it with elemental power. He no longer knew if it came from Asboel or one of the lesser elementals. He doubted that it mattered. Fire now came easily to him, flowing from him more freely than any of the other elements. He thought it from the fact that he'd bonded to Asboel, but he wasn't certain. A nagging part deep within him worried that there was some residual effect from the way fire changed him. The nymid had restored him, but it was possible that fire still influenced him.

"I think I will do fine if needed."

Her shaping built faster than he could react. As it did, Tan's connection to the elementals was cut from him, sliced like a knife across his mind. A panic raged through him and he wrapped each of the elements together, binding spirit, and slammed it against her shaping. Her shaping snapped away from him.

"What was that?"

She fixed him with a dark stare. Flint gray eyes met his and didn't look away, still carrying the intensity and vibrancy he'd noticed the first time he met her. Her one concession to her captivity, letting her silver hair hang loose and wild around her shoulders, magnified the effect. "You rely on the elementals when you need to learn to rely on yourself. A time may come when the elemental power is unavailable." Her eyes softened, but only a little. "You have the power within you. I sense it, as does Amia. You lean on the elementals as a crutch."

"I don't 'lean' on them. That's how my power works."

She tipped her head toward the pulsing orange fire glowing in his hand. "You think your power is confined to the elementals? You shape fire easily enough, unless there's still a part of you that's lisincend?" She cocked her head at him, waiting to see if her comment riled him up, before pulling her chains to get more comfortable. "The elementals may augment your power, but you provide the spark."

Tan sighed deeply. If that were true, that meant he didn't need to bind the elementals together to reach spirit, but he knew no other way to do it. With the elementals, he could draw on their power, use it to help his shapings. That power could be bound together, woven to form the shaping of spirit he'd used to release himself from her when he'd been trapped in the archives, but it was a form of spirit that was nothing like what she shaped. The effect was often the same, but not always. After all the practice, he suspected he wasn't meant to shape spirit in the same way.

"Your way of shaping spirit doesn't work for me."

"Because you haven't taken the time to learn. Spirit is universal. All shapers have the capacity to reach it in *some* way, however vague."

Tan stared at the fire burning in his hand. The flames danced over his skin, leaving him unharmed. There was the sense of elemental power in the flames, the weak draw of saa in even that much fire. It wasn't only Asboel guiding fire for him. Someday, he hoped to reach the other elementals as easily. "Why do you say that?"

"It's the reason for our power. We are connected to the power that drives this world in ways others are not. Spirit is the binding force for that. Those of us who shape spirit may be able to use it more directly, but all shapers can touch it." She shrugged. "Most never bother to try."

"What of the warriors who've never managed to reach spirit? Theondar can't shape spirit. Lacertin couldn't either." Unless they simply had never learned the trick of binding them together. Could it be that *all* warrior shapers could shape spirit if they understood how?

A troubled look crossed over her face and she twisted on the floor to stare at one of the walls.

"Do you know why they can't shape spirit?" Tan asked.

"Not why they can't, but it has long troubled me that shaping—that the use of the elemental power of our world—has diminished. Spirit has long been rare, but the others? When your kingdoms were no more than separate lands, shapers were plentiful. The elementals bonded willingly, teaching those shapers their power. Now? Elementals ignore us." She fixed Tan with an appraising stare. "Or they had. I am uncertain why that would change."

Tan had learned to listen when the First Mother lectured. In trying to protect her people, she might have done terrible things, but she had an archivist's knowledge. "Some think power simply fades from us. Others think the elementals have abandoned us," Tan said, repeating something Roine had once told him.

The First Mother looked down at her hands. "The elementals have not abandoned all. And this power is fundamental to our world. It would not simply fade."

"Did the archivists search for that reason?"

She pulled on her chains again, dragging them across the floor. An annoyed look briefly crossed her face before disappearing. "When they first came to Ethea, it was to learn and study. Few managed to shape spirit, even then." She met his eyes. "What you do, the way you bind the elements together, is a different form of shaping. Perhaps weaker." She shrugged. "They came to study and understand. Only later did they begin to recognize the shift."

"A shift? Even in the last generation, shapers have been more and more infrequent."

"As has the connection to the elementals. They are not as unrelated as you might think."

Tan struggled to find a more comfortable seat. "I'm not saying they aren't related. Only that I have no idea why. The draasin doesn't seem to know." And if he did, would Asboel tell Tan? The draasin had once been hunted by shapers. Why wouldn't he want to keep them from the world?

"Then you need to find the reason. This place," she motioned around her, indicating the university far above ground, "once searched for knowledge and understanding." The chains rattled as she waved her hands. "Now it's nothing more than a way to power. There is a difference."

Tan couldn't argue with that. When he first came to the university, the Master shapers were barely willing to teach. Only when Tan's connection to the elementals was known had other shapers offered to teach.

She pulled on her chains again. "Enough of this talk. You are wasting your time with me." She gave Tan a pointed look. "Don't think I don't know how Zephra will react if she knew you were down here studying with me."

"Zephra would prefer I stayed out of all harm. She still thinks me the child from Nor."

The First Mother snorted. "Even in the time I've known you, you've done a poor job of staying clear of harm. But you are capable, Tannen Minden. That is the only reason I proceed with this. Now. You should focus on spirit alone. Your shapings grow more skilled, but they remain blunt. Until you manage to reach spirit without binding the elements, the shapings will always be that way."

"Most of my shapings are blunt," he said.

"You have exquisite control of fire," the First Mother commented. "There is no reason your other shapings could not be the same."

"I speak to the draasin. Some of what I've learned possible is from what I've seen from the elemental."

"You speak to all of the elementals, Tannen. Do not exclude them simply because you've bonded to the draasin. Perhaps that is why you fail to progress with the other elements."

Tan shifted. The stone beneath him made his legs ache, especially after sitting as he was for so long. "I don't speak to the others as I do to the draasin."

He wondered if he should share so openly with the First Mother, but she had knowledge about shaping that others didn't. As much pain as she'd caused, she remained willing to teach, if only in her own way. She had no remorse for what she'd done, but Tan didn't really expect such emotion of her. Her reasons had been pretty clear: she had done everything she thought necessary to protect the Aeta, even if it meant working with Incendin.

"Only because you do not listen."

"What does that mean? I listen to the elementals. How else would I have learned to speak to them?"

She tried reaching and pushing her hair out of the way, but the chains holding her prevented her from doing it easily. Instead, she blew on the loose strands of gray hair. "You think that speaking only to the great elementals makes you powerful? It makes you *weaker* to be so reliant on them. Think of how many draasin remain in the world. And not only fire, but think of water. Will you be able to reach udilm in the middle of Ter?" She tossed her head. "What you've managed with the elementals is impressive. Now try it with the others."

"I don't know that I can speak to the lesser elementals."

She flipped her hand at him. "Why should it be any different with the others?"

Tan bit back the argument that came to mind as he thought about what she was saying. He hadn't really tried reaching for elementals other than the great elementals. Here in Ethea and in the mountains near the place of convergence, they were easy to find. That was the reason King Althem had wanted the artifact that Tan now stored in the lower archives. But would he find the elementals as easy to reach outside of those places? It had been Asboel who led him to udilm for Elle, not anything Tan had done.

Then there was the issue with the lesser elementals. With fire, he thought he drew partly on the power of saa as he shaped fire, but what if it was all from Asboel? Would he be able to use the other lesser elementals the same way?

There was so much for him still to learn and it felt like not enough time for him to understand what he needed. For the safety of the kingdoms, he needed to master this. Now that the barrier was down, Incendin could attack at any time. Alisz, the twisted lisincend, might have been destroyed, but they didn't know how many of the lisincend remained.

"I can see from your face you finally see wisdom," the First Mother said.

"There's so much to learn," Tan admitted. "And I don't know if I can do it."

She shuffled closer to him, pulling the chains taut. "You need to embrace your abilities. There will always be things you don't know. That's the nature of using the elemental power. Accept that. Recognize that *someone* will always know something you do not. Even working with an element for fifty years will not protect you from that uncertainty."

Tan found a hint of unexpected kindness in her eyes and swallowed back the lump forming in his throat. "I'm sorry for what happened."

The First Mother took a shaky breath. "Not as sorry as I am," she whispered. She ran one hand over the chains, pressing down as if trying to break the connection. "It keeps me awake, you know."

"What does?"

"Who will lead the Aeta? Who will guide them now that I am gone? Always before, we had a succession in place. The First Mother would step aside as another Mother was raised to replace her." She looked down at her hands, real uncertainty coming to her voice. "When I first met Amia, when I felt the strength she would one day possess, I thought I'd finally found that person. Now there is no one."

"The Aeta have survived for centuries," Tan said, repeating the words Amia told him when they spoke about the Aeta. If the First Mother was fishing for him to commit Amia to again serving the Aeta, she really didn't know Amia. "You might have held them together during your time leading them, but another will come forward."

"I wish I believed that."

Tan leaned back, studying the First Mother. Defiance had once come through in her tone and the strength in her back when she spoke of the Aeta, but now she looked a broken woman. Her thin body no longer seemed to have vigor and instead simply looked frail. Her gray hair had lost its luster. Even the occasional steel in her voice was more and more rare.

"What can I do?" he asked.

She looked up and shook her head. "You needn't lie to me to convince me to continue working with you. I have said that I will. It helps pass the time. But don't try giving me false hope, Tannen. That is beneath even you."

"You know how I feel about Amia. I would do anything to help her."

"She has abandoned her place with the People."

"Only because she lost faith in your leadership. She loved her family. Losing them devastated her. For her to learn that the First Mother—the person who should have been responsible for guiding the Aeta and keeping the People safe—had betrayed her family to the lisincend, well that alone would have changed her. But to learn that the archivists had been Aeta, that they had known about her and chosen to bring harm to her, that took away all that remained in her of the Aeta. She may have been one of the Wandering People, but it wasn't until they abandoned her that she became homeless." The sense of Amia surged through his connection to her, strengthened as it often was when he thought of her. "I see how it pains her when we speak of the Aeta that still wander. I see how she wishes there was something for her to do. The Aeta don't have to hide. They can come to the kingdoms and we will help them find safety."

The First Mother sniffed. "All the time you've spend with Amia and you still know so little about the People. We do not *want* to have a place where we're kept. There is freedom to the wagons, to the wandering. That is the way of the Aeta."

"Maybe you're the one who doesn't understand your people," Tan suggested, thinking of the way the Gathering had felt. There had been relief in the Aeta at having a place to be together. Amia spoke of it with a sense of joy. “Does the wandering keep the people safe? You struggled simply bringing everyone together for the Gathering. Wouldn’t it have been better to have safety?”

The First Mother lowered her eyes. “*I* was to provide safety. That has always been the role of the First Mother. That was my reason behind everything I ever did.”

“And now? Seeing what you’ve done? Do you have any regret for the choices you made?”

She didn’t look up as she answered. “It’s all I have left.”

CHAPTER 2

A Mother's Love

TAN STOPPED NEAR THE UNIVERSITY after leaving the First Mother. What had once been impressive stone buildings had crumbled, layering the ground with little more than rubble. The air still stunk from still-raging flames. He forced himself to ignore the stink, never knowing if it was burned buildings or something worse that he smelled.

He moved carefully through the stone, wondering what it had once been like to learn and study in here. This was where his mother and father had met, two of the countless shapers who had trained here over the centuries. Many had become warriors, so it was that much harder to view the pile of rock the storied institution had become. Although the draasin had done more of the damage, some had come from when Althem had let the lisincend wander freely through the city.

A pair of shapers picked through the rock. Tan felt the pressure of their shaping and recognized that they used an earth shaping to slide rock that would otherwise have been too large and heavy to lift by hand. It was a slow and steady attempt to rebuild the university. It would take time to bring it back to what it had been, if it was even possible. So much had changed. Part of him wondered if the Masters were even the right ones to teach anymore. They focused more on where the shaper came from and the threat they might pose rather than on what the shaper might be able to learn. As the First Mother had said, they focused on gaining power rather than on gaining understanding.

Yet, as much as Tan might want to help with the cleanup, there was little he could do unless golud helped. Earth shaping remained difficult for him. He could do little things, use a weak shaping of earth to tie into what he needed for spirit, but nothing of much strength. Not enough to help rebuild the university. Once it was done, he thought he might be able to help. Golud infused the stones beneath them, working through the bones of the city. If he could coax the earth elemental to strengthen the university, maybe it would hold better if there was another attack.

And another attack was inevitable. Tan felt that with nearly as much certainty as he felt the need to learn as much as he could about the ancient scholars. They had knowledge that had been lost. What could he learn from them that had not been seen in the world for a millennia?

Would he understand what it meant to bond to one of the draasin? Asboel thought the bond was all for Tan's protection, but Tan wasn't as certain. There had to be a benefit for Asboel as well, but he hadn't discovered what that might be. From Asboel, he learned control of fire, how to make delicate and intricate shapings of fire. From Tan, what did Asboel learn? Not how the world was in the centuries since he'd been frozen beneath the lake. Tan had been shielded from the world of shapers and warriors by his parents so that he barely knew that world. What, then, was the benefit to the draasin?

"Still staring like some backwoods village boy?"

Tan turned to see Cianna watching him. Her bright orange hair spiked away from her head and she wore a shimmery shirt that nearly matched her hair. Black leather pants clung to her figure.

"I *am* a backwoods village boy. And I was lost in thought, I guess."

"Well, I'm sorry you lost your thought. You know, I never really knew you to have one." She laughed and waved to the earth shapers moving the stone. Only one of them waved back. The other looked over long enough to glare at her, as if the destruction of the university was her fault.

"I don't understand them," Tan said.

Cianna shrugged. "Them? They're just mad fire burned down the city. Some are stupid enough to blame us fire shapers, as if *we* are strong enough to make the shapings that burned though here. The Great Mother knows I once felt power like that." Cianna's eyes went distant and she shivered.

Like Tan, she had nearly been lost to fire, though in her case, the shaping had been forced upon her. Tan had welcomed it almost willingly, doing what he needed to save Amia. It had changed him, giving him power unlike anything he'd experienced. But serving fire like that had a cost. There was a loss of control when you were pulled so closely into fire, and Tan had wanted nothing more than to let fire burn. It was what the lisincend felt with their transformation. Amia had managed to save him, finding a way for water to restore him. He still wondered why the lisincend chose the transformation.

"Do you miss it?" Tan asked.

Cianna's face turned serious. "I didn't have it long enough to really miss it, but there was an ease to it. A caress of fire." She shivered again in spite of the heat radiating off her. "But there was no control. It consumed me. I can't imagine what it must be like for them." Her eyes turned toward the archives, where the lisincend captured during the attack was still held. No one had wanted to move him, and three shapers were with him at all times, though golud maintained his capture.

"They serve fire willingly," Tan said.

Cianna forced a tight smile. "*I* serve fire willingly. What they do… that is something else. They have the illusion of control."

Not for the first time, Tan wondered what it was like for the twisted lisincend. As different from lisincend like Fur as the lisincend were to fire shapers, they had used spirit in the dark shaping that had created them. Following her transformation, Alisz had kept some rudimentary ability to spirit shape. Using the First Mother to teach her had increased her skill, leaving her likely more capable than Tan was now. But like him, what she managed was blunt. It wasn't natural to her, but forced.

"We should rid ourselves of that creature," Cianna said.

Tan had something else in mind for the lisincend, and though he didn't know if it would work, it would be time to try soon. Roine wanted time to try to interrogate him, as if the lisincend would give up anything useful. Tan suspected his way had the best hope of success. "Have you tried to see him?"

She shook her head. "I can't. Not after…" She didn't finish. She didn't really need to.

He touched her arm, feeling the warmth glowing beneath her skin. She burned with it, closer to the lisincend than she let herself believe. He might burn the same way now that fire called to him.

"What was it like before?" he asked, looking around the university. "When you studied here, what was it like?" His time had been achingly brief, only long enough to learn how little he really knew. And then the attack came and he left, shaped toward Incendin to find healing for his friend Elle. Had the Great Mother kept her safe? Had she reached the udilm, and did they keep her safe?

Cianna's eyes tightened slightly. "It was a place of learning. There have always been those with much power here. And then there were those who wanted power." She shrugged. "Maybe we can do it better this time."

"Which were you?"

Her smile returned and a playful light burned in her eyes. "A bit of both?" she suggested. "Though had I wanted real power, I would have gone south to learn."

South meant Incendin.

Tan closed his eyes. The distant sense of Asboel was there, as it always was. Reaching for the draasin was easier than it once had been. He could pull through the connection with the draasin, reach for the power Asboel commanded, but more than that, he could see through Asboel's eyes. Images flickered to him as he focused, those of bleak hot lands sweeping beneath him. Fire burned somewhere to the right, an orange glow in the midst of red as Asboel searched for movement while hunting. There was a contented feeling from Asboel, but a hint of worry, too. Tan wondered about that.

"You reached for your draasin, didn't you?" Cianna asked.

"He's not mine, but yes. I reached for the connection."

She laughed. "He's as much yours as anyone's. Creatures like that don't bond, at least not that I've ever heard. It's been over a thousand years since the world has seen one and you manage to make him your pet."

"I think he'd object to being considered a pet."

"Then are you *his* pet?"

Tan laughed imagining asking Asboel the question. He knew the answer pretty quickly. "He'd tell you yes."

"You still owe me a ride," she said. She pressed closer to him, the heat from her body making his skin dry, but not in an uncomfortable way.

"Sometime," he agreed. "If he chooses not to eat you, that is."

"Thought your girl shaped him so that didn't happen? Wasn't that why Theondar let him fly freely?"

Tan glanced to the sky. He could almost imagine Asboel soaring along near the sun. "If you think Roine could stop one of the draasin from flying freely, you haven't seen the draasin in its full power."

"Only because you refuse to let him."

Tan looked at her. "You haven't been paying attention if you think I control the draasin."

The serious expression returned and she lowered her voice. "Maybe you keep that to yourself," she said, eyes flickering to the two working shapers. "If you *don't* control the draasin, there might be some frightened people if they find out."

"They're elementals—"

"But elementals we can see. The others? We know they're there. With saa, I see it only in the way the flames dance. I suspect ara brushes against my skin when it blows. Golud is there, deep beneath the earth. I can't see or feel it, but I *know*. But the draasin? They're different. They always have been." She ran her hand up his arm, more a caress than anything comforting. A gust of wind caused her to look up and nod. Tan turned to see his mother coming in on a steady shaping of wind. "I would like that ride sometime," Cianna said, then smiled broadly at him before leaving him standing alone in the remains of the university yard.

His mother landed in a swirl of dirt. She seemed to whisper something to herself as she did—likely talking to ara—before turning to face him.

Zephra wore a heavy grey cloak and a hood pulled over her head. She pushed it back, letting her dark hair fall loose around her shoulders. A familiar irritation in her eyes looked something like an admonishment. "Tannen. You should be helping with the cleanup."

Tan glanced at the remains of the university. "I'm doing what I can to help."

"By speaking to the prisoners?" She was small but when she pulled herself up in front of him, she seemed to tower over him as she had when he was a child. Then she'd held a spoon or sometimes a pen and had tapped it in her irritation. At least now, her hands were empty. It didn't make her any less imposing. "I know all about the time you spend with the Aeta."

"Amia or the First Mother?"

His mother snorted. "Both."

"What is your issue with Amia? Had she not saved me—"

"I struggle to believe that a spirit shaper had no idea what her people were up to. Not only did you nearly die because of it, you almost became one of the lisincend."

"And she thought enough of my abilities to see me restored."

Zephra's eyes narrowed. A flurry of emotions flickered across them. "Why do you continue to risk yourself with the First Mother? Hasn't she done enough?"

"I don't risk myself. I'm using her to learn. How else will I understand the ancient runes found in the lower archives?"

"You still haven't managed to open the inner doors?"

Tan shook his head. He could open *some* of the doors in the lower archives, but there was one that remained locked, even with his ability to shape spirit. It remained the mystery he could not solve. The runes on that door were such that he couldn't even get them to glow as he could the others.

"Perhaps it's best. We don't have the knowledge those ancient scholars possessed. I wonder if there are things we're not meant to know."

"Why should we fear knowledge?"

His mother turned to him. "I'm surprised you wouldn't understand."

"What does that mean?"

She turned and looked at the clouds. "It was a time of war, the kind we haven't seen in centuries. Your draasin were hunted then and the shapers had power we can't even imagine. Their scholars created the artifact. What else might they have done?" She surveyed the city, hard eyes taking in the damage as she did. "It's a wonder we survived that time."

Tan had never known his mother to be scared of anything, but the way she spoke left him thinking that she was afraid and didn't share everything she might know with him. It wouldn't be the first time she hid things from him.

"And now you seek to learn from her," she went on.

"The First Mother did what she thought necessary for her people."

"She's convinced you of that? How surprising that another spirit shaper has managed to twist you to her view."

Anger surged in him and he pressed it back. "How little you still think of me, Mother. You don't think I can protect myself from a spirit shaping? I've learned how to *shape* spirit."

She sighed and started away from the remains of the university. "Is that what it is? From what I've read, you shape something akin to spirit, but maybe not spirit itself. Either way, I think you're letting your heart lead you. It places you at risk."

"Like your didn't let your heart lead you with Father?"

"That was different."

"Was it? I'd like to know what Althem promised you that made you think Nor was the place to settle."

Tan followed her as she left the university behind. He suspected she headed for the palace, but couldn't be sure. Roine would be there. Since Althem's death, Roine had taken command of the kingdoms.

"I told you that we'd done our service to the kingdoms."

"Strange that a spirit shaper like Althem would release you like that."

She glanced over and shook her head in irritation. "We served our commitment to the throne, Tannen. Peace was our reward."

"Only Father never really had peace, did he? Why was he summoned and not you?" In the time since he'd learned of his parents' real connection to the university, they'd never had the chance to have this argument.

Zephra stopped and fixed him with a withering glare. "Tannen, careful with what you say."

"Why? You've found it awfully easy to accuse Amia of trying to drag me into some Aeta plot, never minding the fact that I *chose* to help her."

"Only after she shaped you," his mother reminded. "Isn't that what you told me?"

"Her shaping had nothing to do with why I'm still with her. I would have helped her as much as I could regardless. The shaping has done nothing more than—"

"Connect you to her." She cocked her head. "Yes, I'm aware of that as well."

A translucent face drifted quickly out of the soft breeze before fading. Tan studied ara, wondering if the wind elemental would ever respond to him the way it did for his mother. Zephra had a connection to the wind he would never really know. And he couldn't be upset by that. She was a wind shaper, after all, while Tan was… well, a wind shaper also, only without the same degree of ability with it.

Why *wouldn't* ara respond for him the same as it did for his mother?

"I believe you've been keeping secrets from me far longer than I have with you," he said. "Had Roine not shown up, would you ever have told me about your shaping? Would I have learned who my parents really were?"

She reached for him, but he pulled away. The hurt on her face nearly made him reconsider. "You've always known who your parents were, Tannen. Learning we are shapers changes nothing."

Tan sighed. "Had Roine not come to Nor, there wouldn't have been a reason for you to tell me about yourself. I would never have learned *why* Father was summoned to serve, why he needed to be the one to go. All that time, I'd wondered. I understand now. And Father will never know."

His mother closed her eyes. Wind swirled around her head, pulling on her dark hair. "You've said it yourself. Had you not gone with Roine, you would never have learned what you were capable of becoming. You have gifts the kingdoms have not seen in hundreds of years. All I want is for you to have the chance to develop them. Learn from the Masters, understand your shaping. Those are the things you should be doing, not risking yourself where others are better suited."

"I've only done what was necessary. And there might not be anyone better suited. Not after what we've been through. How many shapers have been lost? Dozens? How many of them can speak to the elementals? How many have bonded one of the draasin?" Tan caught her eyes. "The barrier is down and those who remain are stretched thin. It leaves us vulnerable."

"Which is why you need to study. You're untrained—"

"*You* could train me. Teach me what you know of wind shaping. Help me speak to ara."

She hesitated, looking back at the remains of the university, as if imagining Tan trapped within there. "I… I'm not certain that is the right answer."

"Didn't you just say I should learn to shape the wind? That I should learn to master my abilities? In that, you and the First Mother agree."

She let her breath out slowly. "If you'll commit to learning from the other Masters, not only from the First Mother, I will do what I can to teach you about the wind when able."

Tan thought that learning from his mother might actually be good for them. After all the deceit between them, getting to know her—*really* getting to know her as Zephra—was needed. And she needed to know him, to understand who he was becoming. So much had changed between them since they had last spent any meaningful time together.

And he never had a chance to study with her, not as he did with his father. His father had taught him everything he knew about earth sensing. Tan suspected that was why he had such strength and control with earth sensing, though he only wished he'd managed to learn how to shape with the same degree of skill. As it was, shaping earth remained a challenge for him. Golud helped, but would the great elemental help when he was outside a place of convergence?

"Fine. Ferran has also offered to teach. I will go to him for additional instruction. Cianna will help with fire." Amia might not like it, but Cianna was a Master fire shaper. "And I'm sure I can find someone to teach me water shaping."

His mother nodded. "It's settled then. Now, Tannen, Theondar is expecting me before you attempt this."

The sudden change in topic made him pause. "If the others haven't changed my mind, neither will you."

"It will fail, but I will let you learn that lesson on your own," she answered. Then she patted him on the arm like she had when he was a child and started away, hurrying up the street. Tan stared after her, wondering if anything had really changed.

CHAPTER 3

An Attempted Healing

THE SHADOWS IN THE LOWER LEVEL of the archives surrounded Tan. The air held the musty odor of ancient books and even more ancient artifacts. A thick, plush rug woven in reds and blues stretched out on the floor in front of him. A simple wooden chair was angled across from him. The chair he sat on was made of stout oak and nothing like the other one. Tan had carried it down from the upper levels of the archives, unwilling to risk damaging anything on this level.

Pale white light glowed from shapers lanterns inset on the walls around him, giving enough for him to see. Runes glowed softly on the door he left propped open, just enough for him to leverage his fingers to pull all the way open if needed, but he didn't really have the need, not with golud worked into the walls and ara blowing through the archives. There was another door beyond that one, and he left it closed for privacy. This level of the archives was only for shapers like him, though there was still the one door he couldn't reach. Maybe he never would.

He couldn't admit it to his mother, but Tan still wasn't entirely certain *what* he was. He could shape like Theondar, the only other living warrior in the kingdoms now that Lacertin was dead, but he could also speak to the elementals and use that connection to weave each of the basic elements together, fusing them to reach for spirit. With the connection to spirit, he had managed to open the door to this level of the archives.

As far as Tan knew, none like him had been here for hundreds of years. The layer of dust hanging on everything attested to that. The heavy, musty odor in the air told the same. He hadn't known what to expect in this level of the archives and should not have been surprised with what he'd discovered: row upon row of books.

Part of him had hoped to find other items like the artifact, and if he could ever open the remaining door, it was still possible that there would be things like that. The archives were much more extensive here than he'd expected. So far, the books had kept him busy.

Tan turned back to the book resting open in his lap. He scanned the page, the *Ishthin* the ancient scholars had used difficult to translate, even with the gift of understanding Amia had given him before he'd nearly lost her to the archivists. This had been the only book on the shelf where he'd found it. That made him wonder how important the book had been to those scholars.

The first two pages consisted of a large map. The kingdoms were marked in the center, small labels marking the ancient nations of Galen, Ter, and Vatten, before they were bound together under a single throne. Nara looked as if it were still part of Rens when this map had been made. Now Rens had been divided, leaving part of it within the kingdoms and the rest annexed by Incendin. Beyond Incendin lay Doma, the thin stretch of land jutting off into the sea. A series of islands was drawn on the edge of the map, each island larger than the next.

Tan had seen Doma once, though he hadn't known it was Doma at the time. And what memories he had of the rest of Doma were faded, twisted by his time changed by fire.

The door pushed open and Tan looked up. Amia entered the room. Her golden hair was pinned up behind her ears and she wore a simple gold band around her neck, a replacement for the silver band that she'd once worn as a mark of her people. Roine had given it to her as a gift, a way of thanking her for service to the kingdoms. There was a certain defiance to the pride with which she wore it.

"You've been here a long time," she commented. She held a rune made by Tan, one of the first he'd attempted after learning of their potential from the First Mother. With the rune stamped into what had once been a coin bearing the face of the king, she could access this room. He'd managed to link the coin to the door, a shaping the First Mother had taught him. Amia had the only such coin.

"I'm sorry. I…"

How to explain to her the compulsion to understand what he was that kept him away from her for hours at a time? It was the reason he spent so much time with the First Mother, the same reason he would go with his mother, or Ferran were he to teach. Few shapers knew what it felt like to speak to the elementals, and none of them knew what it was like to stare at the udilm or feel the rumbling of golud in your bones. None had ever imagined riding one of the draasin. Tan had done all of those things.

But then he didn't have to explain any of that to Amia. With the shaped connection between them, she *felt* it, as surely as he felt the affection she had for him. She leaned over him, eyes taking in the map, and pointed to the page. "That's not quite right," she said, motioning toward the edge of the map.

"Why?" He knew little of geography outside of the kingdoms, a failing his mother had admitted to facilitating, but what he did know of Doma was that it jutted off from Incendin as depicted in the map.

"Doma isn't as large as what you see here. And these islands," she said, pointing along the edge, "are smaller. Par might be larger, but I'm not sure."

Tan shifted her finger over to point at the kingdoms. "And the kingdoms were different. Ethea had to be claimed from the sea. That's why the nymid infuse the rocks nearly as much as golud." That was part of the mystery he hoped to better understand by searching through these forgotten texts. "The book on the draasin mentioned it. I think it was better known then. But this," Tan said, pointing to the map. "I don't think this is a map of the kingdoms as we know it. I think it maps it as those scholars planned it."

Amia bit her lip as she studied the page. A strand of hair slipped free and Tan reached up to push it back and away from her face, brushing her cheek as he did. She pressed against him and sighed. "What do you hope to find?"

"I don't know. Explanations. Maybe answers. Why did the ancient scholars even make the artifact?" It was the question that troubled him the most. There seemed no reason for that much power to be used by one person. "That much power is not meant for anyone, not even the elementals. Holding that power, I could have done anything, shaped the world anyway I chose." He shivered. "I felt as if I could have returned my father. Your family. Everything." He hadn't admitted that to Amia before. Admitting that he'd considered and then rejected that much power made him worry how she'd react. He suspected she would have agreed with him, but what if she didn't? What if Amia would have wanted him to change things?

"What would have happened if you had?"

Tan thought about what could have been. Flashes of it, little more than hints of memories, remained. Nothing he could act on, just enough to make him aware of what he missed. "You would be Daughter, I suppose. In time, you would become Mother. And then, with enough experience, you would become First Mother."

"And you?"

That had been the hardest, and the first question he'd thought to ask. What would have happened to him?

When he'd stepped into the pool of liquid spirit, he'd known answers to anything. But he'd also held power unlike any that he had ever imagined. With it, he'd saved Amia and the youngest of the draasin, Enya. Tan recognized the power was not for him, just as the power of the artifact was not for him. That didn't mean it didn't make him wonder.

And while holding the artifact, he had *known* what would be if only a few things were changed. Were his father not to have died, would he have been driven to face Incendin? Had Amia not lost her family, would she have gone with Tan and rescued the draasin? Had Tan not wanted to save Elle, would he ever had secured the bond with Asboel?

Only the Great Mother knew for certain. And in that moment, Tan had held a piece of her power. No man was meant to experience that much power. Why, then, had the ancient scholars created the artifact?

There must be an answer here. Everything in his being told him there was. Those ancient scholars commanded so much more strength and skill and knowledge that it seemed impossible to him that they had no reason other than a search for power. Even the First Mother thought they sought understanding, not only power.

Tan closed the book. Answers would come in time, but not today.

He looked over to Amia, not certain whether he was prepared for what was next. "Is he ready?"

Amia squeezed his shoulder and stepped away. "Are you certain you should do this? Roine thinks it should be destroyed."

Tan shook his head. "What would have happened had you destroyed me when I'd changed?"

"That's not the same."

"Isn't it? I did what I thought necessary to save you. To protect you. Can't the same be said for him?"

Amia gripped the gold band at her neck and stared at him. "You don't know what it has done."

"He," Tan corrected. He stood and replaced the book back on the shelf where it had sat alone. This area of the archives had managed to protect the book against the dampness that threatened to stretch in. Likely some shaping, though Tan couldn't detect it. "And you're wrong. He's done no worse than I did. And perhaps there's a reason he transformed."

"You..." Amia trailed off with a shake of her head. "Even when you changed, there was still a part that remained. I don't know if I could have helped you were there not. I don't know if the nymid would have helped otherwise. With the lisincend... they went to it willingly. They only wanted power while you wanted to help. That matters, I think. With them, nothing good remains of the shaper."

Tan knew what it felt like to be consumed by fire. He knew some of what the lisincend had experienced. And if there was anything he could do to help it like Amia had helped him, shouldn't he try?

A small crowd surrounded the lisincend in the broken palace courtyard. The shapers guarding him had brought him out of the archives so whatever Tan attempted could be better contained. Once, the courtyard had featured scenes from each area of the kingdoms, but since the last attack—since Althem had destroyed it—it looked little like it had. In time, they might be able to shape it back into some semblance of what it had been.

The palace itself served a different purpose, as well. Since Althem had passed without leaving an heir, there was need for leadership. All had looked to Theondar—now known as Roine, the last remaining warrior. He had moved the remains of the university into the city and agreed to serve until a replacement could be found.

That was the reason Tan thought saving the lisincend was especially important. They could use what the lisincend knew, discover some way to prevent another Incendin attack, maybe understand *why* the Incendin fire shapers risked death to become lisincend. It had to be about more than power.

But it required first saving the creature.

Chains of stone infused with golud bound the lisincend's wrists and ankles in the center of the yard, anchoring him to the ground. His massive wings were furled in and held by another loop of chain. His leathery skin radiated with a surge of heat, as if fire struggled to escape from him. Narrow eyes watched as Tan approached.

Tan remembered what that vision had been like, the way everything seemed to burn, the seductive ability to see clearly in the dark. He shook away the thought.

Amia pulled away from him as he approached the lisincend. Tan stared after her but felt her irritation through the bond. After what she'd gone through with her people, first losing her family, then abducted and tortured by the Aeta, and finally to learn how the First Mother had been complicit the entire time, Tan didn't blame her. He just hoped she could learn forgiveness.

He shifted the sword hanging from his waist, still growing accustomed to wearing it. He no longer doubted he had the right to it; he was almost as much warrior as Roine, only without the same experience. The runes worked along the edge of the sword were similar to those he'd studied in the lower level of the archive. From what the First Mother explained, with those runes, Tan could augment his shapings.

A gust of wind whipped at his hair and he turned to see his mother land next to him. The translucent face of ara worked in her shaping. Ara seemed to dart around him, tugging playfully at the heavy overcoat that had replaced his worn traveling cloak, before disappearing again.

"Mother. You don't have to be here for this."

She studied the lisincend, tightness in her eyes betraying her concern. "When we spoke earlier, I hadn't known that it was today."

"It was Roine's deadline."

She sniffed, eyeing the lisincend. "I am unconvinced this is the right thing to do. Or that you should even attempt it."

"So is Amia."

She glanced over her shoulder at Amia. "In that, at least, we agree."

"I think you agree on more than you realize."

Roine approached, dressed in more finery than Tan had ever seen the warrior wear. A sword much like the one Tan wore was strapped to his waist. "Let's get this over with, Tan. The others will hold their shapings in reserve, but if I sense danger to you—"

"All I want is the opportunity to try and save him."

"Him? You know what you're talking about, right, Tan? This is one of the creatures that attacked Amia's family. The lisincend attacked this city. They were the reason Lacertin died!"

"Should they not have the chance for redemption?"

"Redemption? These creatures have been attacking the kingdoms since before you were born. There can be no redemption."

Tan stared at the lisincend. Locked in chains as he was, he didn't move. "You would have said the same about Lacertin once."

Roine frowned and bit back a retort. The emotions conflicting on his face said enough. Without Lacertin, they would not have defeated Althem. Tan wondered what Lacertin would have said, knowing what Tan intended.

Roine's jaw clenched. "I have not objected to your attempt, Tannen, but only because after everything you've done, you deserve the benefit of the doubt. I can't say I don't think this is a folly."

"All I ask is the chance."

"And if you succeed?" he asked, staring at the lisincend. The heat that would normally roll off the creature was held in check by the kingdoms' shapers. "Will you trust that you can release him?"

"Amia released me," he reminded.

Roine sighed. "There were other reasons behind that, you know. I seem to recall you sharing the fact that a bond has formed between you. I think that bond would inform her of whether she needed to fear you."

That, and the bond between him and Asboel, but Roine knew little about that bond.

"There are ways to destroy it humanely, Tannen. You wouldn't have to even be involved."

"Humanely? You don't think they'll take a little pleasure from destroying one of the lisincend?"

Roine lowered his voice. "Didn't you?"

Instead of answering, Tan took a slow breath and patted Roine on the shoulder as he stepped past, moving to stand in front of the twisted shaper.

Shapers ringed the creature, all now more familiar to Tan than they were when he first came to Ethea. They treated him differently as well. He said little, but Ferran spoke to him as almost an equal, asking questions of golud and listening, as if what Tan said couldn't simply be found in the archives. Alan, another wind shaper, nodded to him almost respectfully. From the moment they'd met, Tan recognized the regard Alan had for Zephra. Now that she had returned, she had taken her place at the head of the wind shapers; none rivaled her in skill, and none could speak to the great wind elemental as she could. He knew the water shapers, Essa and Jons, less well, but they would be instrumental in what he intended. He remembered that he needed to ask one of them—likely Jons—whether they would be willing to work with him.

And then there was Cianna. She stared at the lisincend, standing before it with a curious expression. A shimmery copper shirt clung to her, as did the deep indigo leather pants she wore. She turned as Tan approached. "It has not spoken since we brought it out from the archives."

"I don't think he said much even while there, did he?"

Cianna shrugged. "I already told you that I refused to go. Theondar is right, you know. He should be destroyed. What you offer is more than he deserves."

What did any of them deserve anymore? Weren't they all twisted in some way? "He suffers," Tan said. The thin barrier of spirit surrounding the lisincend shielded the creature from accessing fire. That didn't take away the call, the draw of fire. Tan remembered all too well how fire seemed to demand his attention when he'd been shaped. There had been only so much he could resist.

Cianna grunted. "You think it should not suffer after what it has done?"

"I am not sure anything should suffer." He turned to the other shapers. "Are they ready?"

Cianna gave Tan a half-smile and shifted her focus to the other shapers. "They are ready."

"Theondar has given me only this one chance," Tan said. He didn't think he could ask for another opportunity. If this failed, Tan would have to trust Roine and let the lisincend be destroyed.

Cianna touched his hand. Fire streaked with an uncomfortable familiarity beneath her fingers. Annoyance surged through Amia behind him. "I don't think it will work," she said.

"If it doesn't work, then we can destroy him." Better that than releasing the lisincend to attack once more.

"You keep calling it a him."

Tan nodded tightly. "And you keep calling him an it."

He stepped away from Cianna, steeling himself for what was to come. He had learned to control his access to spirit, but that didn't mean he had the same level of skill as the First Mother, or even Amia. Tan would have to be ready for whatever it might try to do to him once the spirit barrier was lifted. Had he trusted the First Mother, she should have been the one to lead this attempt.

He faced the lisincend and stood with arms crossed over his chest. The lisincend's eyes drifted to the sword at Tan's waist. Tan shook his head. "I don't intend to harm you."

A long, thick tongue slipped out of its slit of a mouth. Scaly lids blinked. "You should finish me and be done, warrior."

"It might come to that," Tan admitted. Better to be honest than to lie about what might be to come.

"Whatever you think you will accomplish will fail. You think Alisz was the only one of power from the Sunlands?"

Tan hesitated. He'd not heard Incendin referred to that way before. "Fur is gone. I defeated him."

The lisincend laughed. "You? You think highly of yourself, little warrior."

Tan jerked back at the comment, so similar to what Asboel had once called him.

The lisincend worked its long, thick tongue over its lips again, thin eyes flicking around before stopping on Tan. "You will fail. These kingdoms will fall. Fire will burn once more, as it must."

Tan leaned toward the lisincend. "Fire tried to consume me once. *It* failed," he whispered. "And I can free you as I was freed, only I can't promise it won't hurt."

"By freeing me, you only place yourself in greater danger."

Tan twisted to see the other shapers watching him. All of them doubted he would be able to do anything, that he would even manage to save the lisincend, but how could Tan *not* try? "Freeing you puts the kingdoms in less danger."

The lisincend wheezed out a dry laugh. "You are a fool if you believe that, little warrior. When the lisincend are gone and the fires fail, you will see how little you know."

Roine watched him impatiently. Tan closed his eyes. Heat radiated off the lisincend in a way that left his skin feeling tight. Tan ignored the sensation, focusing on what he needed to do. With a whispered summons, he called nymid, golud, ara, and draasin, binding the elementals together as he had learned to do. It was possible that he shaped them without needing the elementals, though Tan no longer knew the difference. The power of spirit formed within him, different than the other elements. Taking this power, Tan shaped it atop the draasin.

Spirit held in place.

Tan reached to the nymid. *Nymid!*

The great water elemental infused the bones of Ethea, worked deep beneath the city in greater strength than Tan would have thought possible. He didn't have the same connection to the nymid as he had with Asboel, but he was better connected than with any of the other elementals. As far as Tan knew, there were individual nymid, but he didn't only speak to the same one each time, not like he did with Asboel.

He Who is Tan.

Tan let out a tense breath. Everything he intended depended on him reaching the nymid. Standing in the palace courtyard, he hadn't been certain that the nymid would respond.

He gathered his thoughts. With the nymid, it was best to be direct. *Twisted Fire. Can it be healed?*

Why would you heal Twisted Fire?

I would restore him if it's possible.

Twisted Fire consumes the shaper.

It once consumed me.

You were not so far gone that you could not still feel.

Is that the key? Tan asked.

The nymid didn't answer.

Tan took a deep breath. *Will you help?*

There was more of a sense of great thought. Then, *We can try.*

Something about what the nymid said tripped an idea for Tan. They were right: when he'd been consumed by fire, he still had felt something. The bond with Amia had been there, but weakened. She had held onto him; her affection for him had preserved him. And because of that, he had risked failing in order to return.

Pulling on the focus with spirit, Tan surged through the lisincend. There had to be something—anything—that he could reach that might allow him to save the person he had once been. Spirit was difficult for Tan. He found nothing within the lisincend other than the draw of fire and a vague sense of fear. Nothing that would allow him to reach who he had been.

Nymid?

The nymid pressed up through the ground, drawn up by Tan's command. They moved hesitantly, sliding over the lisincend. Power rushed through Tan, power to shape and control the water, power to heal.

He pushed this through the lisincend.

The creature howled. Pain surged through the spirit connection Tan now shared with him. Fire beat at the connection, straining for freedom. Tan and the nymid fought back, resisting. All he needed was an opening, something to reach through. But he found none.

Nymid pressed, sensing Tan's need. The sense of the elemental roared through him, filling him with an awareness of their power. Combined with spirit, Tan knew he could save the lisincend, that he could shape the creature back into the man he had been.

The lisincend howled again.

Stone groaned as the lisincend strained at the chains binding it. Fire consumed the lisincend, as it had once consumed Tan, coursing through the creature with an intensity he couldn't match.

The spirit barrier failed.

In a moment, the lisincend would be free to attack. Those watching might be injured, all because he had been arrogant enough to believe he could save this creature. Amia was in danger.

Fire surged, roaring from the lisincend.

Someone screamed behind him. Tan felt Amia's alarm. He would *not* risk her.

Asboel!

The sense of the draasin roared through him. Asboel was always nearby in his mind but could slither quickly to the forefront.

Twisted Fire!

You are a fool, Maelen.

As Asboel spoke, the surge of power roared through him, the great fire elemental pushing on the fire consuming the lisincend. Asboel had not the strength to draw it away, but he could augment it.

In that moment, Tan knew what he had to do.

Pulling on water and air, he created a barrier around the lisincend as flames consumed the creature. A surge of joy raced through the lisincend as fire consumed him, drawing the flames out of the barrier, pulling more fire than he would have shaped on his own. Dark laughter worked through Tan's mind from the spirit connection.

Then it immolated. Flames burned to nothing, overwhelmed by fire.

Tan stared, unable to look away until it was nothing more than ash.

Amia came from behind him and touched his arm. He shook her off as he turned away and staggered from the courtyard, ignoring the stares he knew followed him.

CHAPTER 4

The Bond and the Hunt

A GREAT FLAPPING OF WINGS whipped the air around him. Tan shouldn't have been surprised that Asboel would search for him after what happened but still felt relief that he had. The shadow of the draasin loomed large, heat steaming from its massive sides. Long spikes protruded from his neck, one broken off and not restored when Tan had healed it following the battle with the king. Sharp talons gripped the earth as it landed, and Tan felt the weight of the draasin gaze, though he no longer knew how much of that came from its presence within his mind.

Tan looked over at Asboel. *I'm sorry.*

The draasin snorted. A gust of flames came from his nostrils. *You apologize for our bond now, Maelen? You have never abused it.*

I presumed to use your power.

You thought to heal Twisted Fire. I am not certain such a thing can be done.

Tan couldn't shake the image of the lisincend burning itself to death, or the joy it had felt as it happened. *There has to be a reason. No shaper would embrace that willingly.*

There are always reasons, Maelen. You simply must ask the right question.

Tan sat cross-legged on the ground, a rocky outcropping nearly a league from the city. He hadn't mastered his connection to the wind like his mother, but he'd learned enough to basically toss himself into the air, careening in a deadly fall toward the ground. At least he could escape the accusation he'd seen in the eyes of the shapers.

Sitting here, with the sun descending over the copse of trees, some unnamed stream bubbling behind him, he could almost feel like he was back home in Galen rather than lost in a city that would never—could never—be his home.

Only, Nor was gone. The rest of Galen was changed. Everything he knew had been destroyed. The only home he had remaining was with Amia, and she was different since learning that the First Mother betrayed the Aeta.

Asboel settled to the ground, lowering his massive head down so he could meet Tan's eyes. *Do you feel them?*

Tan frowned at the suddenness of the change. *Feel what?*

Asboel grunted. *Feel the power you have restored.*

Tan shook his head. *I have restored nothing.*

No? Then why does Enya fly so easily? Why does Sashari soar through the skies?

Tan had known Enya's name. Standing in the pool of spirit, he'd learned her name as he freed her from the twisted shaping the archivists had used on her. But he hadn't known the name of the other draasin, Asboel's mate.

You shared her name, he said.

Names were important to the draasin. They gave a certain level of power over them. Not like sharing the bond that Tan and Asboel shared, but enough that he recognized the hesitance to use their names. Even the first time Asboel had shared his name, he had done so cautiously.

If you are to share the bond fully, Maelen, then you are to know our rightful names.

Why do the draasin have names but the other elementals do not?

Asboel snorted. *Are you so certain they do not?*

He hadn't really considered. The nymid had seemed to be much the same, but when he'd first met them, one had been more connected to him than the others. And with ara, weren't there faces hidden with the wind? Tan never really saw golud, only felt the powerful earth elemental.

No. But something is different about the draasin.

We are more powerful.

Asboel didn't say it to boast. He said it matter of fact, as if there would be no arguing. From what Tan had seen, the draasin *might* be more powerful than other elementals. *More powerful than ara? More powerful than golud?*

In these lands and in this time, we are.

Tan thought the comment strange. *Why is that?*

Asboel cocked his head and blinked, yellowish gold eyes seeming to glow. *All are born from fire.*

Even golud?

The ground rumbled as if the golud heard Tan's question.

Asboel pawed at the ground, tearing at the earth with massive claws. His tail switched around him, slamming into the small trees nearby as if they were nothing. *Golud may think earth came first, but always there is fire. It is life. It is everything. Without heat, there can be no rock.*

And golud, do they have names like the draasin?

Asboel snorted. *Ask golud.*

Tan had never really gotten much answer out of the earth elemental, but then again he'd never tried, not as he had with Asboel. There was a bond between him and Asboel, different even than there was with the other draasin. Could he even bond with another elemental? It felt strange to even consider it. With Asboel, he knew his mind, sensed his thoughts.

Tan might be able to touch on the thoughts of Enya or Sashari, but it wasn't the same. Whatever he reached of them likely came through his connection to Asboel anyway.

Did his mother have the same sort of connection to ara as he had with the draasin? He hadn't thought to ask and it seemed to him that ara was abundant, but what did he *really* know about the wind elemental? Could ara be like the draasin, with each having a name, a sense of self? Could the nymid? Or were they simply parts of the greater elemental power?

Tan wished he understood. Maybe then he could understand why *he'd* been given the ability to speak to the elementals. What did the Great Mother intend for him? Surely it was not simply to stop Incendin. There must be more for him.

Did you have a bond before?

He almost asked about before Asboel had been trapped in the ice, frozen at the bottom of the lake, but caught himself. Nearly a thousand years had passed while Asboel had been trapped, long enough that the world had changed, that the threats of Asboel's time had become something different. Then, there had been no twisted fire. Incendin had been nothing more than another land, one filled with fire shapers but not dangerous and deadly.

Asboel sat on his haunches and twisted his head around, practically resting it on his forelegs. *There has been no bond.*

None?

He snorted and a spray of steam burst from his nose. Tan had long ago learned that the steam spouting from Asboel's nostrils did no more harm to Tan than the heat of his spikes. He wondered if the flames from his mouth could harm him. Part of him doubted that they would.

The bond between draasin and your kind is rare. It is not easy for my kind to form these bonds. There were those who would try, but the draasin are fierce. None succeeded.

It is easier for the other elementals?

Asboel clawed at the ground as if trying to pull golud from the earth. *The others are less choosy and they forget easily, so it is rare for the draasin to bond.*

How rare?

I have lived many cycles, but I have only heard of it once before. If the bond fails, I will be weakened.

Weakened?

Asboel's tail switched from side to side. *I cannot explain it any better, Maelen.*

Does it limit you? Tan asked.

Not any longer.

Tan laughed. Now that Amia's shaping forcing the draasin to avoid hunting man had been lifted, he'd wondered what would happen, but so far nothing had changed. Maybe that was the point. The draasin *could* hunt man, but they had no interest in it. They hunted to eat, not for sport.

That's not really what I meant.

Your question doesn't deserve an answer.

Tan sighed, thinking of the lisincend. He'd been convinced he could save him, that his ability to draw upon spirit would give him some insight about how to return the fire shaper who had sacrificed himself to become the lisincend, but maybe Amia was right. Unlike when Tan had nearly changed by fire, the lisincend had gone voluntarily—willingly—chasing fire for greater power. Tan had only done what was needed to save Amia.

He pulled his legs in and sat, staring at the rock scattered around him. *I thought I could save him. Fire consumed him too brightly.*

It is difficult to return from fire.

You survive. I survived.

You barely survived, Maelen, and the draasin are *fire.*

Tan ignored the comment about him. *The same as saa? The same as inferin?*

They are fire as well.

Tan couldn't get the image of the burning lisincend out of his mind. He'd been so certain that he could restore him. Maybe his mother was right that he needed additional training, but why did it feel the other shapers knew less about some things than him? *Why can't they be saved?*

They chose their fate. I have been away from this world too long to understand, but they embraced fire too closely.

Asboel turned his head away, staring through the trees, focused toward the south, toward Nara. It was where the draasin had settled after Tan had saved them, where Asboel and Sashari had gone to raise the hatchlings. But the world had lost two more of the draasin, stolen by the lisincend and destroyed.

How did they take the hatchlings? Since the attack in Ethea, since defeating Althem, Tan hadn't asked. The subject was too sore for Asboel, too fresh and raw.

Asboel breathed out slowly, steam spilling from wide nostrils. *The draasin are weakest when young, before they learn to control the flames, before they learn to climb the wind. Twisted Fire found where Sashari hunted. They took that safety from the hatchlings.*

Will there be others?

There will always be draasin.

Tan felt that wasn't much of an answer. The world had missed the presence of the draasin. Maybe that was the reason shaping had become so rare, though if that were the case, then why was it that *all* the elements were affected? The other elementals of fire that Tan knew about, saa and inferin and saldam, were not nearly as powerful as the draasin. They hadn't replaced the fire elemental in the draasin's absence.

But then, there were other elementals where two shared strength. The nymid and the udilm were both powerful water elementals. Tan once believed only the udilm to be the great water elemental, but experience had taught him otherwise. Could the same happen with the other elements? Were there other strong elementals of wind and earth? And if not, why with water?

So many questions and never enough time for answers. Between Incendin remaining a threat, Doma shapers still trapped, and the barrier needing to be rebuilt, there simply *wasn't* time to learn what he needed.

Tell me, Maelen, why have you come to this place? Asboel asked, pulling him from his thoughts. *What do you hope to learn here?*

There is much I need *to learn. There's so little I understand of the other elementals, but I didn't come here for that. I needed to get away. I… I thought I could do something I could not.*

Asboel seemed to smile. With the draasin, it looked like a turn of his long jaw and the flash of sharp teeth. *It was not the first time for you, nor will it be the last. You are fearless. You are Maelen. That is why I chose to accept the bond.*

Maybe Tan had tried controlling power he was never meant to control. Using the elementals to form spirit was one thing, but controlling the Mother meant a different type of power altogether, power that he had turned away from when he decided the artifact was not meant for him. But then, had he used the artifact, he *could* have saved the lisincend. With the artifact, he could have done many things. He'd seen what he could have done, almost as if he were sitting among the heavens, gifted with knowledge of the earth and stars.

I wonder if I should have restored the hatchlings when I had the chance.

Asboel turned to him and fixed him with eyes that seemed to swallow him. Concern formed a thick line down the center of his long snout. *You cannot change what you cannot control, Maelen. Even the draasin know there are limits to power. Danger comes when you reach for more power than you are meant to possess. Even small changes have consequences.*

Tan looked at his hands. Roine and the others had been right. He shouldn't have tried saving the lisincend. After what they had done to the world, they didn't really deserve saving.

Come, Maelen, let us hunt together tonight. You will forget.

Tan shook the dark thoughts out of his mind and stood. *Let us hunt.*

They soared high overhead, the city of Ethea growing ever more distant, nothing but a darkness far behind him. Villages streamed past, but Asboel never flew close enough to be a threat. Knowing what he did of the draasin, how had shapers ever felt the need to hunt the great elementals? They wanted nothing more than to hunt, though Tan didn't understand why they should need to hunt and feed when he'd never gotten that sense from ara or the nymid. Perhaps the draasin really *were* different from the other elementals. Tan wondered why that should be.

Clouds drifted past and it would have been cool if not for the heat radiating from Asboel. Tan held tightly to one of the spikes on his back, settled comfortably atop him. He felt a moment of peace. How many people could ever say they had ridden one of the draasin?

Awareness of Amia surged through their bond, worry gnawing at her. He sent her the image of him soaring with Asboel, using it to reassure her. She seemed appeased by it and Tan released the immediacy of the connection.

Where would you hunt? Asboel asked.

Nara, Tan sent. He formed the image of the map he'd seen in the lower archives, and Asboel understood. How much of the map had been accurate when Asboel still hunted, before the time he'd been frozen in the lake? They banked, turning hard as his massive wings beat at the wind, sending them higher and higher until at last Asboel lowered his head and dove.

Wind swirled around them. Mist shimmered from the heated spikes, sending moisture spraying onto Tan's face. Translucent shapes like faces appeared and then disappeared rapidly; Tan had always seen the wind elemental when he rode the draasin.

The air changed as they flew, growing warmer. The greens and browns of Ter, the flowing expanse of fields and small farms, shifted, slowly sliding into burned orange of the sandy desert that covered much of Nara. Like Incendin, Nara was a hot land, one tormented by the sun and lack of moisture, a place where fire thrived.

Asboel swooped, circling a shadow moving along the ground. The image of a deer-like creature darting across the ground filled Tan's mind. Asboel dove for it, reaching the animal before it could even register that it had been hunted, and grabbed it in massive claws, pulling it apart and eating as they climbed.

Asboel seemed content. Another shadow appeared, the dark shape sliding through the sky. Tan looked over and saw the other draasin, Sashari, as she flew alongside Asboel. Tan focused on her and felt the distant sense of her within his mind, though it seemed to come more from Asboel than from any connection to her.

And the youngest?

She hunts, Asboel said.

There was a hesitancy Tan only felt through the connection. *She does not need to hide from me.*

Enya had no control. That is unusual for the draasin. It frightened her. That is another thing that is unusual.

Tan hadn't seen her since the archivists used the shaping Amia placed on the draasin to keep them from hunting man and twisted it, turning it so that she was under their control. To save Asboel, she had released that shaping, at least for Asboel. Tan had never given much thought about if the shaping remained upon the other draasin.

Are the others still constrained?

You ask if the Daughter's shaping remains?

Yes.

It remains.

But not for you? Tan asked.

No.

Would you like it removed from them?

Asboel snorted. *The shaping is not as limiting as you would believe, Maelen. We still hunt. We fly. That is all the draasin require.*

They flew for a while longer. *Why did they hunt you? The ancient warriors, I mean. Why did they hunt the draasin?*

Not so ancient, Maelen. The draasin experience the world in a way you will never fully understand. We serve fire. We protect fire. We are fire. Can you stop fire from burning through the dry grass? Can you stop the brightness of lightning? Can you turn off the sun? Such are the draasin. We are. We hunt. That is enough.

Tan hugged the spike. *There is more to it. Why did they hunt the draasin?*

You ask the draasin why your kind would hunt mine?

Firelight danced in the distance and Asboel turned toward it. Tan heard the vague sense of alarm and realized it came from Sashari.

What does she fear?

Asboel sent an image to Tan.

Tan sat rigid atop the draasin. The vision Asboel provided him more than enough information to know what happened: Incendin burned.

Tan didn't know exactly what he saw, but flames anchored against the night, shining against the coming darkness in such a way that he felt them. There was a draw to the flames, the same way as when he'd been changed by fire, nearly twisted into one of the lisincend. Asboel felt it too. The draasin did not have to fight the pull of fire in the same way Tan did, but the draw was there just the same. Power erupted from the flames, more than Tan could imagine.

What is it? Tan asked.

Fire.

I can see that.

No. Asboel pushed through the image of the fire in the distance again. This time, Tan truly saw it, could see through the flames, and recognized the dark lines worked within it. The Fire Fortress.

He'd heard of it. Lacertin had lived within the Fire Fortress for years, secluded to prove to Incendin that he could be a loyal fire shaper.

Had he not, how much would have been lost? So many years were spent with Lacertin viewed as a traitor to the kingdoms when he was actually a hero.

Does it always burn like that?

Asboel turned, arching his body again away, twisting so they departed Incendin lands. *We have watched Fire in these lands many times since our release. Always it burns atop the towers, but this is the brightest it has ever been.*

What does it mean?

A warning.

What kind of warning? Tan wondered.

Asboel either couldn't—or wouldn't—answer.

The return flight was much faster. As they flew, Tan felt a sense of agitation from the draasin. Asboel might not admit to it, but something about the fires in Incendin upset him. Tan suspected the draasin still hadn't gotten over the pain of losing the hatchlings. He didn't understand—couldn't understand—what it was like to suffer such a loss, but he had known loss in his life. His father. His home. His past life. Except Tan suspected the loss Asboel had suffered throughout his life made Tan's pale in comparison.

The draasin landed atop the rocks where he'd first found Tan. Sashari circled overhead, not landing. Tan felt a distant sense from her as well. *Hunt well.*

Asboel twitched his tail. *Maelen.*

Tan recognized the hesitation. If he didn't ask, he would regret losing the opportunity. *What is it? What did you see?*

Asboel sighed with a gust of steam from his nostrils. *Fire burned brightly in that place before the hatchlings were destroyed. Now it threatens again.*

With Incendin, I suspect fire always threatens.

This is different.

Tan turned and faced the south, toward Incendin. Were he still atop Asboel, he might be able to use the draasin's sight and see the Fire Fortress, but here, on the ground, he could see nothing more than trees. The darkness stifled him, making him feel limited. Times like these, he wished for the sight he'd known when fire had twisted him.

Can you explain?

Fire consumes. You know this, Maelen. You nearly lost yourself.

You keep telling me that the draasin are *fire.*

Asboel lowered his head and shook it. *The draasin are fire. But fire is the draasin. I cannot put it in terms you would understand.*

Try.

Asboel stood on his back legs, towering over him. Heat radiated from his body, pressing out between spikes and scales. In the cool air of the evening, steam misted from him, leaving a soft layering around the clearing, almost like a cloud settling from the sky.

I must learn what this is. If Twisted Fire thinks to attack again, I will know. You must not interfere, Maelen. I cannot guarantee your safety.

Asboel. Let me help.

The draasin took to the wind with a powerful beating of wings. *This is not yours to fight. I do not fear Twisted Fire. Fire cannot harm the draasin. You need to remain here. Protect your kingdoms from Twisted Fire. Grow stronger. Then we can hunt.*

Asboel didn't even give Tan the chance to respond. He turned and headed south once again, leaving Tan standing and staring after his bonded draasin and Sashari. Questions rolled through him. Why would the Fire Fortress burn brightly? What did it mean that it had when the hatchlings were killed?

Were Lacertin still alive, he might have answers he needed, but Alisz had killed him during the assault on Ethea. Now they had to figure it out on their own. And because of him, the one creature that might have answers had been destroyed.

Chapter 5

Lessons in Shaping

AMIA MET HIM AT THE DOOR as he returned. They'd taken over the small home where Elle had hidden the night he first met Sarah. The upper levels were sparsely furnished, little more than a few chairs and an old table, but the home was solid and secure, far removed from the destruction that had affected the rest of the city. Roine had suggested they stay in the palace with him, but Tan didn't feel comfortable doing that. The reminder of what he'd been through—what his family had been through—because of Althem would be too much for him. Had it not been for Althem, Tan might still have a father.

She barely waited for him to come in the door before she rounded on him. "What is it? What did you see?" She took his hands and pulled him into the room. "You saw something that troubles you."

Likely she felt it through the bond they shared, the same way he knew the annoyance she felt and the mild unease with his absence.

"I went with Asboel. I needed..." he started and then shrugged, "time away. Silence. Something."

Amia squeezed his hands. "You blame yourself for what happened? Roine was going to have the lisincend destroyed! You're the one who convinced him to give you a chance to try and save it."

Tan closed the door behind him, leaning against it as he looked around the small room. Amia had a lantern glowing with a soft, warm light near one of the chairs. A book was folded open and he realized she'd taken it from the archives. The hearth crackled with a warm fire. Curtains that normally covered the window were open, letting in the smells of the city. A hazy smoke still drifted over the city from the youngest draasin's first attack. An occasional shout rang out and drifted up to them.

Tan walked across the warm hardwood floor to the window and let the heavy curtain fall, drawing away the sounds and the smells of the city.

"It turns out my mother—and the First Mother—were right. I thought I could save him," he said. "And maybe I could, but I don't know enough." He lowered himself into one of the chairs next to the hearth and grabbed the book resting on the arm, flopping it onto his lap. The ancient map stared up at him as if expecting him to understand its secrets. Amia must have brought it here to study, maybe to help find answers together.

Amia rested a hand on his shoulder. "There's nothing you could have done. He didn't want to be saved."

Tan flipped the pages in the book and tried to push out the image of the lisincend burning himself to death. The stench as the flames tore through the creature had been nearly more than he could stand. He closed the book and looked up at Amia. "I know that. Asboel knows that. It doesn't make it any easier."

She squeezed. "I'm glad." When he frowned, she explained, "You've said your mother worries about the fact that you were changed by fire, that you nearly transformed. I know you were restored. The Great Mother knows I can *feel* it. But they remain unconvinced that you're entirely the same."

"I'm not entirely convinced I'm the same," he said. "I can reach fire more easily than before. It's not like that with the other elements."

Amia's mouth tightened. "It will be in time. Your mother is right in that much at least. You need practice. And maybe it was good for them to see how hard you tried."

"And failed?"

"But you tried. That's more than anyone else can say. It shows them that you're still you. You're still Tan, not some early stage lisincend."

Tan laughed and pulled her down next to him. "Not that they could do much if I was. I'd end up bursting into flames like the lisincend."

"That's not funny."

"No, it's not. And I'm not certain it would do anything to me anyway. Fire doesn't effect me the same. At least, Asboel's fire doesn't burn me. Saa doesn't burn when I shape with it."

Tan pulled on fire and it flickered into a tight spiral above his hand. As he held it, he felt the slight draw of the fire elemental to the shaping. Saa was there. He might not have the same connection to it as he did with the draasin—and Asboel in particular—but that didn't mean there wasn't a connection.

He stared at the fire in the hearth, watching the flames leap and twist. He reached for the fire, shaping it, practiced sending it dancing one way or the other. When shaping, he had the distinct sense of power drawn out of him, pulled from some deep reservoir within him. His shapings would be limited by the power he could command. It was different with the elementals. By speaking to them, he could ask them elementals for assistance to increase his own power.

He sent a request to saa. The lesser elemental floated about the flames, either made of fire or drawn to it. There was a vague sense of the elementals swirling about. With Tan's request, saa sent the flames billowing up.

"I didn't know you spoke to saa," Amia said, slipping her arm around him.

"They're always there. At least, in Ethea they are."

"Because we're in a place of convergence."

Since battling with Althem, Tan had come to realize that elementals were drawn to Ethea, which was a place of convergence like the place in the mountains where he'd first met Asboel. What Tan didn't understand was why these places of convergence existed.

"That's why Mother worries so much about my shaping. Outside of Ethea, when I'm away from such places, will the elementals even answer? Asboel will, but the others may not come when I summon them. Without the elementals, there's not much I can do to help."

She gave him a tight squeeze and kissed him on the cheek. "You've always underestimated yourself, Tan. And you've always been stronger than you know."

"Asboel doesn't want me to come with him. I think he fears I'm not strong enough for where he's going."

"And where is that?"

"He showed me the Fire Fortress."

She tensed and twisted to fix him with a hard, blue-eyed stare. "You went into Incendin?"

"Barely to the border. We were in Nara, moving to the east, when Asboel saw flames burning more brightly in the Fire Fortress."

Amia pushed off his lap, moving to the chair across from him.

"Burned? As in the fortress itself was on fire?"

"There were flames, but it wasn't like they consumed it. This was different. Asboel said they had burned brightly before the hatchlings were killed. I didn't tell him, but that was about the time the twisted lisincend appeared. What if Incendin is making new lisincend?"

Amia's face went blank. Tan wanted to pull her back to him, to comfort her, but there was nothing he could say that would provide the needed comfort. It required the sacrifice of spirit shapers to make the twisted lisincend.

"And you saw it?" she asked. "You saw the fortress burning?"

"What I could. When I communicate with Asboel, some of it comes in images rather than words. He showed me what he saw through his eyes, but he didn't explain what it meant."

"We never traveled all the way to the fortress. Mother kept us along the borders for the most part. Until she decided to drag us into the heart of Incendin. That's when the hounds got our scent and followed us. I remember seeing bright flames in the distance but not knowing what they were. What if that was the Fire Fortress?"

"I don't think anyone has ever really seen the Fire Fortress. Lacertin said he was trapped there for years, but other than him, no one really knows anything about what it's like in Incendin." Tan glanced over to the window, the curtains now closed and blocking most of the sound from the street below. Some wind whistled through the window and left the lower part of the thick curtain swirling on the ground. "Had I not made a mistake with the lisincend, we'd have him to ask."

Amia reached across the distance between them and touched his leg. "Do you really think he would've answered?"

Tan sighed. Was that what the lisincend had warned about before burning himself up? Had he known what Incendin planned? "I don't know. With enough spirit shaping, it's possible."

"Those twisted lisincend used spirit in their creation. It resisted any attempt I made at learning what it knew. There was no shaping we could have done that would have helped us."

"That's not the reason you wouldn't try," Tan said.

Amia wouldn't look at him. "I won't shape like *she* did." She took a deep breath and sat back in her chair. "There's something more that you're not sharing. What is it?"

"Incendin should be defeated. Fur was stopped. Alisz after him. They no longer have the First Mother to turn the Doma shapers. In spite of all that, the Fire Fortress burns brightly. If they're not creating new lisincend, what else could Incendin be doing? And now Asboel goes for vengeance, unwilling to bring me on the hunt with him."

"Good," Amia said. When Tan gave her a look, she shook her head, golden hair spilling down her shoulders as she did. "Let others worry about Incendin for once. Haven't you done enough?"

"Now you're sounding like my mother." He didn't mean for it to sound like an accusation, but it came out that way regardless. "And they're not defeated. Incendin still has its fire shapers. Lisincend remain. And the barrier no longer protects us from the hounds." With everything they'd been through, it felt as if they were in greater danger than ever. "We don't know anything about what Incendin will do next. Without the barrier, we're exposed. You've seen how hard it is to stop even one of the lisincend. If they continue to create more—"

Amia leaned toward him, heat flashing in her eyes. "We *will* stop them. And there are only so many fire shapers able to make the transformation."

Tan understood the draw of the power the shapers sought, but there was risk involved. From what Lacertin had shared, only about half the shapers survived the transformation. "Power can't be enough, not for that."

"Sometimes there is no why, Tan. Sometimes darkness and hate comes without reason. Can there be a reason why my people were destroyed? Why my mother was burned in front of me? Why the Aeta tortured me?" She shook her head. "If there's a reason, I don't want to hear it. After everything we've been through, we deserve a chance to find peace. *Both* of us deserve that. You've lost the same! Your home was destroyed. Your father was killed fighting Incendin. Even your king—"

Tan cut her off. "Althem was never my king."

Amia took a calming breath and swallowed, closing her eyes as she rested her head on her hands. "I wish we could stop running and fighting. I wish I didn't have to feel afraid anymore."

Tan pulled her toward him and wrapped his arms around her. He kissed her lightly on the lips. "I'm tired of being scared, too. The thought of losing you terrifies me."

She hugged him back and rested her head on his chest. "And now you want to find out what Incendin plans."

"The alternative is worse. If we wait—if there's something to the fires burning atop the Fire Fortress—we need to know. And Roine can help."

"He's too busy with the minutia of running the kingdoms."

"Then the other shapers. But I'm the only one who speaks to the elementals. There's a reason the Great Mother gave me this gift. I can't simply choose not to use it, not if I can keep others safe from what happened to me."

That had to be the reason he'd been given the ability to speak so easily to the elementals. From Asboel, Tan had the sense that there was a reason he'd bonded to the great fire elemental. From the nymid, he had the sense that there was a reason he and Amia had been brought together.

"What of my gift? I used to think the Great Mother blessed me to help the People, but now I have no people," Amia said.

They fell into silence, neither of them with answers.

The knock on the door startled him. Tan jumped to his feet and hurried to the door, pulling it open. His mother stood on the other side, her dark hair streaked with highlights of gray was pulled in a tight bun. Her gaze slipped past Tan to stare into the room, coming to rest on Amia. She sniffed silently.

"Mother? What time is it?"

"Time to begin your lessons," she said. "Come."

She started away without waiting for Tan or saying anything to Amia. He glanced back to see Amia nod but felt the sadness through their connection. Then he hurried out after his mother, taking only the time to grab a light cloak to protect from the evening chill.

His mother made her way down the street. The buildings here had not seen the same destruction as elsewhere in the city. Most were made of aged and faded brick and stone, though some were painted wood. A chill hung on the air and a few gusts of wind swirled around his mother's feet, almost as if ara worked playfully with her. Light burned in a few of the open windows, enough to see occasional shadows. Tan noted that saa flickered around the flames, as if drawn to them. He could almost *see* the lesser elemental, not only feel its presence.

When they reached an open area, Zephra grabbed his arm and, without a word, leapt to the wind with a quick shaping.

Tan had traveled with his mother's shaping before, but this time it was different. A face of ara flittered in and out, as if spying on Tan. As he watched, it seemed the face took on the same shape each time. Could she have bonded a single elemental much like he had with Asboel? He thought she spoke to *all* the wind elementals, but maybe that wasn't the case.

"Where are we going?" he asked as they traveled. Wind buffeted him, leaving him cold, nothing like when he traveled with Asboel. Then, he had the heat of the draasin's spikes, the warmth of his back, the solid connection. He had none of that now.

"After what happened earlier today, I'm taking you someplace where you can't harm yourself while you learn."

"I think I have enough control to keep from hurting myself."

"Fine. Prove it." She released his arm.

Tan tumbled from her, the protection of her shaping leaving him spiraling toward the ground. Wind streamed past his face. Tears streamed down his cheeks. He screamed, fumbling through the terror and chill as he reached for ara and failing. The wind elemental ignored him.

A patch of green came toward him frighteningly fast. He covered his face, praying to the Great Mother. Tan reached for golud, thinking to soften the ground, and tried for a shaping. This failed, too. Before crashing, he tried one more shaping, one of fire, attempting to press a burst of flame and steam away from him, but nothing seemed to work.

Then he slowed, landing with nothing more than a soft thump. His mother danced to a landing, giving him a satisfied smile as she did. "What was it you said about not hurting yourself?" she asked.

"I would have been fine had you not kept ara from me."

She snorted. "You think *I* can keep you from the elementals?" She strode over to a tree, now covered in shadows. Thin streamers of moonlight filtered through the branches of the tree, not enough to see more than shades of darkness.

Where had she taken him? Not far enough to get away from Ethea. The city glowed softly far in the distance, far enough away that he felt isolated. The connection to Amia came to him as a distant sense, as if his mother's shaping had severed the intensity of his connection to her.

A few scattered trees rose around them, but otherwise, they were surrounded by brown grasses with splashes of green muted in the night. Tan reached out with earth sensing, straining to learn where she'd taken him, and was surprised to realize it was Ter. He'd been through here one other time, when returning to Ethea with the kingdoms' shapers. Then, Ferran had led the group and Tan still had the hope that the king could be saved and that maybe he'd learn how to control his shaping.

"The elementals choose their connection, Tannen. I don't know how it is with fire, with your draasin, but ara must make a choice. Why do you think it took me so long to know whether I could return to help the kingdoms after the lisincend attacked Nor?"

"I thought because you'd died."

She turned to him and jumped the distance between them on a breath of air. The easy way she shaped still amazed him. She had control over the wind that he only dreamed of having. The closest for Tan was his ability with fire, but even with that, he struggled compared to what he saw from his mother.

"Must we continue to go through this?" she asked.

Tan took a deep breath and shook his head. "You needed to reach ara before you could escape from Nor?"

"I didn't think ara would respond to me. Not as it once had."

"Why?"

His mother tilted her head and Tan had the vague sense that she spoke to ara. Then she nodded. "I was bonded once."

"Once? As in before?"

She nodded. "When I served the kingdoms. You asked me why I was allowed to remain in Nor rather than being drawn back to Ethea? My bond was severed from me. The pain of it nearly killed me. Without your father, I think it might have." All these years later, there was pain in her words.

"How was it severed?" The idea terrified him. He'd grown so accustomed to feeling the presence of Asboel, of Amia, that he didn't know if he could tolerate the solitude.

"Elementals can die, Tannen. They can fight with us, but they can die with us, as we can die with them. The breaking of the bond in either way is devastating for the one who remains. Some scholars think that is why the elementals no longer bond as they once did."

"How? I mean, how did your elemental die?"

His mother moved on a cloud of air, hovering above the ground. "It was a difficult time. The war with Incendin… there were shapers lost on both sides. I was lucky, if you can call it that." She sighed, looking out into the night. "So when I learned that hounds had come to Nor, know that I understood what it meant. There was little I could do until I bonded again."

"You can do that?"

She turned and seemed to talk to the air. A slight smile came to her mouth. "I had been Ephra for so long that I didn't know, but ara remembered Zephra. I was too late to save Nor, but I can still save you. That is the reason ara allowed me claim another bond."

"I didn't know."

She sniffed. "There is much you don't know." She swept her arm around and wind rustled the leaves of the trees. A steady drawing to the air told him how she shaped, as did the constant pressure in his ears. "You've worried that you won't learn shaping without the elementals. And I understand that fear. Without my connection to ara, I'm not the same shaper. I would not have been able to disguise myself from you. I wouldn't have survived as long as I did in Incendin. I wouldn't have managed to withstand the king's shaping."

"You didn't withstand it," Tan reminded her but wished he hadn't, suddenly wondering if it would change her mind about helping him learn to shape.

His mother was a proud woman, and understandably so. Few matched her ability with wind shaping. Still, Althem had used her to get to Tan. Had Althem known about Zephra, he might not have tortured her, he might not have forced her to rely upon Tan saving her, the same as he had saved Roine and Cianna.

"I did not. You're right. Had I more strength with wind shaping alone, I might not have been as helpless when the First Mother severed my connection to ara. I've become reliant upon the elemental. Once, it might not have been the case, though I've always used my elemental connection to help with my shapings, but now I truly depend on it." She crossed her arms over her chest. "I should like you to not be quite as dependent as I am on using your elemental. I know you can shape without them. That power is within you. Ara has told me that most of your wind shapings come from you without their aid. That is what I will teach."

"Not how to speak to ara consistently?" That might be even more useful to him than anything else. Were he to manage speaking to ara with a better consistency, he might not need to worry about shaping. He had come to grips with the fact that he wasn't a shaper, not like those trained in the university. Didn't his ability came from the elementals?

"That might be the lesson you want, but it's not the lesson you need," she said. With a shaping, the wind died down.

Tan couldn't tell if it came from what she did or whether ara aided her. Either way, the sudden change was jarring. And impressive.

"I would like you to focus on your feet," she said. "Call to the wind. You may have to chase it in order to catch it, but let it swirl around your feet. I will know if you try to reach for ara."

Unlike Cianna, she implied. With the fire shaper, Tan had managed to replicate many of her shapings using the elemental power. What his mother expected of him was different.

Tan wanted to learn. He agreed that he *needed* to learn, especially after what he'd seen in Incendin. There was a part of him that wanted to tell her what he saw, but doing so risked her trying to keep him from it. And he couldn't deny that what he'd done so far had felt more like luck than anything else. For him to be effective and be able to help the kingdoms against Incendin, he'd need to really master his shaping. That meant knowing how to use both his shaping and that which the elementals let him borrow.

As his mother instructed, Tan focused on his feet. Wind could be difficult for him. Often, pulling a shaping of wind meant that he had to reach for the wind elemental for assistance. The only times it had really come easy was when he attempted to bind the elements together to make a spirit shaping. Then, his intent was different. He did not want to use the shaping of wind, but to use it to make the shaping of spirit.

The dust settled on the ground didn't move as he focused. Tan tried pulling on the wind, attempting to draw the shaping through him as he knew he needed to do. Pulling from outside of him would only use the elementals. With his mother here, he wasn't even certain he'd be able to use ara. Would ara respond to him when Zephra stood by, determined to have him master his own shaping, or would the wind elemental bow to Zephra's request?

Tan focused on what he had to do to simply speak to ara. That came on a breath of air, a delicate way of speaking that he had to be certain he didn't push too hard or he might upset the wind elemental. There was a playfulness to the elemental, different than what he noticed with the others, but could he use that knowledge to help him find the shaping he needed?

The shaping didn't come. As much as he wanted to pull from inside him, the shaping wasn't there. Tan could feel the draw of ara: were he to speak to it, there would be power at his fingertips, but the shaping wouldn't respond to him.

"I can't reach it," he said.

His mother sniffed. "Can you reach fire without speaking to the draasin?" Tan nodded and she frowned. "Why must it be different with wind?"

"I don't know. You're the Master shaper. Why can't you tell me why it's different for me? I hadn't even known how different my shaping was until I realized that almost everything I did was powered by the elementals. That was the only way I was able to stop Althem."

She ignored his frustration as easily as she had when he had been a child. "Try again. This time, focus on your breathing. Listen to the sounds of the wind around you."

"There *is* no wind around me."

"No? Then why can I hear it in every breath you take? How can I hear the way the leaves rustle softly? How can I hear the blades of grasses bending ever so slightly? Wind is always around us. More than any of the other elements, it is wind that gives us life."

Tan focused on his breathing. At least he could control that. At first, there was nothing but the steady sounds of his breathing. But with each breath, he recognized more. Slowly, he began to feel the air moving in and out of his lungs, the way it moved through his nose and mouth, sliding across his teeth. There was an almost imperceptible sound it made as it whistled through his nose.

He listened for other sounds of wind as his mother asked. There was the sound of her breathing, different than his. Her breaths were slow and steady, but he recognized the pattern from growing up around her. He shifted his attention to the sound of the wind in the trees. The air around him felt still, but was it? If she could hear the way it pulled at leaves, could he?

At first, no. Then, slowly, he noticed a distinct faint shimmering sound to the air. Tan focused on this, on the wind that might not be *moving* around him but that nevertheless moved.

With a breath of a shaping, he pulled through him, tying the connection to his breathing to the wind rustling around him. Leaves fluttered with a little more force and then the wind returned, blowing steadily.

He turned to his mother and smiled. "Like that?"

"That's better, but you take too long with your shaping."

"It's not natural to me to focus on my breathing before forming a shaping."

"And it's natural for you to simply push fire from yourself?"

"There's the bond with the draasin," he said. "That's why I can use fire."

"Hmm. I'm not certain it's quite so simple. You use fire easily, Tannen. I'd like you to have the same skill with one of the other elements. I can teach you wind. You understand the concepts, so I think you'll be able to reach for it more quickly each time you do. After a while, you'll gain enough practice that you won't rely on the elementals. There may come a time when they don't respond as you'd like." She took a leaping step on another gust of wind. "Now. Try again. This time, you will need to hold your focus while I try to prevent the shaping."

"You weren't preventing it before?"

She shook her head. "I simply caused the wind to fail. This time, I'll work against you. For you to gain strength, you'll need focus and speed. Failure of either around a more skilled shaper could put you at too much of a disadvantage."

"But I can shape *all* the elements."

She fixed him with a strange look. "Then show me. Stop me using any of the elements."

A sudden gust of air caught him off guard. She wrapped wind around him, holding him tightly. Tan pulled fire through him, burning the wind away. His mother glared at him and with a renewed shaping, lifted him to the air. Tan shifted his focus, this time reaching for the earth. The shaping didn't come and golud didn't respond. Tan reached for fire again, shaping the wind into a funnel, but his mother released the wind, drawing it away, drawing *fire* away, before again wrapping him in wind. This time, it nearly suffocated him.

"Enough," he managed to say.

His mother squeezed him again for good measure before releasing the shaping. "You rely on fire when another elemental would serve you better. You can fight wind with wind. You could have used earth against me. Even water would have worked. But always you reach for fire."

"I didn't want to hurt you."

She waved a hand as she laughed. "Fire can't hurt if it can't burn." She shook her head and fixed Tan with another hard look. "If I do nothing else, I will break you of the belief that you can only use the single element. Now, let's try again."

CHAPTER 6

Wind Elementals

TAN SAT ON THE STREET ALONE, exhausted from working with his mother. He knew he should return to the room with Amia and get some rest, but after the repetitive practice with wind shaping, he needed time to get his mind right.

Firelight danced in a few windows, and a few lanterns were lit along the street. A cool wind blew in from the north, but there wasn't much bite to it. Cold didn't bother him as it once did. Was that the connection to Asboel or was that from the fact that he'd learned how to shape? A hint of the moon peaked from behind dense clouds. The haze that hung over the city remained, but less intense than before. At least now, the stink of everything burning no longer overwhelmed him.

He couldn't shake the unease he felt at what was happening in Incendin. Even the practice with his mother hadn't shaken his concern. For the first time, he wasn't sure he *should* be the one to go into

Incendin. He might be able to speak to the elementals, but when his mother took him from Ethea, he had lost much of that connection. Only fire had responded. What would happen in Incendin when only fire *could* respond and he met shapers much more capable than him? What advantage did he have?

He sighed, letting out a breath of air, focusing on his breathing as his mother had instructed. This time, with a whisper, he called to ara. The wind elemental ignored him. That was always the chance he took with his type of shaping, the reason his mother wanted to teach him to master his shaping rather than depend on the elementals for assistance.

Tan still questioned his connection to the lesser elementals. Saa seemed to respond to him. With a quick shaping, he pulled forth a finger of fire, letting it dance over his hand. Once, this type of control would have been beyond him. This time, he actually *saw* saa flickering through the flame, adding to it. With an easy request, saa sent the flame swirling higher. Likely this was how he had shaped when working with Cianna so long ago. At the time, he thought maybe Asboel helped, but the distant sense of the draasin wouldn't have been enough to help guide his control.

Tan released the connection and then reached for it again, drawing forth fire, letting it flicker on and off. The dancing flame came without a challenge.

Why fire? Earth should be the easiest of the elementals for him. He'd known he was an earth senser first, long before ever learning that he could speak to the nymid or draasin. Earth *should* be the element that he shaped most easily. With wind, he never quite knew if it would respond. Ara treated him with a hint of respect, but nothing like what he sensed for his mother. Zephra was practically revered. Other than with Asboel, the only elemental he'd actually spoken to easily had been the nymid. After the evening of lessons, wind came easier, but still not easy. Would he ever manage the casual ability with the wind that his mother had?

Tan glanced up at the house. Amia would be there. He sensed her resting, warm by the hearth. He imagined her with a book spread across her lap, taken from the lower archives, one that she studied and tried to better understand.

After working with his mother, he had the urge to understand the elementals, all of them. The greater elementals might not respond to him outside Ethea, but would the lesser? If he could speak to them the same way he spoke to the greater elementals, he wouldn't need to depend on being in a place of convergence. Regardless of what his mother intended with her instruction, Tan wanted to ensure he could reach any of the elementals if needed. They would augment any shaping ability.

Tan started down the street, listening to the wind as he went as his mother had taught him. Ara was there, he was certain of it. The wind elemental might choose not to speak to him tonight, but that didn't mean he wouldn't try.

He closed his eyes as he felt a particularly strong gust. *Ara*, he called to the wind elemental. *Has Zephra forbidden you speaking to me?*

It whistled along the street before coalescing into a translucent face. *Son of Zephra.*

Were you watching today?

Ara seemed amused. *You have much to learn from Zephra.*

She thinks to teach me control so I don't need elementals to shape.

You have much to learn to match Zephra's control.

Tan laughed bitterly as he continued down the street. Another gust of wind hit him, this time a little warmer than the others. He focused on the way it played across his face and how it blew along the street. A hint of different aromas mixed on this wind.

Are there are other elementals of wind? Tan asked.

He worried about being too direct. With ara, there was always the risk of offending the elemental and losing the connection, but if he didn't try anything direct, he could spend the entire night simply trying to get a reasonable answer.

You don't want to speak to them, ara said.

At least that was answered. *They don't listen anyway.*

No, ashi and wyln are too serious. Ilaz should not be trusted. The face twisted, swirling around his head before settling alongside him.

Tan wondered what would make wind too serious or what might make an elemental untrustworthy, but couldn't come up with anything. What he needed was answers. If ara wouldn't provide them to him, he might need to find them on his own. That meant going to the archives. He should be exhausted after everything today, but he was too alert to be able to sleep.

Can you take me to the archives? Tan asked.

Ara pulled at his jacket for a moment and then leapt toward the darkness overhead. *You don't need ara for that, son of Zephra.*

Then ara disappeared, leaving Tan standing with wind drawing around him.

He tipped his head, focusing on the soft breeze and thinking of the lesser elementals ashi and wyln. Could he reach to them as he had with saa?

Tan whispered into the wind, murmuring for ashi, focusing as his mother had taught him earlier to use the steady swirls he felt within the wind and asking for the gusts to pick up. If they were anything like saa, they wouldn't be able to draw the same level of power as ara.

A sudden burst of warm wind struck him, lifting him off his feet so that he hovered in the air. Tan had the faint impression of a voice, almost as if talking to him. That was different than when he spoke to saa.

He whispered a request to be lowered to the ground. The wind elemental lowered him slowly and he stepped back onto the street. The breeze working around him shifted, now coming from the south. It felt a touch warmer, though that might only be his imagination.

Would it be the same with wyln? He let out a breath of a request, trying the same as he had with ashi. At first, nothing happened. Tan wondered if wyln would even bother answering. Maybe it was too weak to offer much assistance. No answer came. Finally, he tried the other wind elemental ara had mentioned, ilaz, not knowing what to expect. Probably nothing.

A steady, sharp wind tugged at him as it blew in from the east, hissing in his ear. It was a painful sound, almost angry. Tan sent a request for it to stop, but it didn't. Instead, it increased, pulsing against him.

Tan grabbed his head. *Ara*, he breathed.

The hissing, painful sound continued for another moment. Then it began to taper off, pushed back by a gust of cool air. A translucent face appeared briefly, as if admonishing him, and then disappeared.

With a shiver, he continued down the street, wondering if the other wind elementals served different purposes than ara. He would need to take the time to study and understand. Why was it that ara helped him and his mother, but ilaz seemed interested in tormenting him? Why had ashi lifted him but wyln did nothing?

He hadn't tried reaching the other lesser fire elementals to compare. Saa responded to him, but would inferin or saldam? Maybe they weren't even found around the city, though in a place of convergence, he expected to find *all* the elementals here.

Then there was golud. The earth elemental barely spoke to him. It rumbled responses but never really gave him reason to believe it did much more than answer him. Golud had helped several times, though. Using the earth elemental, Tan had managed to hide Asboel from the kingdoms' shapers. He had managed to ask golud to help put out the flames throughout Ethea. But could he actually speak to golud as he did the other elementals, or would he always be left with nothing more than the rumbling sort of response?

Tan reached the archives. He hadn't really intended to make his way here, but the questions coming to him seemed to guide his feet, drawing him toward the only place he might find understanding. He hurried through the upper levels of the archives, quickly lighting a few shapers lanterns as he went, before reaching the stairs leading down to the lower depths. He followed them down as they descended beneath the city. At the bottom of the stairs, he considered the doors, almost opening one only someone able to shape with all of the elements could open, but turned instead to a door that remained a challenge to him.

Made of a rich, dark wood, it took up most of the center of the hall, filling it. Tan had never managed to figure out the secret to opening it. It didn't respond to his shaping each of the elements, nor had it responded when he had pulled on the elementals he could reach.

Tan rested his hand on it. Runes were carved into the surface and up to now, he hadn't managed to get even a single one to glow. He tapped on the surface, hearing the dull *thunk* as he did before turning away. Now wasn't the time to go and try to understand how to open doors in the archive that failed to respond to him.

He debated going into the separate archive, the one where he had to bind the elements together to enter, but he wasn't much in the mood to read through the book there. Instead, he turned to the door leading to the underground tunnels beneath the city. With a shaping of spirit, Tan opened it and stepped inside.

Using a shaping of fire, he held a glowing light in his hand and made his way through the tunnels. He'd explored part of them since Althem's death, making his way to and from the palace through them, but hadn't really felt compelled to search how far they went. From what he'd seen, the tunnel extended past the palace, reaching deep beneath the city. Tan passed the pool of nymid where Roine had been destroyed, and barely glanced at the door which would take him into the palace dungeons.

The tunnel began to curve around. Smooth stone arched overhead. The ground was slick with green-tinted water. The constant sense of elemental power pressed on him, that of golud and the nymid. Here, beneath the earth, it was a constant sense.

At one point, another door opened off to the right. Tan paused and looked at it. He'd seen it before. Like the one leading into the palace, it was made of a plain oiled wood. The rune marking for spirit was carved on the surface. Tan touched it but did not shape it open. This led to an empty basement and out into the city. It was nothing more than a way for the archivists to move unseen.

He went on, following the slow curve. Darkness stretched before him, pushed away by the fire he held out in front of him. Tan pulled this shaping from himself, but it would have been a simple thing to ask saa to maintain it. As soon as he started the shaping, he felt saa drawn to it.

Was it like that with *all* shapings? Were the elementals drawn to them like saa was with a shaping of fire? He hadn't paid attention in the past, but then, he hadn't known enough about his abilities before. But how could elementals be drawn to all shapings? As far as he knew, spirit had no specific elemental, nothing but the pool drawn by the presence of all the elementals.

With a quick thought, he sent a request asking for saa to hold the shaping and released the effort he pushed into it. The elemental took it over willingly, holding fire in place without objection, almost as if it had only been waiting for the chance.

A steady breeze pulled through the tunnel, rustling his hair and sending the flame flickering slightly. He thought about asking ashi to draw along the wind, but he didn't know what would happen were he to ask that of the wind elementals. The power was so different than what he knew with fire. When his mother returned, he could ask her.

A little farther down the tunnel, he came across another door. This time, it was on the left side of the tunnel. Tan paused and studied the dark wood, reminded of the one back in the archives. A massive rune was carved into it, but not one that he recognized. The door was wide—much wider than any of the others—and taller than him, almost as if made for some massive person. Tan ran the hand not holding the flame overtop the surface. The wood was smooth and slick, as if the dampness beneath the earth left it saturated. There was no handle or any way that he could find to open it.

He turned away from the door and continued down the tunnel. The ground sloped slightly, leading him lower, though the ceiling appeared to remain at the same height. Tan frowned, pausing to glance up, but not finding any real reason for the changing slope. A few bits of rusted iron hung from the wall in places. He stopped at one of them and ran his finger around it. It crumbled as he touched it. There was a familiar sense to it, though it couldn't place what it was.

Further down the tunnel, there was another door, this one as large as the other. Like the other, only a single rune marked its surface to give any clue as to how to open it. Tan rested his hand on it, trying to listen for elemental energy, thinking there had to be *some* way for the door to open, but he sensed nothing.

He went onward. Gradually, a soft hissing mixed with the steady thud of his feet on the stone. Tan saw nothing that would explain the sound, but it reminded him of the uncomfortable sound made by the ilaz when he'd summoned it. As the sound intensified, Tan finally stopped, unwilling to go on any further.

How far had he walked beneath the city? How much farther would the tunnels reach?

He'd need to take more time. And perhaps not come down here alone.

The hissing came louder, as if sensing his unease. Tan stared into the darkness, looking for some explanation, but saw nothing. Debating whether he should continue onward and explore, he decided that he should not. As he turned, starting on the long walk back toward the lower archives, it seemed the steady hissing taunted him, a reminder of how little he knew of the elemental power he sought to control.

CHAPTER 7

Withdrawing Fire

LATE THE NEXT DAY, Tan sat in the archives, staring at the stack of books around him. A shapers lantern gave the room a soft light but he rubbed at his eyes, debating whether he should try another shaping of fire. He was tired from another lesson with his mother, and reminded again of how little he really knew. He'd managed to shape more effectively this time and had even whispered a silent request to ashi, wondering if his mother would notice him using a different elemental. Tan wasn't sure whether she did.

Why should he be able to open this door and not some of the others? He hoped he would find some way to understand the runes on the doors, but so far had not. The First Mother had taught all that she knew of the runes. That meant there was something else he hadn't discovered, whether it had something to do with the elementals or something else. The shelves around the room held texts—most older than anything he'd ever seen—that had somehow survived their time locked in the archives away from anyone else, but none that he'd gone through had anything that he could use to explain what he'd found.

He rubbed his eyes. How long had he slept? An hour or two, long enough to feel a little more alert but not enough to feel rested. He should return to Amia, but there should be something—*anything*—in the archives that could help him.

He sighed, listening as he did to the sound of his breathing. It was different from his mother's, with a unique rhythm and pattern all its own. Tan had no other way to explain it other than that. He reached for ara, but the wind elemental ignored him. It was there—he was certain of it—but it simply chose not to answer.

What of the others? He wouldn't try ilaz again, not without better understanding that particular elemental, but what of ashi? It had responded each time he reached for it, though it might not have spoken to him like ara did. As far as he could tell, none of the lesser elementals spoke to him, though that might simply be from lack of trying. Tan had learned how to speak to the greater elementals out of necessity, but couldn't the same be said for what he needed to do with the lesser elementals now?

Ashi.

Tan whispered the name. It came out on a soft breath, tied to the memory of how the wind elemental had felt. For a moment, Tan didn't think anything would happen, but then a soft tugging of a breeze flowed around him. It was warmer than anything he'd ever recognized with ara, reminding him of the warmth he felt when soaring with Asboel.

He waited, thinking the elemental might speak to him, but it didn't.

Tan sighed and shook his head. The wind eased before dying completely, leaving him sitting in silence once more.

He stood with a groan and shuffled, stiff, over to the shelves. There, he found a solid box made of marble and etched with runes. It had originally been in the lower archives when they had first opened the door. A soft lining of red satiny fabric lined the inside of the box. Tan had chosen this box to hold the artifact, laying it at an angle.

The top of the box was heavy and he shifted it to the side, setting it carefully down so as not to break it. Inside, the artifact rested, the runes along its surface glowing with a faint light. Since Althem had used it, the runes glowed constantly. Tan still didn't know the purpose of them all, but he knew that most tied the artifact to the elements used in powering it, but not all of them could be explained that way. Some were strange, even to the First Mother. He'd hoped there might be answers in the books in the archives, but he hadn't found any answers yet.

He stared at the artifact, resisting the urge to lift it and use it. Its power wasn't meant for him. It might not be meant for anyone. Why had the ancients made it? What did they know? Had there been something they hoped to save, or were they simply like Althem and the lisincend, driven by power?

With the artifact, Tan would have answers to any question he might ask. He could do anything, but that was the way to corruption. He already knew what would he do to protect those he loved: turn to fire for power enough to save them, practically change into one of the lisincend for it.

Tan pulled the cover back on the box, unwilling to keep looking at it.

He scanned a row of shelves lining the wall. Answers might be in one of the books sitting here, but he'd need to take the time to find them. He thought that was what he wanted—that having nothing but the time to sit and study these ancient volumes would make him happy—but he found himself getting restless. Incendin remained a threat.

Tan closed his eyes. *Asboel.*

Asboel pulsed in his mind, a steady presence. Once, the draasin had clawed through him as it fought for access, but now Tan had a peace with him. Asboel wouldn't overwhelm him. Perhaps he could not, now that Tan understood the connection between them.

Maelen. You should not have called.

Tan pressed through the connection to Asboel, trying to see what he saw. *Why should I not have contacted you? Are we not bonded?*

There came a delay. *We are bonded.*

Something strained Asboel. Tan caught flashes of landscape around him. Brown rock and a bleak expanse of land. No fire. Tan had only visited once before, but he suspected it was Incendin.

You shouldn't attack Twisted Fire on your own. Let me hunt with you.

You are not ready for this hunt. There are more than before. The draasin will cleanse Twisted Fire from these lands.

There is danger in those lands. You were the one to show it to me.

There is more danger than you know.

What is it?

Tan wasn't certain Asboel would answer. Then he let out what came through their connection as something like a sigh. *Fire.*

An image of the fortress burned suddenly bright in Tan's mind, flames leaping from it. What did it mean for fire to return to Incendin with such intensity?

You should not return. Twisted Fire is dangerous, Tan said.

This is more than Twisted Fire.

I don't understand.

Nor do I. We will learn. Then perhaps you may hunt with us.

The bond conveyed more, a hint of emotion that Asboel sought to hide from him.

We are bonded. You must share. I might be able to help.

The irritation surged more brightly. *You cannot help with this, Maelen. It is Enya.*

Tan's heart fluttered. The last time the youngest of the great fire elementals had been involved with anything, part of the city had been destroyed, burned while the archivists controlled her. Had something similar happened?

Twisted Fire? Tan asked.

They do not have her.

What is it then?

She seeks revenge for the hatchlings.

And you do not?

Not like this.

Another image came to Tan. In it, he saw fire burning across already desolate plains. The ground was scorched and twisted, destroyed by time and the effect of fire, but made worse by whatever Enya had done. It was not simply a fire shaping, but something different and darker.

Is that fire? Tan asked. The way the earth seemed shifted and changed by the shaping of fire left him uncertain. He couldn't imagine the power that would have been necessary to create such a shaping. More than what he'd seen in Ethea after the attack, though there had been Incendin shapers involved as well.

That is Fire.

To Asboel, it was clear there was a distinction.

What does she do?

She seeks to withdraw fire from these lands.

Can such a thing be done?

Asboel went silent for a time. *Not easily, but it can be done. If she succeeds, it will be my fault. I shared with her the process. Doing so makes her stronger, but changes her as well.*

As fire changed me?

It is different, Maelen.

Tan wondered if that were true. Fire changing Enya seemed not all that different from what had happened with him. *Where is she now?*

She remains in the waste.

An image of Incendin came through the connection. *In Incendin?*

I will keep her away. Remaining is too dangerous.

You don't want revenge for what happened with the hatchlings, too?

Vengeance will come in time, Maelen. Asboel paused. *You must stay away. If she withdraws fire, it could damage one like you connected to fire.*

Would she hurt me?

Tan sensed the uncertainty in Asboel. *Not intentionally, but you would not be safe. With what she does, it is possible she would manage to withdraw fire from you as well.*

The bond would not protect me?

Not from this. Your other gifts from the Mother might help, but I am not certain.

What can I do? There must be something, Tan said.

You must stay away. Even I must stay away as she does this, or I risk the same damage. Now you must not interfere. What I do next is difficult.

And if you fail?

Asboel seemed amused by the idea. *You distrust me so much as that?*

You know that I don't. Tan wished he could help, wished there was something Asboel would let him do, but without having mastered shaping the other elements, anything he could do would be limited. *I will be ready to help if you summon.*

There was a pause before Asboel answered again. *I will be careful, Maelen. Do not fear for me. I have survived much worse than you will ever imagine.*

Then Asboel receded, leaving him with only the most distant of senses of the draasin.

CHAPTER 8

Earth Master

MASTER FERRAN STARED AT TAN, his lean face unreadable. "You lose focus easily. Earth does not answer as quickly as some of the elements."

Tan doubted that Ferran knew how earth answered compared to fire or water, both of which would respond to him more easily. Yet he was an earth senser first. It was the one gift his father had left him with, knowledge of how to stretch out with his senses and listen to everything around him. He had been an earth senser far longer than he had been anything else. Why was it so *hard* for him to reach earth for a shaping?

They stood in Ter, brought away from Ethea on a shaping of wind, Zephra dumping him almost in an attempt to prove how much he relied on the elementals while in Ethea, but even there, golud did not answer as quickly as the others. Tan *felt* it there but sometimes struggled to reach it, to speak to it even as he did with ara.

A wide field of flowing grasses, now drying in the autumn air and turning to brown, pressed against the wind. Hills rolled around him and trees dotted the hills, nothing like the thick forests of Galen. The wind blowing out of the north held an edge to it, a cold bite that slipped through his heavy cloak. Tan resisted the urge to shape fire and warm himself.

"My father never taught me shaping of earth," he told Ferran.

"You still know of it. That is enough, I think. You are a skilled earth senser, if you take the time to reach for it."

Tan didn't miss the implication. Even Ferran thought he went too easily toward fire.

"To become the warrior you are capable of being, you will need to master all of the elements. Zephra tells me wind is coming along. You have shown promise with water. And we know how well you manipulate fire."

Water came along only because Tan had connected to the nymid first. Despite the lack of an active bond with the nymid, Tan shared a connection to it that was unique, and nothing like what he shared with the other elementals. It granted him the ability to shape water more easily, not requiring the same strain that he felt when trying to shape wind or earth.

"Zephra taught me to focus on my breathing. What is your trick?"

Ferran looked offended by the question. "Trick? There is no trick with earth. Earth is everything. It is power and creation. It is life."

Tan noted that shapers of each element felt the same way. Perhaps they were each right, in their own way. "How do you shape, then?" he asked.

"Earth shaping is within the shaper. It lies deep within you, tying you to the land. When you feel it—when you can easily reach for it—you will understand and the shaping will come. Golud will not always be present, Tannen. That golud lives within Ethea is a boon, but not one that must be counted on."

He'd found golud outside of Ethea, but then, he'd been at another place of convergence. What would happen when he went searching for earth elementals outside of Ethea and they didn't answer? Would it be as his mother suspected, or would he manage to reach one of the other earth elementals, one he had yet to learn of?

He tried reaching for golud, sending a slow, rumbling sort of request to the earth elemental, and waited. There came no response. Maybe this was the elemental's way of teaching him that he needed to control his shaping or he'd run the risk of not reaching the elemental when needed.

Tan took a deep breath and thought about what Ferran had said. If earth was found deep within him, could he draw it out much as he drew out fire? He was still not certain fire wasn't tied to him by the elementals, but there was no doubting the fact that he could shape fire easily. Even here in Ter, far from Ethea, he only had to reach and fire would answer. How could he do the same with earth?

What would his father have said? All of his early lessons with sensing had come from his father, not his mother. For so long, Tan had thought it because his father was an earth shaper while his mother was a wind shaper, but if she'd lost her connection to the wind, if that bond had been severed, she might not have been able to teach him. The thought of losing the connection to Asboel left him feeling nothing but emptiness.

His father had taught to stretch out his senses around him, to *listen* to the earth. Tan did as his father had instructed all those years ago. It seemed so long since he'd actively used his earth sensing. As he did, he felt the connections stirring around him, the sense of everything blooming around him. The grasses, the insects crawling along the ground, the rabbits and field mice burrowing, himself and Ferran disturbing the earth around themselves. Could he use that connection to shape earth without needing the elementals?

The first attempt he made did nothing. Neither did the second. Both left him feeling weakened from the effort. On the third attempt, he did nothing more than try to bend the grasses flat around him.

The earth rumbled softly in answer.

"Good, but was that you or the elemental?" Ferran asked. He performed a quick shaping, sending the earth heaping around him so that he rose to stand taller than Tan.

If Ferran could shape like that, how was it that it took so long for them to rebuild the university? Strength like that should give him the ability to pull the stones and stack them back into place, building up what the draasin had knocked down.

"That was me," he answered. How long had it been since a shaping of earth—one of any substance that he had done on his own rather than a shaping meant to bind with the other elements—had come from him rather than through golud? Tan couldn't really remember.

"It is a start. Do you know what it is that you did?"

"I started with sensing, connecting to everything around me. Once I did that, then I was able to use that to create the shaping."

Ferran used another shaping and the earth smoothed again, looking as if nothing had changed. Tan thought he could sense what it was that Ferran had done. It was much like when Cianna first taught him fire. The more often he paid attention when a shaper was working with the shaping, the easier it was for him to create.

"You must practice," Ferran said. "Shaping of plants or even trees requires little power. It is moving and manipulating the earth itself that really tests the shaper. Your father had a particular talent with it."

"I wouldn't know," Tan said.

Ferran's face barely changed, but the earth seemed to rumble softly beneath Tan's feet as if in answer. "You know the lessons he taught you. They were the lessons that helped you survive against Incendin when you first went with Theondar. I believe you told me how you managed to evade both hounds and the lisincend? Even a powerful senser would struggle against such odds."

Ferran twisted so that he looked toward distant Ethea. The faint lights of the city were only just visible. "And then you managed to hide the draasin from me. Golud may have helped, but that doesn't change the fact that without training, you still managed to hide one of the elementals from a Master shaper. I would say that Grethan's lessons served you well. My hope is that what I can teach will build on that and perhaps give you a way to reach for earth without the elemental power, as Zephra continues to work with you on wind."

Tan agreed that he needed to become more skilled with shaping. If he hoped to be of any use to Asboel or even the kingdoms as they faced whatever it was that Incendin planned, he would need to have complete mastery.

"What do you do when you begin your shaping?" Tan asked.

Ferran nodded, as if pleased by the question. "I begin each shaping as you described. The shaper must be connected to earth to have any control over it."

"How do you do it so quickly?"

Ferran made a motion with his hand, sweeping it all around him. "I've learned to never lose the connection to earth. As soon as I do, the shaping changes."

The fact that Tan no longer knew how to remain in constant contact with his earth sensing told him how much he had changed since first leaving Galen. Back then, he had used his earth sensing to track through the mountains. It had been a game for him and his father, and then later, it had been how Tan managed to hunt and serve as one of the most skilled trackers in Nor. Cobin always had some talent, but not the same as Tan or his father.

Not for the first time, Tan wondered if Cobin and Bal had managed to find safety. The last time he'd seen them, Cobin had provided part of the distraction that had enabled Tan to reach Amia. Without that distraction, would he ever have become the person he was now? How had they adjusted without Nor? When everything finally settled down, Tan vowed that he would find Cobin, but so far there had not been the time. Maybe there would never be the time to find his friend. Given how much had changed, perhaps that was best. And what of Lins Alles? Other than Bal and Cobin, he was the other survivor from Nor. Had he gone to Incendin or did he find some small village someplace in the kingdoms to hide?

Tan shook away those thoughts and stretched out with his earth shaping again. Muted by lack of use or the fact that Tan relied so heavily on fire, it was a different sense than it once had been. Then, it had been all that Tan had known. Now, other senses competed. Water and wind might not be as powerful for him as fire, but he could sense them as well.

The sense of the earth around him was solid. He tracked along, pressing through the grasses and rolling hills and stretching as far as he could, moving into the flatlands. He lost the connection there. Once, he would have managed to reach all the way into Nara, but the sense was weak now, nothing like what he needed. With practice, Tan hoped to regain some of that skill.

His mother had instructed him to focus on his breathing to reach for the wind; how was this any different? Fire was no more difficult for him than drawing it through him, but maybe that was because he was in constant contact with it. He didn't *have* to sense fire; because of Asboel, it filled him.

As he held the contact with earth, he sensed a change around him. Wind blew with more force than it had before. Tan pulled back his connection, drawing it in, and realized that the wind was shaped. Zephra returned.

She glanced from Ferran to Tan as she came to land, the wind stirring the leaves around her. "I'm sorry to disturb your lesson, Ferran, but I would like your assistance with something."

His eyes narrowed and Tan felt his shaping build. It lingered for a long moment and Tan sensed its intent, how it was made to listen, augmenting Ferran's ability to sense. "Yes. I think Theondar would appreciate my help," he agreed. He turned back to Tan. "Continue to practice until I return."

"I can help," Tan started.

His mother cut him off with a shake of her head. "You are the student now, Tannen. The university may have fallen and the Masters may not be as powerful as they once were, but that much has not changed."

She waited for Ferran to step next to her and then lifted them on a shaping of wind.

Tan stared after, watching them disappear. At least there was no one around to see how angry he was that his mother had again chosen to leave him, as if he were completely incapable of doing anything to help the kingdoms. He had shown his worth over and again, and still she thought to shield him.

But it wasn't even that fact that bothered him the most. It was the possibility that whatever she needed Ferran's help for had to do with whatever kept Asboel silent. Since warning him of what Enya planned, Asboel had remained completely silent. That didn't necessarily mean anything; there had been many times since they bonded where Asboel had gone silent, but this felt different in some ways.

As Tan watched the wind carry off his mother and Ferran, he decided he had to know.

Did he dare attempt a shaping that would bring him toward Incendin? Maybe he didn't have to reach Incendin itself. From Ter, he could reach Galen and peer over the border from there. He knew shapings that could help, if only they would work.

He started with fire. Not only because it was the easiest, but the chill air left it difficult for him to fully concentrate. When he mastered a shaping of warmth around him, he focused on his breathing, slowing and pulling on wind. It came slowly at first but seemed drawn by the warmth he had shaped, lifting him with a gust of wind that held him much like he'd been lifted by the lesser wind elemental. Tan used earth to stabilize himself.

Roine had once shown him how warriors traveled, but Tan knew he wasn't ready for that sort of shaping. This might not be as quick, but he could use it.

The shaping took him up. With a little effort, he realized he could direct the wind, drawing him over Ter and sweeping high over the countryside.

He had passed the border of Ter when the shaping faltered. The wind slowed and died. Tan flailed at it, using the shaping of fire to keep him aloft, but even that began to leave him and he tumbled to the ground. All around him were trees, the hills of Ter starting to slope upward into the mountains of Galen.

Wind suddenly whipped around him and he looked up to see his mother come in on a shaping of air. She glared at him as she landed. Ferran was with her and stood behind her, watching Tan with an unreadable expression.

"What do you think you were doing, Tannen?" she demanded.

Any answer would like draw her ire, so he went with the one that fueled his concern. "The draasin is in danger. When I last spoke to him, he warned me of what was happening—"

She sniffed and waved her hand to the south, toward Incendin. "The draasin? You fear your draasin? From what I saw, the draasin is fine. The lisincend the little one chose to attack might be another matter."

Lisincend? Asboel would have reached out to him were the lisincend involved, wouldn't he? And if it were Enya attacking… then maybe Asboel had stopped whatever she intended.

"I would think that if your draasin wanted your assistance, he would have come for you. That he hasn't means that what he intends does not require your help," his mother went on. "And seeing how easily I managed to prevent you from traveling, I think that is for the best."

She turned to Ferran. "I will return Tannen to Ethea and then come for you. You and I will continue what we had begun."

"If you wish, Zephra," Ferran said.

Zephra came over to Tan and grabbed his arm.

"Mother, I can help."

She shook her head. "You have been lucky so far with what you've managed to do, Tannen, but I will not have you getting yourself killed simply because you're too stubborn to recognize what you don't know."

They lifted into the air, the shaping of wind whistling around them and carrying them back toward Ethea. Tan didn't even fight; it would have done no good had he tried. Zephra's connection to the wind was too strong for him to counter it.

"You wonder why I don't approve of Amia, but if she truly cared about you, she wouldn't let you attempt this either."

With that, they moved too quickly toward the city for Tan to answer. He wouldn't have known what to say anyway.

CHAPTER 9

Zephra's Return

TAN STOOD IN THE UNIVERSITY YARD, practicing wind shaping, ignoring the earth shapers struggling to repair the courtyard. Unlike the archives and the lower parts of the city, golud didn't infuse the walls of the university, at least not with enough strength to keep it standing. But the central stone area where warriors had once landed with regularity remained intact.

As his mother instructed, he focused on his breathing first, listening to the sound of his breaths, each one moving through him steadily. Since returning him to Ethea, there had been no more sessions with her. Days had passed and he still hadn't learned what she had found in Incendin, and Asboel remained painfully quiet. Neither had tamped his anger with her.

Instead, he practiced shaping on his own, determined not to let her control him again. He fixated on the way the wind flowed around him as he breathed, the sense of the breeze playing along his skin and hair. The shapings came, each time with less difficulty. He was tempted to draw on the elementals, but he would do this on his own.

He breathed out a sigh, thinking of ashi and how the wind elemental responded to him better than ara. With the thought, a warmer breeze gusted in from the south. Tan held the connection for a moment. As he did, he could feel the control available to him, a shaping that he would only have to push away and he would have it mastered. He let it go.

Why should this wind elemental work for him when ara did not?

Perhaps his mother could answer, though after the way she'd been treating him, he hesitated going to her with questions about the elementals. She wanted him to master shaping without relying on them, but Tan suspected it was all tied together. Hadn't he learned to shape fire better *because* of his connection to Asboel rather than in spite of it?

Tan turned Tan turned to Amia, who sat atop one of the rocks that had fallen. From its enormous size, it looked like it had come from one of the lecture rooms. She stared blankly, a distant look in her eyes. She'd been that way since he began working with his mother.

"You don't have to wait for her," Tan said.

"No. This is something you said you must do. I'll be here with you when she returns."

Tan had spent the better part of two days angry with Zephra. Now he would have answers. "I will find out what she knows about Asboel." His silence had bothered Tan as much as anything. "He's family now."

He regretted mentioning anything about family almost immediately.

"It's fine," she said.

He touched her arm and tried to pull her toward him in a hug. She resisted for a moment. "You're family, too," he said.

She rested her head on his chest. "You know I feel the same way. But I wonder what else is there for me? I'm a spirit shaper who was meant to lead the People, only there aren't a people for me to lead."

"There are many ways you can still serve."

"Not where I'm trusted. If your mother won't, what makes you think anyone else will? What will I ever do that's useful?"

Tan wanted to tell her that she would be useful, that there were many things she could do, but he had many of the same doubts. With Asboel telling him to stay away from Incendin, his mother treating him as if he'd never left Nor, and Roine not willing to meet with him to discuss his concerns, he felt as impotent as he had before he'd learned any control over the elemental powers. He held Amia, hoping she understood.

Where was his mother, anyway? When he had found the rune glowing on the coin, he knew she'd be returning soon.

Finally, a gust of wind swirled around him. Tan looked up to see her land on a thick pillow of air. Wind whipped around her, pulling at her dark hair. Wrinkles pulled at the corners of her eyes and her mouth twisted in an expression Tan recognized as disappointment. He wished she had not given it to Amia as well.

Tan clutched the small silver coin in his hand, the rune marked across its surface distorting the image of the king's face that had once been there. The summoning rune glowed softly. It hadn't taken Tan long to determine where to find her. There were only a few places in the city where it was safe for a shaper to land, otherwise too much force and energy would be thrown around, leading to the sort of destruction the city had too recently faced.

"Tannen," she said. Ara flittered about her head, barely more than a translucent face that faded as the wind died.

Tan studied her clothes, noting the thin wool pants she wore and the scarf she had wrapped around her neck. A leather satchel hung from her shoulder. "You left the kingdoms again."

"You're questioning your mother?" she asked.

"I'm questioning Zephra."

She sniffed and started down the street toward the palace. "Is that any different? I seem to recall that *I'm* the Master shaper. You were to be studying anyway. Is that what you're doing here?" His mother started away from the university without waiting for his answer, and Tan followed. Amia remained silent as she walked at his side. She held his hand but fixed her gaze straight ahead, focused on the palace in the distance, unmindful of everyone they passed.

"Have you found Elle?"

His mother shot him a look. "What makes you think I went searching for her?"

Tan nodded toward the satchel. "That was hers, I believe. I seem to remember the way she stuffed it full of books."

His mother's frown softened. "It was her grandfather's. I used to see him with it all over the university. He was much like Elle. Loved the archives, even if he didn't understand why the archivists wouldn't allow him to reach the lower levels."

They continued toward the palace, the streets becoming increasingly empty the closer they came. Here, in the center of the city, the destruction had been most severe. This hadn't been done by the draasin. That attack had affected other areas of the city, leaving the university damaged, but the palace had been well protected by Ethea's shapers. When the lisincend came, invited by Althem in his attempt to control the artifact, a different type of destruction had taken place.

"You summoned Roine. What did you find?"

She fixed him with an annoyed expression. "Yes. Roine. Not you."

"You won't keep me from what's happening in Incendin. If the draasin are involved, I *need* to know. Besides, I'm a warrior shaper."

"Not yet. You might be something else, but you are not a warrior yet." She said it with such emphasis that it felt like a slap to Tan.

"Then what exactly am I?"

She hesitated as she met his gaze. The corners of her mouth tightened. "You can be too much like your father at times."

"I'll take that as a compliment," he said.

"You should."

She turned toward the palace. Here, the destruction was worse than in other parts of the city, even when compared to the city surrounding the palace. They were forced to climb over piles of rock to make their way. This gave a certain protection to the palace not afforded to the rest of the city. The shapers attempting to repair the city had not done much here. The rest of the city needed what strength they could offer first. Zephra lifted onto a finger of wind, drifting in a controlled fashion above the rock.

Tan shot her a look and took Amia's hand.

When he caught up to his mother, he saw that ara swirled around her, aiding in her shaping. "You use ara nearly as much as I use the fire elementals," he said.

"Only because I know how to shape wind, even without ara," she said. With a quick step, she took to the air and spun to face him. The translucent face of her bonded elemental again appeared near her cheek. "In time, when you master your shaping and if you bond to wind, you will learn the subtleties that it can offer."

Amia shook herself and turned to Zephra. "You only speak to one of ara? How is it that you can shape as you do?"

His mother considered Amia for a moment as if debating whether to answer. "Ara can take many shapes, many forms, but the wind is powerful and my own shaping ability adds to what ara allows me to do, giving me even more strength." She frowned at Amia. "How else do you think I managed to take on another's face for so long?"

Her face rippled, the translucent form of ara shimmering around her. Sarah appeared, bearing similarities to Zephra. Now that Tan knew what he did, he could see how she hid her features, but it was subtle.

Zephra settled back to the ground and her face reappeared as they stepped into the wide courtyard surrounding the palace. The grounds had been completely destroyed here, the earth heaved by Althem's shaping and that of the warriors chasing him, but time and Roine's shaping had restored much of it to what it had been. It still wasn't as Tan had first known it to be, with images and scenes from each area of the kingdoms, but there wasn't the reminder of the death and destruction that had come through here.

The shaping that had once prevented others from shaping within the courtyard had lifted as well. Tan wondered if the shaping had been over the courtyard or whether it had covered the entire palace. Either way, it was gone, left as nothing more than a memory.

Servants led them inside the palace and guided them toward a narrow room on the first level, passing a row of portraits of the previous kings. Tan had seen them before, had spent time speaking with Roine about their significance. He was surprised to see the portrait of Althem hanging on the wall, eyes that once attempted to look warm and inviting now nothing more than hard and calculating.

How much damage had been done because of his spirit shapings? Tan paused and studied the portrait, thinking of all the terrible things Althem had done. All to try to reach the artifact, to control power. It had all been rendered futile with one snap of Asboel's jaws. Maybe the Great Mother had welcomed him back, but Tan hoped not. Let him wander in the Void, let him be claimed by the emptiness the priests spoke of for those undeserving of the Great Mother.

Amia touched his arm. "Tan?" she whispered.

He took a deep breath and turned away from the portrait. "I'm sorry."

"I sensed… darkness within your thoughts." She kept her voice low and pulled him to the side. Zephra walked ahead but her posture made it seem as if she listened.

Tan glanced over at the portrait of Althem. "I thought I was over what happened, but maybe I'm not."

Amia gripped his arm. "I'm not sure we'll ever have the answers we want, Tan. Why did the First Mother abandon the core beliefs of the Aeta? Why would she use her abilities to force others to serve Incendin?"

"At least she could claim she protected her people."

"Could she?" Amia asked, pulling him to a stop. Zephra kept going before realizing they had stopped. She turned to shoot them a look. "I'd argue that she put the Aeta in more danger because of her actions. She sided with Incendin, against the kingdoms. Far better to have made bargains with people who wouldn't take you and torment you as part of some twisted ritual to serve fire."

Tan hesitated, wondering if he should tell Amia about the regret that filled the First Mother. "She wishes she had done things differently," he said.

"Don't we all."

Tan took her hands. "You should speak to her. Maybe it will help you find—"

"Find what? Peace? Forgiveness? The People are scattered now and there is no one to lead them. That is on her."

"The People should not suffer for what she did."

"But they do. Can't you see that? Even were there someone able to lead them, they suffer. There is no more Gathering. There are no more Aeta." She turned away from him and tried to let go of his hands but he wouldn't let her.

"Then you should lead," he said.

She tensed and stopped pulling. "I'm not sure I can. Or that I want to."

Tan didn't need to feel the pain through the bond to know what she was feeling. It was in her voice and the way she hung her head. It was the pain that had plagued her since learning of the First Mother. "I will help you with whatever you need," he said softly.

She looked over and a sad smile came her lips. "I know you will."

They continued down the hall toward his mother. Tan held tightly to Amia's hand. Whatever else was happening with Incendin, he had to figure out a way to help her, too. Only, he didn't know how.

Roine emerged from a door at the end of the hall. His hair had grayed in the last few weeks, but it gave him a more regal appearance. He wore a thick green jacket, plain and without any embroidery, and black pants tucked into his boots. A weary smile greeted them.

"I hadn't expected all of you. You said Tannen was taking time to learn shapings."

Tan shot his mother a hard look. Had she been the reason Roine had kept his distance?

Zephra made a point of not looking over at him. "It seems that one made certain to attune to my rune."

"I did nothing but copy it," Tan said.

His mother gave him a disapproving look, one he'd seen so many times growing up.

"How are you, Theondar? You look tired," Zephra said.

He motioned them into the room. High ceilings towered over walls of smooth white alabaster. A long table filled the middle. Shapers lanterns hung on columns spaced evenly throughout the room and for a second, Tan mourned the loss of knowledge of how to build them.

Roine stood behind a wide chair carved with shapes of the elementals and pulled it away from the end of the table. It served as the throne for the kingdoms, the seat of power. And now it was Roine's. He waved for everyone to take seats of their own. Zephra arched a brow, and he smiled back at her sheepishly. "I never wanted to sit in this chair," he said.

"It suits you, Theondar. Maybe it wouldn't have suited Roine, but it does you."

He shook his head. "I will lead until an heir comes forward."

Zephra used a shaping of wind to position a different chair near enough for her to sit in. Tan and Amia took seats on the other side of the table, facing them.

"Do you think another will come forward? Althem was not known to have any heirs," Zephra said.

Roine snorted. "Perhaps not officially, but he had his dalliances, as his father did before him."

Zephra rested her head on her hands. For the first time, Tan noticed how tired she looked. What had she been doing that kept her away from the kingdoms? It was about more than searching for Elle, he was certain of that.

"Ilton was devoted to Queen Asinna," Zephra said.

"While she lived," Roine agreed. "But after her death, he was a little less discreet. Most in the palace knew."

"You weren't in the palace. Not like Lacertin."

Roine's face still clouded slightly at the mention of Lacertin's name. "No. I wouldn't have been, but Althem had a loose tongue and shared with me what took place within the palace." He shook his head. "Regardless, Althem began to take after his father, sneaking serving girls to his quarters at first. From what I've been able to determine, he began moving on to more difficult conquests." He said the last with disgust.

"If Althem told you about his father, how do you know you can even believe it?" Tan asked. "Everything we know about Althem could be a lie. With his ability to shape spirit, he could have made you believe whatever he wanted and you'd be no wiser to it."

Roine sighed as he turned to Tan. "That's been the hardest part of agreeing to lead. I've been forced to try and separate what was real and what illusion Althem had created through his spirit shaping. I'm still trying to understand." He leaned back in his chair and crossed his legs.

Tan wondered if he realized that it made him seem more regal. Perhaps Theondar had never really left. Maybe he'd have to stop thinking of him as Roine.

"You mentioned other conquests," his mother said. She seemed to struggle to keep her voice even. "What conquests do you know of?"

Roine glanced at Tan before shifting his attention to Zephra. "I knew of the serving girls. For years, I'd always looked the other way. I assumed they thought the idea of being with the king too enticing. Few ever made any noise, and I suspect Althem never gave any the reason to believe they would ever be anything *more* than what he used them for."

Amia tensed and Tan felt her irritation through the bond. "You mean he shaped them."

Roine's face fell. "I understand that now. I can't imagine the horrors he has done throughout the years without any knowing."

"It's why spirit was closely monitored," Zephra said, making a point of looking at Amia.

"Those of us blessed by the Great Mother have been taught to use our gifts for our people. Not for something like... like *this*."

"There seem to have been many ways spirit shapers have learned to use their gifts," Zephra started. "The archivists sought to use them on our shapers. The First Mother used them on Doma shapers—"

"Enough, Mother," Tan snapped.

She opened her mouth and then closed it again, pulling her eyes off Tan and almost forcing herself to focus on Roine. "There is more?"

Roine scrubbed a hand over his face. "That's the part I'm having the most trouble with understanding." He looked at Amia. "Maybe it's good that you came. I might need your help to know exactly what happened. At some point, Althem must have become bored with servants. He seems to have moved up to those with more power. Daughters of merchants. Local land owners of power. Sensers."

Tan already suspected where Roine was going. "Not only sensers."

"I'm not certain, but I think so. I don't have any way to prove it without Amia." Roine looked at her. "I'll need your help. If anyone can help me untangle this mess, it is you."

Tan felt a fluttering of uncertainty through their bond. "I… I'm not sure I can do what you ask. After seeing what *she* did, I haven't been willing to use my ability." She fell silent, looking down at her hands. Tan reached for her but she pulled away.

Zephra cocked her head as she studied Amia. "He sought an heir who could shape?"

Roine breathed out with a sigh. "I think so."

"Why?" Tan asked. "What would it matter if he did this to someone who could shape or not? It's disgusting either way."

"Horrible, yes, and the reason for it was that we've always known shapers were more likely to bear shapers. And when two shapers come together?" She nodded toward Tan. "Well, much power can come."

Roine sat up and looked from Tan to Amia. "I don't know how many shapers were used. Maybe I'm wrong. The Great Mother knows

I hope that I am, but if I'm not and there *is* an heir out there, I can't sit and pretend I didn't know."

"Does it change anything?" Tan asked. "After what Althem did, why should their bloodline remain in power? Why not you, Theondar?"

Roine shook his head. "That's not how it works, Tan. There has been little unrest so far, but if word begins to spread that there's an heir and I've ignored it, it could lead to a fight for the throne. The kingdoms have known peaceful succession for hundreds of years and without knowing what is going on with Incendin—"

"Or Chenir," his mother said. "I don't understand; Chenir is active in ways I have not seen before."

"What of Doma?" Roine asked.

"I didn't reach Doma. After what I saw in Incendin," she glanced at Tan, "I didn't take the time to visit Doma. They have always been somewhat protected. The narrow connection between Incendin and Doma keeps them safe."

And, Tan noted she didn't say, there was some hope that Elle had reached the udilm. If the water elementals intervened, she would be able to keep Doma safe, as it always had been.

"What did you find in Incendin?" he asked.

"The draasin attacked the lisincend. Perhaps they will do our work for us. Other than that, Incendin is afire, but what else is new?" she asked.

"The Fire Fortress burns more brightly than it has since they created the twisted lisincend," Tan said. "Does that matter?"

Zephra turned to him, anger flashing on her face. "How do you know that the Fire Fortress burns?"

Tan pushed away from the table. "You're not the only one bonded to an elemental, Mother. Regardless of what I've learned of shaping, I'm not the child you still remember me to be."

"That's not an answer."

"No more than you answered me."

"Easy," Roine said. He set his palms on the table. "Incendin is active. We know that much. And you're right, Tan. From what we can tell, the Fire Fortress burns brighter. Were Lacertin still alive, we might know what that means."

"The draasin are nervous," Tan said. "I'm not sure what they know about the flames, but they worry that Incendin is active."

He said nothing about what Asboel told him of what Enya attempted. His mother hadn't mentioned anything other than an attack, so maybe there was nothing more to it. From what Asboel said, there was nothing Tan could do, not without risking himself needlessly.

Roine and Zephra looked at each other.

"What do you know that you're not sharing?" Tan asked.

Zephra shifted in her chair and made a point of not looking at Amia. "The number of lisincend have increased. When I saw them attacking the draasin, I couldn't believe how many there were."

Increasing lisincend. To create lisincend, it meant sacrificing Aeta.

"None have tried pushing against the border, not as they once did," Zephra went on. "We need to raise the barrier again. Without it, we're at risk for another attack."

"We don't have enough shapers to spend holding the barrier," Roine said. "Too many died in the last attack. We're better served with them stationed along the border. With a few good earth sensers, we can keep track of an incursion."

"Theondar, that's not going to stop—"

"It's all we can spare," he said, cutting Zephra off as he did. "That's the other reason I need to find any of Althem's heirs. If there are shapers—or even sensers capable of shaping—the kingdoms will need them."

Tan hadn't seen this side of Roine before. When he first met the warrior, it had been clear that he was more than the Athan. He had knowledge and skill and insight. Without that, they wouldn't have reached the cave. He held them together, guiding them until they reached the artifact. But there'd always been uncertainty. Now, seeing him sitting here as he was, Tan suspected this was the warrior shaper he had been, the man the world had known as Theondar. But from what Tan had learned, Theondar had been arrogant and quick to anger. This Roine was insightful and calm.

"Our shapers have always outnumbered Incendin," Zephra said.

"And they still might, but we just don't know. Not enough to risk it."

"And if they have transformed? You know what they gain. Enough to challenge a warrior," Zephra said, looking at Tan.

"That has always been the benefit of the transformation. Tan knows better than most what that means."

"I've told you what it was like when fire consumed me." Seeing the way his mother tensed as he mentioned what happened, he made a point of expanding. "Don't worry. Amia made certain that I was healed. The nymid restored me."

"You retain an affinity for fire," his mother said. "Don't deny it, Tannen. I've seen you when you don't think I'm looking. You *play* with fire, as if it's something you can touch and hold. And then there's what you wanted to do with that creature. You tried to save it." She looked at him, an accusation in her eyes. "You wonder why we hesitate sharing what we've learned of Incendin? It's more than the fact that you're untrained. It's because I fear you'll be drawn into it, that fire will call to you again and that we'll lose you completely."

Tan stared at the edge of the table. He couldn't deny his affinity for fire, but surely that had more to do with his connection to Asboel than anything else?

"I'm not 'playing' with fire. I'm trying to understand the elementals. All of them. Why else would I have asked you to teach? Why else would I work with Ferran?"

"And you spend free time studying with a woman who did everything possible to endanger our people. It was her fault you were nearly turned—"

"Is that your issue with Amia?" he asked. "Don't pretend it's not there. I thought it was something about the Aeta, but you blame her for what the First Mother did."

"If you wouldn't have been trying to save Amia, you wouldn't have changed."

"Is that what the First Mother tells you, or ara?" Tan asked. "If not for Amia, I might have remained twisted by fire, but she convinced me to search for help. The nymid restored me, Mother, regardless of whether you believe me or not. And you're mistaken if you intend to keep from me what's happening in Incendin. Without me, Incendin would have had the artifact long before. Without me, Althem would still rule Ethea and you'd be nothing but shaped to his will. If the draasin are involved, so am I."

He stood and slapped his hands on the table. "Regardless of what you want to believe, I'm a warrior now. Maybe not the one the kingdoms would choose, but I am what the Great Mother made. And I will do what is needed."

With that, he stormed out of the room.

CHAPTER 10

A Warrior's Request

TAN WAITED IN THE HALL, staring at one of the tapestries. It depicted a vision of the elementals from a time when many people spoke with them. What appeared to be the face of udilm appeared in a wave splashing along some mysterious shore. The friendliness of udilm woven into the tapestry had certainly not been Tan's experience. He wondered which was more accurate: the tapestry or the dour elemental he had encountered.

"You managed to do something very few people have ever done."

Tan turned to Roine. "What is that?"

He smiled. "You silenced Zephra."

Tan took a deep breath. As soon as he'd left, he'd felt regret for speaking to his mother that way. He'd already lost her once; now that she had returned, he needed to find some way to get along with her. "I'm sorry, Roine. She didn't deserve what I said to her. She's been trying to teach me but she still thinks she can shield me."

Roine clasped Tan's arm and squeezed briefly. It was something Tan's father used to do. "You can apologize to her yourself, if you wish." Roine looked up at the wall hanging, his eyes skimming past the elementals. "You should know that I happen to agree with you. I warned Zephra that she might be wrong, but she claims she knows you too well."

"She hasn't known me since I left Nor," Tan said.

Roine gave him a knowing look. "You're still her son, but in her eyes, she fails to see the man you've become. Oh, she *knows* the things you've done, but I don't think she lets herself understand how that's changed you. And make no mistake, Tannen, you *have* changed. It might not be fire that twists you, or maybe it is. The connection to the draasin started it, I think, but it's become more than that."

"You're wrong," Tan started. Roine cocked a half smile. "It didn't start with the draasin. It started with Amia. None of this would have happened had I not followed her."

"Always a girl," Roine said, his voice going soft. Heartache filled his voice.

"What was it like for you?"

Roine's eyes scanned the wall of portraits as if searching for a memory that had been lost. "For me, the first time I saw Anna..."

"The princess?" Tan asked.

"You probably wonder as I did whether Althem shaped the feeling into me. I'll admit that I spent a full day agonizing over it. It would be a way to tie me to him. But I've come to realize that he couldn't. The first time I saw her—really saw her—was long before I met Althem." Roine started down the hall and Tan followed, glancing back to see Amia watching. She waved him on. "I'd come to the city as a senser. So many came to study in those days that the university dorms were packed.

We'd sleep six to a room. Only when you learned to shape were you accorded rooms of your own. It bonded us, I think. Many of us who lived together remained close. Your father, for one."

Tan would love to hear more about his father, but that wasn't the story Roine wanted to tell. "How did you see Anna?"

"She came to the university on an errand for Ilton. She would have been fourteen, no more than fifteen, and I the same age. I'd begun showing signs of nearly shaping. Wind would soon respond to me and in the coming months, I'd learn to capture it and then water." He looked over at Tan. "Once you can shape two elements, it's little more than a matter of time before the others follow. I would become a warrior shaper. There were few of us, even then. But before then, I saw her. I didn't know who she was, only that her wavy black hair caught my eye. She carried herself with a confidence unlike anyone I'd ever met." He snorted to himself. "Well, except for Zephra. And she's always traveled by her own wind."

Roine nodded at the portrait they stopped in front of. "So maybe Althem shaped me, but I don't think it mattered, not when it came to Anna. I think I'd already decided what would happen with us by the time I met Althem."

Roine turned to Tan with an angry light to his eyes. "His shaping was different than the archivists. More subtle. With the archivists, you knew you were shaped, only there was nothing you could do about it. With Althem…" He shook his head as if to clear the memory. "I'm not certain what he placed on me. There was the affection I felt toward him. Loyalty that I thought he'd earned. It wasn't until the nymid healed me that I recognized the difference." The corners of Roine's mouth twitched. "I'm no longer certain of anything I once believed. For all I know, everything I thought about the world is wrong. Perhaps Incendin is a peaceful and welcoming place and the kingdoms are the dark and dangerous place we've always accused them of being."

"Why are you telling me this?" Tan asked. "Are you trying to keep me from going to Incendin?" Not only his mother, but Asboel as well, though Asboel's reasoning was quite different than his mother's. What did it mean if Roine attempted to do the same? Was he wrong? *Had* fire changed him more than he realized?

"Not Incendin. I'm not your mother, Tan. She and I see eye to eye on many things, but this isn't one of them. You've been through too much to be excluded. Besides, we don't have the luxury to exclude anyone right now." Roine started down the hall again, moving past the portraits. "I see things differently in my new role. Once, like you, I focused on the biggest threat I could see. I was—am—a warrior; how could I not? But it's different for me now. I have different obligations."

He stopped in front of a massive map hanging on the wall. On it were details of the kingdoms, the four surrounding lands that had joined together under a single throne: Vatten, Ter, Galen, and Nara. For as long as the university had been in Ethea, the kingdoms had been united. The map showed Incendin, but as it was, not as it is. Rens was marked along the far eastern border of Nara, stretching up and abutting the mountainous part of Galen. In the time the map had been made, Doma had not existed. It was another part of Rens. North of Rens was Chenir, a land locked away from the kingdoms by the Gholund Mountains, their massive peaks stretching from Galen all the way to the sea.

"How do you think to hold back Incendin?" Tan asked.

Roine tapped a thin strip of land jutting off Rens on the map. Doma. "Doma has suffered because of Incendin and the First Mother. Their people taken, tortured, and shaped to betray their homeland. I would have them returned."

"That means crossing into Incendin to free them."

Roine nodded. "And we are."

Tan hesitated. "As in, you're planning it?"

"Cianna and Seanan and a few others. They will free as many as they can."

Tan hoped they hadn't left while Enya was trying to withdraw fire. He didn't know what that meant, but believed it when Asboel claimed it might be dangerous for a fire shaper. And Tan had other abilities. Cianna and Seanan could only shape fire.

"You will need a spirit shaper," Tan said.

"Not for this. The First Mother showed a way to use the elements to free the shaper."

Tan held back his surprise. He hadn't known that Roine had gone to her as well. "Let me help." Going after them would give him the opportunity to discover what happened with the draasin. "If what she told you doesn't work or if there's another spirit shaper—"

Roine raised a hand and cut him off. "The others will be fine. I do not think the First Mother lied when she helped. She shows real remorse." He smiled tightly at Tan. "Cianna has learned to protect herself from spirit shaping and demonstrated it to the others. They will be enough."

"You don't trust me to go with them to Incendin?"

Roine grunted. "You think that I don't trust you to help, but you're wrong. You could help, but you'd also be conspicuous. The hounds know your scent, and Incendin is their home. You'd be forced to destroy every hound you came across. Cianna and her team can move quickly. And from what Zephra reports, the draasin hunt the lisincend. For that, they have my thanks."

"So I'll stay here?"

Tan began to think of how he would reach Asboel. The draasin might have warned him to silence, but Asboel wanted vengeance for what happened with the hatchlings. He would attack more than simply the lisincend. How long before the draasin went after the Fire Fortress?

"I had something else I wanted to ask of you," Roine said. "It will take someone of your unique talents to do. Were you better trained, I might not be quite so hesitant. Were there any other options, I probably wouldn't ask of you at all."

"You act as if I haven't done anything."

"Not at all, Tan. Only that there's a difference between someone who knows their abilities and someone still learning. You've nearly died every time you've faced the lisincend. If not for the elementals, you wouldn't be with us."

"I seem to remember watching you nearly die, Roine," Tan said. "Had it not been for the nymid, you might not have survived Fur when he attacked you near the lake. It seems to me you've survived twice because of the nymid. How is that any different?"

Roine tipped his head and surprised Tan by laughing. "It's easy for me to forget what you've done, too. And I've only known you a few months. You were so uncertain when we first met. Now?" He smiled. "Now you remind me of myself when I was your age."

"Is that a bad thing?"

"Far from it. Had I known what I was trying to do half the time, I might not have even attempted some of the things I did. That's one of the benefits of youth: not knowing what you can't do. Now, if I think about things too much, I can convince myself it'll be too hard." He turned back to the map and pointed beyond the sea, out past Incendin and Doma. "You heard me tell Zephra that the border is in danger. It's worse than that." He faced Tan and his eyes carried a weariness that hadn't been there before. "When the barrier fell, many of the shapers holding it perished. The lisincend shaping destroyed them. I've told your mother that we have shapers stationed along the border, but they are few." He sighed, turning back to the map. "It's why I need for Cianna to succeed. We need those Doma shapers returned."

"But you don't want me to go."

"I need you to search for other allies. There have always been rumors of other shapers. With the Incendin threat, the kingdom's warriors never had the chance to search for them. We were always so focused on keeping back Incendin. Now that we can't…"

Roine stared at the map. "Zephra searches Doma. That's what I asked of her. And I'd go if I could, but now that I'm expected to lead, people feel I should remain available in Ethea. It's been many years since I've spent much time in the city. You can't imagine how difficult it is for me to simply sit around and wait, letting others do things for me that I should be doing." He turned and looked down the hall, as if wishing he could simply shape himself away on a gust of air and lightning, disappearing as he had so often done. "We've lost so much over the years. When I first came to Ethea, there were dozens of warriors. Over time, they aged and died, disappearing from the world. Other than me, Lacertin was the only remaining warrior I knew." He offered Tan a fond smile. "And now you. But you're different than my ability in a way that's been missing from the world for far too long. Without you, I'm not sure we would have survived Althem and the Incendin attack. It's almost as if the Great Mother has a plan, but it's also why I need to learn whether Althem had a plan."

Twice, Tan had been closest to the extreme power they called the Great Mother. The first time, when standing in the pool of liquid spirit, he'd felt like he could shape anything he put his mind to. There was a sense of knowing that allowed him to save Amia and the draasin. Had he held onto that power longer, he might have been able to do even more. And then, when using the artifact, he'd drawn each of the elementals through it, bringing their power together as he funneled spirit. With enough time, he could have summoned spirit fully, as he had within the place of convergence in the mountains, but he'd turned away from that power, afraid that it might overwhelm him.

Could there be a plan? The elementals seemed to think so. Why else had the nymid come to him, offering to heal him so that he could reach Amia? Had it only been about saving Amia, or had there been another reason? Had Tan died, the draasin might remain frozen deep within the lake. The elemental power of fire might have remained suppressed for longer. Instead, they released the draasin and because they had, Incendin had been thwarted. Perhaps that was the Great Mother's plan.

"Shapers?"

Roine stared at the wall before him. "He had his reasons for what he did, but maybe there was more to it than I realized. What if Althem thought to *create* shapers?"

"It's still horrible what he did."

"More than you can imagine," Roine said softly. "I only hope he was part of the Great Mother's plan."

"I've never known you to be so philosophical," Tan said.

Roine stared at the map as if searching for an answer. "Before... all of this, there was a part of me that thought I could be one of the scholars. Althem discouraged it. Like you, I had so many questions and no answers. Why have we lost touch with the elementals? Why have shapers begun to lose power? When I left the palace, I sought answers on my own."

"Did you find anything?"

"I think Althem never wanted me to find anything. When he recalled me, he begged of me to find the artifact, discover why Lacertin had killed Ilton. I begin to wonder what would have changed had he not summoned me." Roine met his eyes. "You've not known me long, Tannen, but you know me well. I wouldn't ask this of you if I didn't feel it mattered. The kingdoms need help."

Tan thought of the flames leaping from the Fire Fortress and the fear Asboel had tried hide from him when sharing what Enya did while in Incendin. He couldn't shake the sense that he needed to help the draasin. If they had attacked the lisincend, Tan would have heard had the draasin been injured. Besides, this was Roine asking.

"What of finding an heir?"

Roine looked away from the map. The tension in his eyes was clear. He was tired. As a warrior, he could shape anything he needed, could control powers greater than most could even imagine. It hadn't made him nearly this tired. As ruler, he struggled under the weight of his new responsibilities. "That task is mine," he said softly. "If not for heirs, then because if they are able to shape, we owe it to them to teach what we can."

"The First Mother could help find them," Tan suggested.

"That... poses dangers I'm not willing to risk."

"I don't know that I can ask it of Amia, Roine. Given what she's been through, she's struggling with what it is that the Great Mother placed her here to do. If it's not to help her people—"

"I haven't had the chance to tell you, but the Aeta are making their way toward the kingdoms. I've sent word they will be welcomed. This *would* help her people."

Tan wondered what that meant for the Aeta. What would change for them? "Give her time, Roine."

Roine's face twisted in a pained expression. "I hope so."

Tan wished there might be something he could say to Amia, but she had to come around on her own. He turned away from him and looked at the map, thinking about how he would do what Roine asked.

Where would they find allies? Chenir was separated from the kingdoms by a massive inlet of water. It was the reason most trade with Chenir came by sea. Could they find help there?

"What keeps Incendin from attacking Chenir? From the map, it's not clear why Chenir hasn't suffered the same fate as Doma."

"Incendin technically shares a border, but the mountains lining the northern border between Chenir and Incendin are even more impassible than between Galen and Incendin. They had no need for a barrier to protect them. Their traders come to ports in Vatten, as ours go to Chenir. They are a peaceful folk."

"And you think I should go to Chenir?"

Roine sighed. "Chenir doesn't have shapers. Not like Doma. But there are rumors of shapers beyond the sea, past Incendin."

"Why send me?" Tan asked. "Why not Zephra?"

"Honestly? Zephra can shape the wind, but you can travel as a warrior. That's respected, even now."

"You've barely shown me how to travel that way."

"You've seen enough. Wind and fire, water for stability, and earth for strength. As your skills improve, you will manage the shaping fine."

"That's not the real reason you want me to go, though."

Roine turned away. "Your mother really underestimates you. No. I want you to bring Amia with you. With her ability to sense spirit, she should be able to help. Find us allies."

"Not force them," Amia said, approaching slowly.

Roine fixed her with a hard stare. "No. We will not repeat the mistakes of the past."

Amia looked from Roine and then to Tan, where her eyes lingered a moment. "Is this what you'll do?"

Tan nodded carefully, not certain what Amia was getting at.

"You've told me what is happening in Incendin. I agree that you shouldn't be involved. Not so long as he asks you to stay away."

Roine smiled. "Thank you."

"I don't mean you," Amia said. "So if it keeps Tan from Incendin as the draasin requests, I'll help."

Chapter 11

A Friend in Need

MASTER FERRAN STOPPED WORKING with the massive blocks of stone as Tan and Amia arrived at the university courtyard. Chunks of fallen rock stacked high, like some massive puzzle he worked. Sweat beaded his brow in spite of the cool day.

"You're leaving?" he asked Tan as they approached.

Tan glanced at the pack he had slung over his back. At least this time, he'd be prepared. Most of the journeys he'd taken had left him with nothing more than a cloak and the clothes he carried. This time, he had a thick wool cloak for the cold Amia promised they'd find, the pack with a change of clothes, and his warrior sword. He might not feel entirely comfortable wielding a sword—he'd been an archer once although he no longer felt the need to carry a bow—but the warrior sword helped him shape more strongly, much like the artifact.

"Theondar asked of me," Tan said.

"Then it must be done," Ferran agreed. He wiped the sweat from his brow, smearing a layer of dirt and debris across his forehead. Then he glanced back at the remains of the university. "I thought you would have more time with me for training. We could use someone with your strength, you know. Even untrained, there is much you can do."

"I would have liked more time to learn," Tan admitted. Ferran had shown a genuine interest in helping him learn.

Ferran nodded slowly, strangely reminding Tan of the way golud felt as it rumbled beneath his feet. "Since learning of your abilities, I've tried speaking to golud, asking for help with my shapings, but I've heard nothing."

"Maybe when I return, I can see if there's anything I can do," Tan suggested.

"And I will carve time to teach what I can," Ferran said before nodding solemnly and crossing his fists over his chest before turning away and returning to his work shaping the rock away from the university.

Amia's mouth twisted into a frown.

"What is it?" Tan asked.

"Probably nothing. I just never expected to see someone in the city make that greeting. It's a sign of respect." She turned to Tan and rested a hand on his shoulder. "The Aeta have long used it as greeting when meeting another of the family. Maybe Ferran saw it from the archivists." She tapped the stones of the landing circle with one foot. "Are you certain you shouldn't speak to Zephra again before we leave?"

Tan sighed. He hated leaving as he had, but would seeing her change anything? It would likely only make him more frustrated. She saw him as her child, as a boy to protect, no matter what she claimed. Even her attempt at helping him under the guise of Sarah had been intended to get him away from the city, to send him to the place of convergence where he could use the nymid to help Elle. That he'd instead gone to Incendin likely upset her as much as when he'd gone wandering through the mountains of Galen when he was younger. Was her attempt to teach him more of the same?

"I'll speak to her when we get back," he said.

Amia rested a hand on his arm, sending a calming shaping through him. He arched a brow at her. "It's different with you," she explained. "And you don't even know how long we'll be gone. You want to leave it like that with her?"

"I thought you two didn't get along."

"I can't say we're on the best of terms, but I think of what I'd say to my mother were I to get the chance. I won't ever get that chance. The lisincend took it from me."

Tan glanced over to the palace. Perhaps he *had* been a little harsh with his mother. She only wanted him safe. And her teaching of him had seemed genuine. "Maybe you're right." There was time to go back and find her before they left. Delaying only kept them from finding the allies Roine sought, but seeing as how Tan wasn't even sure where to begin, it wouldn't hurt to wait.

"Come," Amia said, taking his hand and starting toward the palace.

Tan let himself be led. As they left the university courtyard, a gnawing sense came to him from someplace distant. It was like a pinprick of pain, deep in his mind. *Asboel?*

It had been days since he'd felt the draasin. What had happened in that time?

Tan reached for his bonded elemental. Searing pain split his head. His eyesight flickered, growing dim. Colors swirled at the edges. Tan strained for the draasin, feared there wouldn't be an answer.

The pain came again, this time like a hot knife cutting through his mind. He screamed and dropped to his knees.

The agony seemed to last an eternity. It overwhelmed him, overwhelmed his ability to push aside anything else. For countless moments, it was all he knew.

Then Amia touched his forehead. A cooling calm came over him, easing the pain.

He blinked away tears that had streamed from his eyes. Remnants of the pain were still there, but less than they had been before it struck him.

"Tan?" Ferran approached and looked from Tan to Amia with concern in his soft brown eyes. "You screamed and the ground trembled as you did."

He hadn't felt the ground trembling, but then, with the pain in his skull, he couldn't feel much else. Even the touch of the wind on his cheek and the heat in the air was lessened.

"What is it, Tan?" Amia asked.

He shook his head. Asboel still hadn't answered. Usually that wouldn't concern him. The draasin remained a distant sense in his mind most of the time, coming to the surface when he wanted to speak to Tan or when Tan called for him. This time, there was no response. There was no sense of the draasin in his mind.

"The draasin," he whispered to Amia. "I don't sense him." He took a step and stumbled.

Ferran slipped an arm around him for support. "Come with me."

"I can't. I need to find out—"

"You need rest," he said.

Amia held his arm, pushing a constant shaping through him. "Whatever attacked you nearly knocked you out. You were screaming and the wind whistled. The air grew warm. And, as Master Ferran said, the ground trembled."

All shapings. Had he done them without intending to? What did it mean if he had?

"Theondar," Tan said. "Find him."

He reached into his pocket and pulled out a summoning rune. He tried to shape it but failed. As he did, the pain in his head returned even stronger than before. The coin dropped to the stone with a soft clatter.

Amia scooped it up and closed her eyes. With a shaping Tan felt as a vague pulsing in his ears, the rune began to glow. "Where can we go?" she asked, looking around at the fallen university.

"The archives," Tan said.

Ferran gave him a strange look and then lifted him easily, carrying him down the street with a shaping of earth.

Tan sat at one of the tables in the upper archives. The lisincend had tried destroying the archives, but someone had been through here and righted all the furniture except the shelves. Books were stacked in most places, though strewn across the floor in others. The air had a musty odor mixed with the faint hint of burned paper.

He rested his head on his hands, leaning over the table. Pain pulsed behind his eyes. Amia touched his forehead again and the pressure eased.

"What is it that you're doing?" he asked.

"Taking away your pain."

"You can do that?"

"Not the actual pain," she said. "Just what you sense of it. When the shaping weakens—which it will—you'll begin feeling it again."

"Can you tell what's causing it?"

"As far as I can tell, nothing is causing it."

The door to the archives opened and his mother flew in on a gust of air. She looked from Amia to Tan and stopped in front of the table. Power surged from her. Tan shouldn't feel it so clearly, but somehow, he did.

Roine followed her into the archives, moving with a determined stride. He wore a worried look on his face that furrowed his brow and fixed Tan with a frown.

"What happened?" Zephra demanded.

"I don't know. We were returning to the palace to find you when he collapsed," Amia said.

His mother shot Amia an annoyed look. "Why would you return for me? Theondar sent you—"

"You knew?" Tan asked, looking up. "You're not upset that he asked me to go?"

She shrugged. "It is harmless enough. It's Incendin that I fear for you, Tannen, especially with what the draasin do. You've faced too much of Incendin. Let others do their part."

"Zephra—" Roine said.

Tan lowered his head, staring at his hands. The pulsing behind his eyes started to return. He focused on it, needing to push it away. Whatever Amia did to ease the pain also separated him from his connection to the elementals. He *needed* that connection.

More than that, he needed to know what happened to Asboel. Why hadn't the draasin answered him? He was bound to Asboel, meant to help protect him, even if he didn't believe he needed protection. Had something gone wrong as he'd tried helping Enya? Or worse—had he attacked the Fire Fortress itself?

"That's why Roine wanted me to go? Because you think it's safe?" he asked as the pain lessened again.

"That's not the reason, Tan," Roine said.

"You're sending the others, but did you really give me this 'assignment' to keep me away? Have I shown myself to be so weak that I need such help?"

Roine pulled a chair away from the table. He glanced at Ferran as he did. The earth Master stood along one of the shelves, studying it silently, no differently than he had stared when Zephra had admonished him. "I have a different responsibility now than I had before," he started. "I told you how I need to look at more than my needs, but the needs of the kingdoms. Protecting you is a need of the kingdoms."

Tan rubbed the sides of his head, trying to push the pain to someplace deep in his mind. "I think you're inflating my importance."

"I don't think so. We haven't had a warrior shaper in a generation, and then you appear. Not only able to shape all the elements, but able to do so with spirit, like the ancient warriors themselves. And beyond that, you can *speak* to the elementals. How much of an advantage does this give us? Even if we lose all of our shapers, we can't afford to lose *you,* Tan. What you can do is irreplaceable."

Tan stared from Roine to his mother. Roine nodded slowly, and Tan began to think that Roine hadn't shared everything about his plan for Tan with Zephra.

"What is this? What happened to you?" his mother asked. "When Ferran sent word, he said there was an uncontrolled shaping."

"That's just it. I don't know." The pain seemed to be easing. "I'm having some sort of pain tied to the draasin."

"Are you certain it's the draasin?" she asked.

With a deep breath, he pushed away the sense of the pain as he so often did when Asboel tore through his mind. The effort left him feeling tired, but the agony he'd experienced receded, as if pushing away his sense of Asboel pushed away the pain. He listened for the other elementals for a moment, searching to see if he could still reach them. Ara fluttered nearby, but so did ashi. Now that he'd used the other wind elemental, he could identify the difference.

"I'm certain," said.

Amia studied him and then rested her hand on his forehead. Her shaping built and washed over him. "What did you do? It's changed."

"It started when I reached for—" he caught himself before revealing Asboel's name "—the draasin. I felt something in the back of my mind, but wasn't sure what it was. So I tried reaching to him. When I did, that's when the pain started. It's better now."

"You closed him away from you," Amia noted.

His mother frowned. "You can do that?"

"I've had to before, otherwise he would destroy my mind. The draasin are simply too powerful. When he speaks to me, if I had no way of pushing him away, I think my mind would be torn apart."

He needed to find Asboel. Whatever had happened was because the draasin was in trouble. That meant something had happened during their attack on the lisincend. Tan felt certain of it. "I need to find him."

"That wasn't what we discussed," Roine said.

Tan glared at him. "You would have me leave an injured friend?" He shifted his attention to his mother. "And you? You know what it's like to lose such a connection. You think I should ignore what I feel?"

"It is too dangerous, Tannen," she said. "You're talking about risking yourself for an elemental power who—"

"Who has done nothing but help every time I asked," Tan said. "And I won't do anything but help if he needs. Roine said the kingdoms need allies. The draasin *are* our allies. If we let anything happen to them, Incendin will already have won."

He stood, shaking off Amia, who was trying to hold him down, and ignoring the hard stares coming from his mother. Master Ferran watched him silently, simply leaning against the massive stone support. His mother looked from Tan to Amia before turning away, her eyes giving away the irritation she felt. Tan took that as his cue to leave.

He stepped into the street, pausing long enough to get a sense of the other elementals. Asboel was a distance sense of pain in his mind.

Were Tan to draw him forward, his mind would explode with pain once again. Ara swirled around his mother, drawn to her in a way he would never be able to replicate. Golud rested beneath his boots, filling the stones of the city. Mixed with golud was the nymid, mingling earth and water, the two building the city's bedrock stronger than either would have managed alone.

He reached the university and pulled Amia toward him. She waited, arm linked in his. Roine might have taught him how to shape and travel like a warrior, but Tan had never attempted it. Now, with Asboel in danger, was not the time.

There was another way for him to travel, if only it would respond. He reached for ara, asking for the wind to aid his shaping.

"This is foolish, Tannen," his mother said. "Stay and learn. The elemental will—"

"Will what? You think I should let him die?"

"Please…" she said.

"I will not lose him," Tan said, but the wind elemental didn't answer.

A satisfied smile came to his mother's face. The translucent face of her elemental slipped around her as if hiding from Tan. "I will not help you in this."

Fine. If ara wouldn't answer, then he would shift his focus. He had already discovered that he needed to learn more about the other elementals. If he could speak with them—if he could use their energy—he would be even more powerful.

This time, he asked of ashi. Ashi answered, blowing around him with a warm gust out of the south, swirling around his head.

His mother's eyes widened slightly.

"You won't keep me from him, Mother," Tan said.

The wind lifted him. Adding a hint of fire drawn from saa, they shot into the sky on a cloud of shaped air. They streaked south and east. Asboel was out there, though Tan didn't quite know where. The pain tearing through his mind kept him from knowing.

Amia tensed. "Are you certain this is what you should be doing? You know what Asboel warned. If what Enya did withdraws fire from you—"

"Asboel needs me. He might not ask for it, but the pain was his way of calling for help."

She gripped his arm tightly as they soared toward the draasin. Tan hoped they would be in time.

CHAPTER 12

A New Bond

TAN HELD THE SHAPING OF WIND for as long as he could. From what he could tell, Ashi fueled the shaping, giving him the strength he needed to pass over Ethea, and across Ter, but he wouldn't be able to hold on much longer. Tan sensed the strength in the elemental, but he wasn't attuned to it well enough to use it with any skill or precision. Instead, he asked the wind elemental to carry them.

With ashi, the farther they went to the east, toward the warmer air, the stronger the elemental seemed to become. Tan needed to use less and less focus to guide them.

As they crossed into Nara, he steered toward a small rocky area and back down to the ground. They touched down on dusty, brown rock. The air held the shimmer of heat, but not quite the oppressive heat he remembered of Incendin. The outcropping had shadows coalescing and a small pool of water beneath it. Had he been drawn to this?

Maybe, but it was more than that. He'd seen it before. Asboel had been here.

Tan looked up at the wind and tipped his head. It blew around him in warm, steady gusts. *Thanks,* Tan sent to ashi.

Something like streaks of color swirled around him. There was a quiet sense of a voice, so distant he almost wasn't sure what he heard. Had he not pushed the sense of Asboel away, he might not have heard it. As it was, the sense was distant and faded, barely more than a quiet humming.

Tan reached for it, straining toward the connection. He wasn't certain it would work, that he *could* pull the sound toward him. Part of him feared what would happen if he did. Would it be like what he'd experienced with ilaz? But if he could reach for ashi, if he could speak to the air elemental as he spoke to ara, how much more effective would his shapings become, especially now that they were away from a place of convergence?

The sense of words and the voice came closer. Tan realized that he somehow shaped spirit as he pulled it toward him, not weaving together each of the elementals to do so. The First Mother would be pleased. It had only taken him to lose the connection he shared with Asboel to find it.

A voice boomed in his head, reminding him of how he spoke to Asboel.

This land is dangerous.

Tan pressed the voice to a manageable level as he'd learned to do with Asboel. The voice wasn't ara. There was nothing of the great wind elemental to the way it spoke. *Ashi?*

Ashi, he says. I am of the ashi, but I am more. I am Honl.

Tan hesitated. Other than Asboel, none of the elementals had ever named themselves. Honl was one of the ashi elementals. *I am Tan.*

I know you, Tan.

There was a welcoming sense of warm wind power from the elemental, a power that Tan had felt before without really knowing what it was. Honl had given him the strength to float above the city when he first learned of ashi. But it was more than that. The swirls of color reminded him of what he'd seen coming off Asboel as he flew. Had it not been ara as he always suspected?

Has it been you, not ara?

Honl seemed to laugh. *Ara helps when it wishes, but they prefer to serve Zephra.*

How long have you…

Tan trailed off, uncertain how to ask the question. How long had Honl been with him? Ever since he'd learned to speak to the other elementals?

Since you summoned, Honl said.

Tan tried to think back to when he might have summoned the wind. Since learning of his connection to the elementals, there had been many instances when he had. *When did I summon?*

Honl swirled around him. *The device was too powerful. Ara helped Zephra. You summoned.*

How had Tan not known he summoned a different elemental? With wind, the sense was different. And ara *was* more interested in serving his mother. That was how she had managed to restrict his shaping the wind at first. Without Honl, she would have kept him in Ethea.

"What is it?" Amia asked. "I can almost hear you, but it's different."

After what happened with Asboel, this almost made up for the terror he felt for the draasin. "What do you know of the wind elementals?"

She turned to let the warm air gusting out of the north blow against her face, swirling in her golden hair. "Ara? Less than you, I imagine."

"Apparently I know less than I thought," Tan said. "Not only ara, but the other elementals."

"I know little of the elementals, Tan." She studied the ground around them, shifting the pack she carried.

"This wasn't ara who brought us here."

"You shaped us yourself?" Amia asked. "I thought you struggled shaping wind."

It sounded like what his mother would say to him. "I've improved, but I still don't have the strength to shape us this far. We would've ended up somewhere in Ter, and that's *if* I managed to reach the wind in the first place. Zephra enjoyed making it difficult for me to reach for wind. She considered it a training technique."

Amia bit back a smile. "Then how?"

"Another wind elemental. Ashi. I thought ashi a lesser elemental, but I'm not sure. A lesser elemental shouldn't have been able to bring us this far so easily."

"Lesser like the nymid?"

That had been his thought, too. "Apparently what I know of the elementals is wrong," he said, wishing he'd had the time to better understand the elementals. "At least, that's what it seems like from talking with Honl."

Amia turned toward the breeze blowing toward them, studying it as if to understand.

How many elementals are like you? Tan asked Honl.

The wind elemental swirled around his head. *Like me? I am me. There is no other Honl.*

Tan surveyed the hot land around him. *Why did you say this is a dangerous land?*

Wind kicked up dust and sent it swirling around Tan. He coughed and covered his mouth.

Can you not taste it? There was pain here. Great pain.

Tan removed his arm from his mouth and let the dust settle in his nose and mouth. As it did, he *could* taste the pain. It was hot and angry… and familiar. The draasin had suffered here.

This was where the hatchlings died?

Honl swirled around him, reaching the ground before flipping back and righting himself. As Tan watched, he had a sense of direction from the elemental, a head and foot. There was a definite sense of a mouth and, if Tan twisted his head just right, almost a face.

Not dead. Broken. Taken.

Tan frowned. Hadn't Asboel told him the hatchlings were killed by the lisincend? *They were dead.*

Not dead, Honl repeated.

Where were they taken?

Honl swirled toward the sky for long moments before returning to the ground. *Toward Fire.*

Fire. Tan had an unsettled feeling. *Did Twisted Fire take the draasin?*

Honl slipped around him again, sliding in a flickering sort of movement. *Twisted Fire? Like Fire when you summoned?*

Tan created an image of the winged lisincend in his mind and pushed it to Honl.

Not Twisted Fire. Fire like this.

A different image came and Tan gasped. "Fur?" In his surprise, he spoke the name aloud.

Amia jerked her head toward him. "What about Fur?" It was because of Fur that Amia had lost everything. The lisincend had destroyed her family, all under the direction of Fur.

"Asboel thought the hatchlings dead, but Honl says they were taken by Fur."

"But Asboel hunted him."

"He did, but Fur escaped. When Alisz gained power, I assumed she'd taken care of Fur. From what Lacertin said, there was no love lost between them."

She looked to the east, toward Incendin. "What does it mean that Fur has the hatchlings at the same time the Fire Fortress burns more brightly?"

"And at the same time as the draasin attacked the lisincend and Asboel now suffers," Tan added.

He crawled under the overhang and stood, letting his earth sensing stretch out. For too long, he'd been dependent on fire. For too long, he'd been dependent on fire. He was startled again to realize how his tie to Asboel had created that dependence.

He sensed where the hatchlings had been. Shards of their thick shells mixed with the sand. Droplets of blood from the attack burned deep into the earth. The tiny insects that crawled along the sand did not dare reach into the outcropping of rock, as if the presence of the draasin kept them away.

Tan paused and took a drink of water pooling beneath the rock. It was stale and had a thin film over it, but tasted cool and refreshing. Even the water held the memory of the draasin.

Could they have lived?

And if they did, what would Asboel have done to get them back? Tan didn't really have to ask; he remembered well the anger Asboel had when he thought the hatchlings gone. If he had learned from the lisincend that they lived, it would explain an attack on the Fire Fortress. It might even explain why Tan couldn't reach him.

But what if Asboel didn't know? What if Asboel's silence had to do with what Enya did, withdrawing fire? Nara showed no signs of anything, but what would it be like when they crossed into Incendin? Would the draasin have changed the land in such a way that the lisincend—and fire—were weakened?

Do you know where the Eldest has gone?

Honl flickered around him again, twisting in a spiral from the ground up to Tan's face. As he settled, features of what seemed a fluid face emerged. It wore a grim expression but didn't answer.

The draasin? He sent an image to Honl of Asboel.

Honl swirled around him with an agitated flash of colors. *Dangerous. Do not follow.*

For a moment, Tan had an image of the Fire Fortress, and then it was gone. He tried to focus on Honl, but couldn't. The wind elemental moved around him too quickly to follow. Tan crawled out from under the outcropping of rock, back into the heat. Amia waited, her brow furrowed in a worried frown.

"What did you learn?" she asked.

"Nothing I didn't know already."

She met his eyes and started shaking her head. "I still don't think you can go into Incendin after the draasin by yourself, Tan."

Considering the pain he'd felt, Tan didn't know if he had any other choice. He *needed* to go after Asboel, if only to ensure that the pain went away. "If I don't do this, who would help? Who else would risk themselves for the draasin? Roine has already said he needs to remain in Ethea to ensure stability of the kingdoms. And my mother? She disapproves of me even leaving the city. The other shapers? After the draasin attack on Ethea, how many would risk themselves like this?"

"They did before."

"Roine shared with me the need to find allies. For the kingdoms to find help. Asboel *is* our ally. They've proven it over and again. And if he's injured because he's attacking the lisincend, the kingdoms need to help."

Amia grabbed his arm and forced him to face her. "What if he's not there? You don't know that he is. For all you know, he's somewhere far to the north of here."

"I'd know if he was."

"The same way you know what happened to you when you started having pain in your head?"

"It's connected," he said. "I don't know how, but it is. Incendin attacked the hatchlings and now I find out they might not have died. The draasin attacked the lisincend. If Asboel learned of the hatchlings, I *know* where he would have gone. It's the only place that would pose a risk to him. Even if he didn't, then whatever Enya has done has injured him. I can't leave him like that, Amia." He held her eyes. "He's a creature of great power, but he's more than that. You know that; you feel the connection as well."

"You continue to view everything as fixable. Maybe this is something you can't fix."

"This is different than what happened with the lisincend. This is *Asboel.*"

Something more troubled her. He sensed it as mixture of emotions surging through their shaped bond.

Tan shaped wind and earth and fire and water, combining them into spirit. This he layered over Amia as she had taught him. A sigh washed over her.

"I'm a fool," he said, understanding coming to him through the shaping. "I shouldn't have brought you."

"You would have left me behind in Ethea? Now you think to treat me as your mother treats you."

"That's not it. It's Incendin. I understand, Amia, and you don't have to come with me," he said gently. "I know how you fear facing Incendin again. After what you've been through, I can't blame you, but I need to do this. He's not just an elemental. The draasin are different than the others. At least, Asboel is different for *me.*"

Amia stared at him for a long time. "You're not going without me. I'm bonded to you as much as you've bonded Asboel."

He brushed his hand across her cheek. "I know you've struggled with your place since learning of the First Mother. But *he's* our family."

She laughed softly. "Not quite the family I envisioned, but you're right." She rested her head on his hand, taking slow breaths. "We don't know enough about Incendin. After all this time, they are still such a mystery. Had we only the chance to ask Lacertin."

It no longer felt strange to think the same thing. Lacertin had sacrificed everything on behalf of the kingdoms and now they were without his wisdom. "He's the only one who's been in the Fire Fortress and returned to talk about it."

Fire is dark in that place.

Tan jerked his attention to Honl, who flickered around him. *You know the Fire Fortress?*

I have blown through there. Wind blows everywhere, Tan, even through Fire. Without wind, Fire does not burn.

Can you guide me once we're there?

Honl took a moment to consider. *You will help Fire?*

Tan had a fleeting image of the lisincend. Of Fur. He shook his head emphatically. *No. I will help True Fire.*

Honl flittered with a little more agitation before settling next to Tan. *Then I must try.*

CHAPTER 13

Green in Incendin

AMIA STARED INTO THE DISTANCE. Across the barren rock, there was heat and fire and death. They had both been through Incendin, though Amia's trek through those lands had been different than Tan's. The last time she'd really been to Incendin, she had nearly died. The hounds had chased her and her people, and the lisincend had followed.

"I'm not certain that I can go," she said.

Tan took her hands, pulling her around to face him. "I'm not sure I could shape you back to Ethea, but maybe Honl can carry you most of the way. There's much you could do in the kingdoms. You could gather the Aeta. They will need leadership. I'll return when I can. Asboel needs me." Tan let his awareness of Asboel's pain rise closer to the surface of his mind. With it came the searing sense of agony. Whatever had happened to Asboel left Tan unable to reach the fire elemental.

Amia closed her eyes and nodded. "*I* need you. I don't know if I can do anything for the People. Not by myself, and not without you."

"I wouldn't ask this for any other reason but Asboel—"

She kissed him on the lips, silencing him. "I understand. It's the same as what you were willing to do for me." She rested against him for a moment. Tan savored the sense of her, the way her body pressed into him. "How will you find him?"

Could Honl help? *Honl, can you help me find Fire?*

The wind elemental swirled toward them. Tan realized that he could see him better the longer they shared a connection. Would he soon be able to see him clearly?

I cannot, Honl answered.

Tan waited for him to explain more, but he didn't. If the wind elemental couldn't help, could Tan reach for him with earth sensing?

He stretched out with his senses, using the skills his father had long ago taught him, attempting a shaping like he'd seen Ferran use. Tan had to focus, using his connection to the earth through sensing, but managed to add to it, to twist it into the shaping he intended. Even with the shaping augmenting him, he couldn't sense Asboel.

He let out a frustrated sigh.

"Let me try," Amia whispered. "You'll have to help. For this to work, I think we'll both need to shape spirit," she said.

Tan took a deep breath and focused on the elements. He shaped each together, weaving them as he did when shaping spirit. Amia shaped at the same time, but frowned at him.

"I don't think it will work like that. Whatever you do when you shape spirit is different when you do that. This shaping must come from you."

"I can't—"

"You've always shaped spirit," she said. "Like the other elementals, it's within you. Had it not been, you wouldn't have survived the pool."

Could he shape spirit without binding the elements? What had it taken for him to shape wind and earth? He needed focus. With wind, he'd learned to focus on his breathing, to use that to connect him to what he intended. With earth, it was different, tied to his ability to sense. What did spirit require?

He could think of only one way to reach spirit within him. He focused on his connection to Amia and sensed it clearly. As he did, he felt something deeper, similar to what he'd felt when seeking Honl.

Tan stretched for it. Something akin to what he'd sensed when standing in the pool of spirit burbled deep within him. Much like with the pool of spirit, he could draw upon it.

He only managed to skim across the surface of what he sensed. It felt different than when he drew on spirit by binding the four elements together. Purer.

Had it always been there? Was this what the First Mother sought him to harness?

Amia reached through their bond. There was no other way to think of it: she pressed through him, into his mind. As she did, their thoughts mingled. He felt her fear at being this close to Incendin. It was a different fear than what he'd expected. Tan thought she was scared for herself, that the hounds chasing her and her people across Incendin had made her frightened of this place, but while there was some of that, what truly terrified her was something different: him.

He felt her try to hide it from him, but as she pressed through him, everything was laid out, no differently than when he'd stood in the pool of spirit.

Amia feared what would happen to him in Incendin. Through her eyes, he saw the lisincend attack her family's caravan. He saw her people taken by the lisincend, turned into playthings for the hounds. He saw her mother destroyed, burned by fire. The pain and horror was dull, muted by time and the mourning she had already done.

Beyond that, he saw the lisincend destroy him, blasting him into the lake. There was surprise when he'd emerged from the water coated by the nymid armor. The renewed terror when the hound attacked. There was the fear she felt as he'd attacked Alisz, risking himself to save Amia but nearly losing himself as he did. She saw fire changing him and, through their connection, Tan finally saw what he must have looked like. Fire had twisted his face, drawing his lips tight, narrowing his eyes, and layering his face with thick, scaly skin. Had he seen himself, he would have thought him one of the lisincend. Then his rebirth, saved again by the nymid, only to suffer and nearly die once more as he faced Althem.

All this came to her mind, the fear raw and real and immediate.

He was her family. After what she'd been through, after losing everything, including the Aeta she thought could be her family when the rest had died, she had nothing else. She had no one else. Only Tan.

Tan understood. She didn't fear going to Incendin. She feared *Tan* going to Incendin.

He touched her arm, running his hand across her skin. It would not make her feel any better, but he would reassure her as well as he could. *I must do this.*

She twisted her face up to him. The sunlight played off her golden hair and reflected in her bright blue eyes. *I know.*

Think of what we'll lose if I don't.

Tan showed her the connections he'd made throughout Ethea. He showed her Elle, terrified and dying as she rode Asboel along with him to find the udilm. He showed her how Asboel had done all that he could to save the youngest. He showed her the friendships they had formed: Roine, Ferran, his mother, Cianna, and Asboel. They were his family now.

I know.

And he sensed that she did. That came through their connection as well.

Steel ran through Amia, a strength she rarely chose to show, but that Tan knew hid within her. Had she not had that strength, everything she'd been through would have crushed her. She would have fallen the first time the lisincend attacked. Or the next. Possibly any of the times they had nearly died. Instead, Amia remained strong, pushing on regardless.

It was this strength that drove her now. She pressed through the connection with Tan, forcing deeper into his mind and thoughts. With any other, he might fear the immediacy of the connection, he might fear that she would shape him. But he trusted Amia. He was laid bare for her.

Somewhere in his mind, she found the connection to Asboel and plunged into it. As she did, the pain returned, rising hot and fresh to the surface. Somehow, Amia kept it suppressed.

She gasped softly. Tan didn't know what she sensed, only that his sense of her faded as she reached through the connection and toward Asboel. She was there, but she was also *not* there.

Then she withdrew, rising back out of his mind, sliding away from him, back through their connection, and out. Amia sagged toward the ground. Tan slipped an arm around her waist and held her up, keeping her from dropping. Fatigue etched into lines around her eyes, and he felt it through their shaped connection.

He felt none of the same exhaustion, which told him that she had done all the work with the shaping. "Did you find him?" he asked. Speaking to her felt wrong considering their connection, but communicating through the bond communicating through the bond required shaping and strength, both of which were energy draining.

She nodded weakly. "He's out there. Possibly injured, though I can't tell with any certainty."

Out there. Tan suspected she meant Incendin, but had to know. "Where?"

"Near the border."

"Not the Fire Fortress?" That had been his fear. Had Asboel gone there, would Tan have been able to reach him? Not without more help than he had.

"Not there. The border." In spite of the heat, she shivered.

Tan held her and lowered her to the ground so she could sit. "You've been there," he said with a new understanding.

"I've been there," she agreed. "We never really traded in Incendin. Not often. The lands are too hard on the horses and the wagons, and none really wanted to head any farther into Incendin than was necessary." Her strength began to return as she sat next to him, but still she clutched his arm, as if afraid he might try to leave without her. Or maybe she wanted to keep him from racing after Asboel. "But the borders were generally safe. We were allowed to trade, and Incendin goods always fetched a premium. Few other traders ever came there, giving us an advantage."

"There was a time you went farther into Incendin," Tan reminded her.

Her eyes narrowed. "And we paid dearly for it."

"I think your mother knew what the First Mother had done to the Doma shapers."

Amia's eyes stared distantly toward Incendin. "I'd been thinking about that too. There wouldn't be too many reasons for us to go so deep into Incendin otherwise. We were practically to the Fire Fortress before we were chased."

"What's it like?"

"The fortress itself is impressive," she admitted. "It rises from the surrounding waste like a finger of darkness. Flames leap around the top. Probably shapers, though with Incendin, you can't put it past them having some other dark power."

Like the bowl with runes carved along the outside. The fire shapers had used that bowl to somehow augment their shapings, to twist and taint what they were able to accomplish and force a dark twisting of the archivist's power. That had been how Alisz managed to become one of the twisted lisincend.

"And the people?" Tan asked.

Amia shrugged. "I've never met anyone who lives near the Fire Fortress. Only those living along the edge of Incendin. And they're like anyone else. Their culture is different, as is their dress, but it's not their fault where they were born."

Tan hadn't really thought of it that way. He always focused on Incendin being a land overrun by horrible fire shapers. The hounds and the lisincend as well as all the shapers they had. But that wouldn't necessarily mean the people of Incendin were like that. They were likely no different than anyone living in Nor or Velminth, or even Ethea.

Amia took a deep breath and stood. "I'm ready. Let's go help Asboel."

Tan took her hand and together, they looked toward Incendin. "You'll have to guide the shaping," he said. "You know where we have to go; Asboel wouldn't tell me."

"I think I'm strong enough for that," she said.

Honl?

Tan called the wind elemental, not certain how quickly he'd respond. As soon as Tan spoke his name, the wind elemental swirled around him, kicking up a hint of dust.

We need to find Fire.

Dangerous, Honl said.

I know. But he is my bond, my responsibility. It is what the Mother would want.

The wind elemental swirled around him with agitation.

Amia will guide you through me.

Honl seemed to shift his attention to her, sliding from Tan toward Amia.

Amia pressed through Tan again. He opened his end of their connection so she could. Tan directed Honl to lift them on a gust of air and they rose with increasing strength. Again, Tan marveled at how easy the connection to Honl felt, almost as easy as it was for him and Asboel. They climbed to the air, riding on a cloud, as Honl pushed them forward.

When they crossed over into Incendin, Tan felt a tingle across his skin from the remnants of the barrier. With it fallen, why hadn't Incendin attacked yet? They had shapers stolen from Doma, so they should have the advantage. Too many kingdoms' shapers had been lost in the recent attacks. The kingdoms were weakened, in danger of falling if another concerted attack came, but none had. Was it because they feared the draasin, or was there some other reason?

They raced across the sky. Beneath them, the barren expanse of Incendin stretched as far as he could see. There were patches of darker brown, practically black in some places, but Tan didn't have enough time to see what they might be. He saw nothing else, no sign of life, nothing that indicated an imminent attack.

They flew east. Slightly to the north was a hint of red flames rising from the Fire Fortress. Tan had only seen it through Asboel's eyes, never his own, and he felt a thrill of fear at how close they had to be for him to see it at all. Then it was gone. They moved quickly, their speed increasing the farther they moved toward the east. Toward Doma, he realized. The last time he'd been there, he'd nearly died.

Amia's concern filled the bond and he squeezed her against him.

Tan reached out with earth sensing. Doing it while airborne was difficult. The connection was weaker this way, but he pressed out anyway. He didn't sense Asboel, and that worried him. Wherever the draasin had ended up, it was probably someplace from which Tan wouldn't have easy access to help. Roine had claimed there were kingdoms' shapers in Incendin. Would they answer the summons on a rune coin?

He pulled it from his pocket. With a pulse of earth and water and wind and fire into the rune, a glow crept into it. They might not need any help, but if they did, he wouldn't be unprepared. Not when there might be other shapers out here, shapers stolen from Doma.

They began to slow as they neared a wide swath of green below. Strange trees rose up from the ground, wide leaves appearing waxy from a distance as they caught the light. Sharp thorns rose from their sides. Nothing but barren waste stretched on either side of the patch of green. Tan sent instruction to Honl to avoid the trees and the green and they landed softly on the hot ground.

Honl's presence caused dust to swirl around them and Tan studied the land beyond the dust cloud. It was different than the other parts of Incendin he'd been through. There, it had been rocky and almost mountainous. This was flat. Wide fissures split the ground in places, and Tan had the sense that if the earth shifted, the fissures would open and swallow him.

All of Incendin was hot and barren, but strange plants still managed to grow. Most had thorns and were twisted. A single stunted tree attempted to grow nearby. Thick, waxy leaves grew in clumps from the ends of branches, and the bark was a deep gray, almost black. Tan reached out with earth sensing and could tell which of the plants were dangerous and likely to attack. From what he could tell, that included most of them.

He looked beyond the waste and stared toward the green. Honl had given them some distance from it. It was abrupt rather than gradual, as if a line had been drawn across the Incendin waste and renewed life suddenly sprang up along lines of demarcation. Trees grew there, sharing some traits with the stunted one, but the leaves were wider and the tree itself another ten feet taller. Strange greenish-yellow grasses grew. A few flowering plants emerged in the spaces between the grasses and the trees.

"What is that?" Tan asked. "I thought it was Doma."

Amia shook her head. "Not Doma. You've been to Doma. It's mountains and sea. There is little else to Doma."

"Then what is it?" he asked.

"I don't know, but that's where Asboel is."

CHAPTER 14

The Draasin Trapped

TAN PUSHED WITH EARTH SENSING toward the patch of green life, so out of place in Incendin. His sensing brought him past lines of poisonous plants and into the suddenness of vibrant plants and flowers. He expected something similar to the danger he sensed all around him in Incendin, that of poisonous plants and insects that wanted nothing more than to attack, but he sensed none of that. The plants did not seem violent and angry. There was nothing but a benign sense. The pointy spines on the plants might catch their clothes, but the plants wouldn't harm them otherwise.

He pressed harder, straining with more strength in earth sensing than he'd used in ages. Once, he had been quite skilled, using earth sensing constantly as he made his way through the mountains around Nor. Living in Ethea took away his practice. Now, what would once have come easily to him required thought and effort.

If Asboel was in danger, Tan had to push forward and find the answer.

Watch over us? he asked of Honl.

The elemental hesitated. *I may be limited with what aid I can offer.*

Tan paused and looked toward the swirling colors he associated with Honl. *Why? Can wind not go everywhere?*

Not when there is another.

He noted the hesitance from the wind elemental. It was not the first time he'd sensed it from him. *Ara?*

Ara prefers I not blow through her lands, but she tolerates me. This one will not.

Which is it?

Honl didn't answer, only drifted forward.

Could it be ilaz? The other wind elemental had buzzed through Ethea, so Tan knew it would be found near here. He was tempted to call to it to know for sure, but he dared not. The last time he'd done it, the painful sound it made buzzing around him had nearly been overwhelming. He might have Honl for help, but unlike ara and how it helped his mother with her attacks, Honl seemed reluctant to do much more than carry him. That meant Tan needed to be careful.

They weaved around the poisonous Incendin plants. Without his ability to sense his way through them, Tan doubted that they would have survived. At least in the other place he'd been in Incendin, there had been a cleared path. Here, it was almost as if the plants had been set so as to prevent anyone from moving safely through.

Amia held onto him carefully. At times, there was no safe way to move through the land and he had to jump on a shaping of wind. His connection to Honl grew stronger the more he used the wind elemental, and he found himself reaching for wind more and more. With it, Tan needed less help reaching his own shaping.

Another jump and they reached the change in the landscape.

The vibrant green grasses grew in an irregular line across the ground, weaving in and out of Incendin plants, almost as if intentionally pushing them back. Trees were set back from the grass line, and a few other plants grew among the trees, sprouting flowers of all different colors. The fragrances were nothing like anything Tan recognized.

He paused and sensed the foliage. He felt nothing alarming from them.

He started to take a step but Amia held him back. "Asboel is in here, but I don't think he's alone."

How would Amia know that if he couldn't sense it with his earth sensing? "Another one of the draasin?" Could Enya or Sashari be with him? Was that why Tan couldn't reach him as he thought he should?

"I don't think so."

"The lisincend?" The last Tan knew, the draasin had been attacking them. If anything were to happen to him, it would likely be from twisted fire shapers.

Amia bit her lip as she frowned. She held onto his hand, her eyes sweeping into the grasses. "I don't know."

Not knowing made the nervous energy rising within Tan even worse. If Asboel were in danger, he couldn't wait to reach him. And if he didn't reach him, what would happen to Tan? The pain searing through his mind remained a distant sense as he pressed it deep down inside him, but what would happen if he slipped and the power surged forward? What would happen if it increased in intensity?

He took the first step across the border. The grasses swirled around his legs, reaching toward him. A pressure built in his ears and it took Tan a moment to realize someone was shaping. Not Amia; he'd know if it were her. But what? The shaping seemed to control the grasses, leading them to twist around him as they caught in the wind. Tan reached for Honl, but the elemental wouldn't respond. With a shaping of his own, he silenced the wind, pushing it down.

"This is shaped," he said to Amia.

"The wind?"

He shook his head, surveying the grasses and the trees. "All of it, I think. It's like what we found in the cavern near the place of convergence, what the ancient warrior shapers had made."

"Did they make this?"

She meant the ancient warriors, but Tan didn't think so. There was something to the shaping that felt newer. If so, that meant someone else had created this shaping, one strong enough that it pressed back the border with Incendin. Whoever had made this possessed skill that hadn't been seen in nearly a thousand years.

He should be excited to find someone with skill like that. Instead, fear left him cautious.

A heavy wave of shaping washed over him. It came as an indistinct sense, slow and steady.

"Did you feel that?"

Amia stared toward the east. "Of course I felt it."

"Do you know what it is?"

"No."

They continued onward. As they did, Tan reached out with his earth sensing, straining through the grasses and trees to understand what had made this and to find Asboel. Something in the shaping impeded him. It reminded him of what he had done when he obscured Asboel from the kingdoms' shapers. Only this seemed intent to obscure everything from him, and over a massive scale.

He wouldn't be able to find Asboel this way. They could wander through here for days and still not find him. Tan needed another way.

"Are you recovered enough to try to reach through me again?"

"I can try. Since we're closer, maybe it will be easier."

The shaping around them likely made it harder, not easier, and was probably the reason it had taken so much strength from her the first time she'd tried reaching for Asboel.

"You'll have to help again," she said.

Tan took a deep breath, focusing on his connection to Amia and using that to reach the sense of spirit. It was easier this time. Spirit welled deeply within him and he skimmed across the surface. Amia pressed through their connection, forced herself through the bond to Asboel, this time not moving with the caution she'd shown earlier. Pain split his head and seemed to last ages before she withdrew.

Amia rested her hands on her legs, panting as if she had just sprinted through the desert. Her eyes were glossy from the effort and she took deep, steadying breaths before she could speak. "We're close. He's hurt. I don't know how, but there's something not right with him."

She led him into the deeper part of the grasses. They ducked beneath the drooping branches of trees, avoiding the spines that wanted to tear at their skin and hair. There was movement to the air, but when Tan tried to reach for it and shape it, it reacted differently. Whatever elemental worked through here resisted his attempt. Maybe it wasn't ilaz, but what other elemental could there be?

They walked for an hour, the sun burning brightly overhead, before he started to sense the change. It came gradually, the steady shifting of pressure on the grasses and a distant sense around the edges of trees. He didn't need Amia to point him toward where they were headed.

As they approached, a plume of fire shot to the sky.

Tan froze. "That was shaped."

"I can see that," Amia said.

"Can you tell who it might be?"

"Can you?" she asked.

Tan tried reaching with his earth sensing, but the shaped land still resisted him. "Not well. All that I can sense is that we're close. There's something else here, but I don't know what."

Another slow wave of indistinct shaping washed over him.

"Asboel is here," Amia said. "I can feel him. I think I retained part of your connection when I pulled back this time. I don't know what I did, but it lets me reach him more easily than I was able to before." She tipped her head toward a clump of trees. Tan thought it near the center of this shaped garden. "Whatever we'll find is in there."

"You should stay here," he warned. "You're tired and weakened from helping me reach him. I don't want you getting hurt."

She shot him a glare. "You're not going to convince me to sit on the side while you risk yourself, Tan."

"We don't even know if I would be risking myself," he said.

"I think we can assume that a shaped garden in the middle of Incendin carries with it some risk."

"I thought you said we were along the border of Incendin."

"Near enough."

"And Doma?" Tan couldn't shake the sense that they should be near Doma, but Amia was right. This wasn't what Doma looked like. There, the trees and forests looked more like Nor than anything else. There were pine and oak trees stretching along the mountainside. Even the scents of Doma were like what he found in Galen. Nothing like these strange trees.

She pointed toward the north, where a dark blur rose above the horizon. "That would be Doma. Much farther to the east and we reach the coast."

Maybe if they were closer to the coast, he could ask the udilm to help. Then again, udilm might not answer. His water elemental connection was to the nymid.

Another shaping of fire shot toward the sky.

Tan prepared to attack if needed by mixing fire and air into a shaping of his own as he started forward. They stepped past a barrier of trees ringing an open area. Shaped flowers filled the clearing. There, in the center of the clearing, Asboel lay on his side. His breathing came slowly and irregularly. Flames scorched the trees around them, but not as much as Tan would have expected from the draasin. Amia held a hand on his arm, keeping him back.

"Can't you sense it?" she whispered.

He shook his head. "Sense what?"

"This was for him. I'm not sure what's happening, but there is power here. Whatever it's doing is holding Asboel in place." She turned to him, sweeping her hands out in a wide circle "Now that I see him, I can sense it. All of this. Everything that has been shaped. *This* is the pain you feel."

A shaping raced toward Asboel and he responded with a spurt of flame, blocking whatever attacked him. That had been Asboel's shapings he'd seen, but Tan hadn't known. Had he pushed him so distantly into the back of his mind that he could no longer sense even that?

All around him, he now sensed wind, but not wind he'd ever known. It mixed with water and earth, circling the ground below Asboel. Fire mingled within it. Tan might not understand what the shaping would do, but he understood the intent.

"Spirit." Someone intended a spirit shaping with Asboel.

Doma shapers, then. It had to be. Other than the stolen shapers from Doma, Incendin didn't have anything other than fire shapers. They must have learned this shaping from the First Mother.

Rage bubbled up from Tan as he began to understand. The attack might not even be meant to harm Asboel. The shaping held him in place, but if they used spirit, they wanted to control Asboel, much like the archivists had once sought to control Enya. In order to do that, they'd have to sever the bond he shared with Asboel. Which meant these shapers knew of the connection. This attack was the reason he suffered along with Asboel.

"Can you find them?" he asked.

"Tan—"

He shot her a look. "I will not sit idle while they attack him."

"As soon as you do anything, they will know you're here, if they do not already. Without knowing how many of them there are, I'm not sure that's the best idea."

Tan stared at Asboel. The only other time he'd seen the draasin injured had been when Althem had blasted him from the sky. Had Tan not intervened, he might have died. Asboel thought himself powerful enough that little could harm him, but in spite of his power, he was still mortal.

Another cycle of shaping rolled through. This was different than before. Wind swirled around Asboel, lifting under his wings. Earth rolled over his front legs, holding him down. Water swirled in the wind. There was enormous strength to the shaping.

Tan realized that he might not be strong enough to stop the shapers.

Asboel roared, but weakly. Steam hissed from his nostrils. He attempted to push out with a shaping of fire, but it failed. Much longer, and his connection to Tan would be gone. Given what Zephra had described from the loss of the bond, that might be worse than dying.

"Find them," he asked Amia. "Send me their location. I have to stop this."

He unsheathed the warrior's sword; he had only used it one time before.

"Tan," Amia started, "please come back to me."

He clenched his jaw, eyes flickering to where Asboel rested. Earth had nearly enveloped him completely. More than anything else, that would hold Asboel. Earth countered fire better than nearly any of the other elements.

Tan began drawing shapings through the sword. Had he not been as angry as he was, he would have wondered if the shapings would work, but his anger fueled the shapings. Fire. Water. Earth. Wind came slowest, but it came.

He looked back at Amia. "I have to do this."

The pained look on her face told him that she wished he didn't, but the shaped connection between them told him that she understood.

CHAPTER 15

Rescue

THE DISTANCE FROM THE EDGE of the trees to Asboel, nearly enveloped by shapings, did not seem that great, but resistance hit him as soon as Tan set foot into the clearing. Grasses twisted and twined about his ankles. The ground trembled. The air felt thick and hot. All of it was shaped.

With a roar, he pressed a shaping out through the sword, severing what worked to trap him. He managed to make it another dozen steps before another attack came. It was as if the ground and plants and air all conspired against him. Tan spun, slicing with the sword, pushing out with a shaping he drew through the sword, but they came quickly.

The trees.

It was Amia's voice and it drifted through his mind, almost as if slowed by the shapings, as well.

Tan glanced to the trees. At first, he saw nothing. A flash of color in one of the treetops caught his eyes. He focused his attention there, briefly ignoring the attack thrown at him. Fire. He was certain of it. When the shaper used fire, he sensed it.

Tan raised the sword. Using earth, he sent a lancing shaping through the sword toward the shaper. Had they been anywhere but this strangely shaped garden, his shaping would likely have simply destroyed the shaper. Instead, it merely knocked him back. That contented Tan.

The shaping attacking him—attacking Asboel—shifted. No longer did fire work through it. Whatever attempt they made using spirit changed, lessening with the absence of fire. Tan shifted his attention to wind. With the connection he'd formed with Honl, Tan thought he might reach wind next, but the shaping eluded him. Whatever wind blew through here kept Honl back. The grasses continued to spiral up his legs. The shaking ground trembled beneath him, threatening to topple him. If he fell, he suspected the grasses would quickly manage to hold him in place.

Can you find them? he asked Amia.

I can't.

They want to sever the bond. They want Asboel.

The ground shook again, throwing his attention away from Amia. With an angry stomp, Tan sent a shaping through the earth, plunging deep as he reached for golud. Would the earth elemental even respond out here?

Stop!

He sent it as a rumbling fashion as he always did when speaking to golud, a demand upon the elemental. The trembling paused and he heard a startled gasp nearby. Tan focused on where he'd heard the shaper and sent a blast of fire through the sword. A grunt rewarded him.

Two shapers were slowed. That left wind and water.

Tan ran toward Asboel. This time, the grasses left him alone. He slashed at them with the sword as he ran. Wind coalesced in front of him, but he pressed a shaping of fire and earth against it, the warrior's sword augmenting the shaping and burning the shaping away. The air became heavy, filled with moisture, and Tan pushed back with fire, burning away the water shaped in the air. Had he more skill, he might have removed the water from the air, but he didn't know how.

Then he reached Asboel. The heat that usually radiated from his massive sides had eased. His breaths came slowly. Tan touched his side, moving past the thick spines on his back. Asboel lifted his head and twisted to look at him with golden eyes that had gone dull. He shook his head once and tried to growl, but nothing came from him but steam.

The attack changed.

The shapers switched their focus from Tan and moved back to Asboel. Water and wind swirled around him. Fire added with it, and then earth. Whatever brief success Tan had in slowing them had failed.

They drew on spirit. It pressed *into* Asboel.

Tan felt the pain of the shaping through the connection he shared with Asboel. It was there, deep and buried, agonizing to the draasin.

Is there anything you can do? he asked Amia.

I'm not strong enough, not after… She didn't need to explain. She'd spent too much strength simply trying to find the draasin. *Can you stop the shapers?*

They're too skilled and I don't know where they are. They stopped focusing on me. They've nearly finished what they intend with Asboel.

He had no idea what they intended by breaking the bond, but it could not happen. It would leave Asboel vulnerable.

And if Amia couldn't help, Tan had to do it himself.

That meant pain. Possibly more than he could tolerate, but if he didn't, Asboel would be lost. For all Tan knew, another could assume the bond.

Incendin. One of the Doma shapers.

Fur.

Tan took a deep breath, but before drawing the connection to Asboel to the forefront of his mind, he reached deep within himself and found the connection to spirit. Each time he found it, it became easier. Tan pulled on this connection, hoping to protect his mind as he plunged through it to Asboel.

Then he reached for the draasin. The pain was immediate and unbearable.

He sunk to his knees. The grasses wrapped around his ankles and legs, reaching for his wrists. He ignored them, unable to focus on anything other than the pain.

Tan steadied his breathing. With the connection to spirit, he pushed toward Asboel.

The pain intensified. He retched, heaving on the grasses. Somehow he managed to keep from falling forward.

Was he wrong? Would this not work?

Distantly, he sensed the increased shaping the Doma shapers worked. The pain intensified. The bond felt like a fragile, frail thing. In spite of the pain, he had a vague sense of Asboel, but it was distant and weak.

Then the pain stopped. The bond severed.

Tan fell to the ground.

In that moment, he pressed through the spirit inside him, reaching for Asboel. A barrier tried to stop him, but Tan knew Asboel. This was his friend, *his* bond. Spirit surged and Tan poured it into the draasin.

Asboel.

The name came from him in a shout. Pain and nausea rolled through him, nearly more than he could tolerate. No answer came. Had he been too late?

Asboel!

Tan pressed everything that he could into the shaped connection, praying to the Great Mother that he could protect his elemental bond. His friend.

Maelen. The voice boomed in his head and came as a satisfied sigh. *I warned you this place is dangerous.*

Are you…

Tan couldn't finish. He wasn't sure he wanted to know if Asboel would die from this attack. The shapers had known about the connection they shared, they had known *how* to attack Asboel.

It will take more than this to end me.

The shapings began wrapping with more intensity around Tan. Grasses cut into his legs and arms. Wind pressed against his face, smothering him. The earth rumbled. With enough time, it would split open and swallow him.

Next to Tan, Asboel struggled to stand, but the earth held him. With a roar, the draasin spouted fire in violent arcs around the clearing. It skirted Tan, not touching or burning him, but it freed him from the shapings. The ground steadied and wind eased.

Tan rose to his feet and held his sword in front of him. The effort of reconnecting to Asboel had weakened him. He could shape, but it would not be with much power or strength. Anything he would manage would require the elementals.

Asboel continued to shoot flames around the clearing. Rage filled him and he sniffed the air as he searched for the shapers. The draasin pawed at the ground. His wings unfurled and flapped, sending a hot breeze circling around him.

The change in the air was welcome to Tan. *Honl.*

The wind elemental swirled around Asboel, coming to pause in front of Tan. *Did I not warn you?* the wind elemental asked. *Danger, I said. Fire nearly lost. These are dark lands.*

Can you help?

Honl hesitated and swirled around Asboel. *Fire is weak. I will try.*

A gust of warm wind split away from them, driving toward the line of trees. Asboel continued to shoot flames around him, but Tan could tell that what Honl said was true. The draasin was weakened.

Cool air mixed with the warm, and Honl was blown back. The elemental fluttered toward Asboel, circling around his spines and using the warmth of his body, but something had changed about the wind elemental.

Danger, Honl said.

The shapers stepped away from the trees, becoming visible for the first time. They wore simple brown leathers that blended into the shaped garden, nothing like what Tan usually saw on Incendin shapers. They approached slowly, a concerted effort, one mixing all the elements, though this time not in an attempt to reach fire, but simply to overpower the elementals and Tan.

Asboel and Honl had failed. He pressed through the ground, reaching for golud with a rumbling request for help, but the earth elemental did not answer this time.

Go, he urged Amia. *Find safety.*

There was no answer.

Had she been hurt? He scanned the clearing, looking for a sign of her, but there was nothing. There was nothing Tan could do against four powerful shapers. All his energy had been spent trying to heal the bond with Asboel. At least the pain in his mind was gone. Reforging the connection had healed that much at least.

Asboel, I am sorry.

Maelen.

The great fire elemental roared. Fire shot from his mouth but was pressed back by a shaping of wind and water. Earth pulled at the draasin's feet, confining him again.

After everything they had been through, they would fall here together. Tan would not have the chance to be with Amia. And Roine would never know what happened.

He sighed.

With the last of his strength, he formed a shaping of all the elements, binding them together. Doing this nearly took everything he had remaining. Tan pushed this energy into the sword. Runes glowed along the surface, burning brightly. Then he dipped into spirit and added this.

Bright light lanced from the tip of the sword.

Asboel roared. Honl swirled with renewed energy.

Other shapings erupted around them. Fire bloomed from the north. Earth rumbled toward him, different than the other earth shaping. Wind gusted, cool and refreshing, reminding Tan of the winds of Galen.

The rune coin in his pocket burned.

Now, Tan.

It was Amia. She wasn't gone.

Ours? Could it be possible? Could the kingdoms' shapers have found them?

The shaping focused on Tan and the elementals shifted, turning away from them. It was the opening he needed. Tan pointed the sword toward the nearest shaper. If these were Doma shapers, twisted by the First Mother, they deserved a chance at redemption.

"Stop!" he shouted.

One of the shapers turned back to him. A shaping of wind built. Tan wouldn't be able to stop it, not without harming himself. Wind began to swirl, pulling on him.

Tan reluctantly turned the sword toward the shaper. Was there nothing he could do? If only he could remove the First Mother's shaping on him, he might be saved.

The wind shaping built. Tan couldn't wait any longer. He sent the combined shaping through the sword. Light shot through the wind shaper, tearing him apart. The wind ceased.

Another shaper turned toward him. With a rumbling, rolling motion, the shaper sent earth toward him. The ground began to split. Tan pointed the sword and the blinding white light tore through the other shaper as it had through the first.

The remaining two shifted their attention back to Tan, who said, "Please. I don't want to—"

He didn't have the chance to finish. The shapers attacked at the same time, mixing fire and water in a swirl of steam.

Tan couldn't react in time. He pointed the sword toward the water shaper, but his effort faltered. All the shaping strength he had failed.

Asboel leaped in front of him, absorbing the shaping. He roared and fell silent.

Tan felt another shaping build but couldn't see anything. Asboel blocked his view. Massive power built, culminating in an attack. Tan leaned against Asboel, waiting.

Nothing came.

Asboel?

Maelen.

Are you injured?

It is temporary, he said.

Asboel shifted, slowly dragging himself to his feet. As he did, Tan held his breath, uncertain what he'd see when Asboel moved. What had happened to the shapers?

Asboel settled himself in the middle of the clearing again, curling his tail around himself. He took deep, contented breaths that matched what he felt through their bond. Heat again radiated from his sides. He would be fine.

"Nice of you to finally choose to introduce me to the draasin."

Tan turned. Cianna stood, staring at Asboel. Her fiery orange hair stood out from her head. She wore a black shirt and pants that clung to her, making her look like an Incendin shaper. She turned to face Tan. "This is what it took, though?"

"What," he began, barely able to catch his breath, "what happened?"

Cianna shrugged and glanced to the trees. Amia leaned against the trunk of one. As he watched, he realized the leaves already began to wilt. The green in the grasses around his feet faded. "You summoned. She found us."

Amia had brought them here. Not only Cianna, but the other shapers sent by Roine.

Tan let out a relieved sigh. "Thanks for coming."

"What was this?" Cianna asked.

"Doma shapers, I think. The ones twisted by the First Mother."

"What did they want?"

He shook his head. "I don't know. They tried severing my connection to the draasin."

Her eyes widened. "Didn't know that was possible for a shaper to do."

"Neither did I."

"Just shapers? Seems like they moved around an awful lot of power."

Tan started toward the edge of the clearing and Amia. "You think they can speak to the elementals?"

Cianna glanced at the ground. "That one. The fire shaper." She pointed to a body lying motionless on the ground. "Had it not been for Alan, I'm not sure I would have been able to stop her. Now, that could just be Incendin training, but I've seen a few Incendin fire shapers in my time along the border. Seems that whatever she did was more than simply a fire shaping."

Could they have used elemental power as well? It seemed unlikely, but not impossible. Tan had seen too much in the time since he'd learned to shape to think anything was really impossible.

Tan hurried over to Amia. She stared at the clearing, her eyes wide. He sensed the fatigue she felt through their shaped bond.

"Are you okay?" he asked.

She nodded. "What you did..."

Tan sighed. "I know. I didn't want to, but I couldn't do anything else."

"What was that shaping?" she asked.

"I don't know. I bound the elements together and used the sword."

"That wasn't spirit."

"No. I added spirit to the shaping."

Amia stared at the sword a moment before turning to him. She threw her arms around his neck and pulled him in a tight embrace. "Thank you."

"Why?"

"For not hesitating any longer. I know you thought you might be able to save them. I felt your hesitation. But there wasn't anything you could do."

Tan looked over her shoulder. Could he have done anything differently?

Not and save those he cared about. Asboel lived. Amia was safe. Wasn't that all that mattered?

Yet he still didn't understand what had happened here.

CHAPTER 16

Search for Allies

TAN SAT NEXT TO AMIA sat along the Incendin shore. Cianna crouched nearby. Warm wind gusted around them, flickering off his face, mixing the scent of salt with the hot sea breeze. Ashi swirled within the breeze, Tan was certain of it now. Honl was there, a translucent figure that practically hung in the air, no longer afraid to show his presence.

Asboel rested on the rocks overlooking the water. His deep golden eyes stared out to the sea. Tan wondered what he saw. He didn't try reaching through their connection to borrow the image. The draasin was still tired and wounded. Whatever shaping had struck him at the end had taken more out of him than he admitted, but Tan could tell he would be fine. In time, he would heal. But for now, Asboel needed to rest.

Amia slept next to him. The shapings she'd been forced to use had taken too much out of her. Tan felt exhausted, too, but his strength returned more quickly. Did he borrow from the elementals, letting him regain his strength more quickly?

"What did you find in Incendin?" he asked Cianna. The other kingdoms' shapers were camped farther down the shore; they refused to remain too close to the draasin. How long would they feel that way around him? Would he ever change that?

She sat cross-legged behind them and flickered fire on and off her palm.

"Nothing. Theondar sent us scouting. He was worried about the Doma shapers. We were to rescue those we could."

Tan pushed away the image of the dead shapers. "They didn't want rescuing."

Cianna's face scrunched in a troubled frown. "No. And they were more skilled than what I expected for shapers trained in Incendin. Theondar will need to know."

"Not all were trained in Incendin," Tan said. "Some went to Ethea to learn before they were captured."

Cianna frowned and cupped a ball of flame in her hand. Tan saw the way she shaped it, how she pulled it from within her and held the shaping just above the surface of her hand. Now that he understood fire shaping better, he thought he might be able to replicate this one. A fireball might have uses.

How much would he be able to learn if he had the time? Would he ever have the time to simply study shaping, or would he forever be chasing ever-greater threats around the kingdoms?

"Can you get rid of that?" he asked, pointing toward the shaped garden. Now that they were far enough away, Tan suspected the intent of the garden. It trapped and amplified power, but only for the shapers who created it. Perfect for capturing one of the draasin.

With a snap of her wrist, she sent a burst of flame back toward the patch of green. Fire erupted along the dry grasses, quickly alighting and glowing with a steady reddish light. It blazed across the garden quickly, confined to the garden without spreading outside the borders of what the shapers had created.

Asboel twisted his head to stare at the flames eating through the remains of the garden. He tipped his head to Cianna. *Tell her that was skillfully done.*

Tell her yourself, Tan said.

Asboel snorted steam at him.

Tan turned to Cianna. "The draasin would like you to know he thinks your shaping skillfully done."

A wide smile split her face. "Tell him thanks."

Tan shook his head slightly. "I think he understands you fine."

"Really?"

Asboel studied her. *This one is interesting.*

Haven't you met a fire shaper before?

None that haven't tried to kill me.

Those were all from Incendin. They work with Twisted Fire.

Not all.

Tan looked out over the sea. Now that he had Asboel back to safety, the draasin needed to know what he'd learned. Tan just wasn't sure how he would react. As weakened as he was, would Asboel be able to do anything? Knowing the draasin, he wouldn't rest until he managed to save the hatchlings—only Tan suspected that they were in the Fire Fortress. There would be too much shaping power to attack there.

Tell me, Asboel commanded.

Tan sighed and looked up at the draasin. Asboel stared back, his enormous eyes practically swallowing Tan. Steam came from his nose but didn't burn Tan. Perhaps unsurprisingly, it didn't burn Cianna either. She sat, for all intents looking unperturbed by the billows of hot air coming from the draasin's nose.

The hatchlings. They live.

That is not possible. I saw them.

You saw them weakened. They were taken.

Tan sent an image of Fur through to Asboel. The draasin roared softly.

How is it you know this?

Ashi.

Asboel's tail lashed from side to side. *So. You have bound another.*

Not bound, I don't think.

Do you know its name?

Tan nodded and Asboel snorted again.

Then you are bound. I did not think you could bind another, not without losing our bond.

Maybe because it had been weakened? Tan asked.

Perhaps. I should not be surprised it is ashi, though. Asboel unfurled his wings and flapped once. Hot air drifted out from beneath his wings, buffeting around him. Translucent swirls moved within the wind and what seemed like faces appeared. Tan had always assumed it to be ara. *They are drawn to draasin. Once, they were stronger. In this time, it is another.*

Honl swirled around Asboel, swaying in front of his wings, working against the flapping of wind.

Asboel seemed to study Honl. *There could be power to this one. You may need to coax it, but it is there.*

I keep learning how little I know of the elementals, Tan said. *When I think I begin to understand, that's when something else shows me how little I know.* And if what Asboel said was true, that meant ara hadn't always been a greater elemental. Had it once been ashi? It was another question he didn't have the time to answer.

Something like a laugh came from Asboel. *There are many powerful elementals.*

Even with fire?

None like the draasin, but fire can still be powerful in other ways. Even saa burns.

Our ancient scholars claimed there are greater and lesser elementals.

Your ancient scholars were fools.

They could speak to the elementals.

And what did that teach them? Only what the elementals chose to share, Asboel said.

Tan hesitated, choosing his next question carefully. *Why do you share with me?*

We are bonded, Maelen.

Tan could sense that there was more to it than that, but he chose not to press. *What of the hatchlings?*

I will find them. If they live, they will return to me.

You will destroy Fur this time?

Asboel tipped his head and fixed Tan with those great eyes. *You would rather I not? You think he can be restored?*

Tan closed his eyes. He no longer knew whether it was possible to redeem something so far gone. *I was restored,* he said.

Your motives were different. You did not simply seek power.

Tan still wasn't convinced that was the only reason for the lisincend. There had to be something more to risk death from the transformation. *Where is Enya?*

She has gone from here. I sent her away after we attacked Twisted Fire. That is how they captured me.

I don't understand.

She attempted to withdraw too much fire. I stopped her before she destroyed herself. Much like you, she sought to do it for reasons other than power. Now she must heal.

Like you.

Asboel flicked his tail to the side. *Like me.*

How did you stop her?

I had to take it from her. It weakened us both. That is how they managed to capture me.

If it weakened her, where did she go?

When they came for me, I sent her away. She has suffered too much. She desires vengeance from Twisted Fire. I have promised it to her in time.

Where is she now? Can you sense her?

If I choose. Fire bonds us.

As it does you and I?

Asboel tipped his head and stared at Tan. *Fire does not bind us. The Mother binds us.*

And now, after what Tan had done to save Asboel, did spirit bind them? *Where is she?* Tan asked again.

Near these lands, but not. Do not worry, Maelen.

What will you do? Tan feared Asboel's next attack on the lisincend. What would happen to him if he attempted to attack before he was fully healed?

Recover. Then I will find the hatchlings. Twisted Fire must not be allowed to bond them.

Could they?

Asboel turned and stared toward Incendin. Through their connection, Tan saw the Fire Fortress burning brightly. *It is possible.*

I could help, Tan offered.

Asboel seemed to hesitate. *Twisted Fire cannot harm us.*

Tan shook his head, pushing back the frustration he felt. *We've seen that it can. And if Twisted Fire has grown more powerful—*

That was not Twisted Fire. Twisted Fire will feel the power of a draasin attack in full.

Tan shivered. Part of him wished he could see it. *You will wait until you recover?*

This time, I will wait. All will be needed. You may hunt with me.

Asboel slowly stood. He stretched his wings, and a surge of power filled the air with steam. He had recovered quickly, but he was still not as powerful as he would be in a few days. Tan sensed that time was needed. Would Asboel really wait?

With a steady flapping of his wings, Asboel took to the air.

Hunt well, friend.

A spurt of flame erupted from his nose. *Always, Maelen.*

As Asboel disappeared, moving quickly north—toward Nara, Tan realized—he looked over to Cianna. He had a few days at most before Asboel was well enough to attack. He would use that time to do what Roine asked, but then he would return to help Asboel. In the meantime, he needed someone to keep watch for him.

"You were planning on scouting Incendin for Doma shapers?"

She nodded slowly. "Why do I have the feeling I won't like what you have to say?"

"I want you to watch the Fire Fortress. I'm afraid that the draasin will attack it soon. They might need help."

"You can be stupid sometimes. Why should I believe the draasin would care about the fortress?"

"Because the draasin had two eggs. Hatchlings. And the lisincend destroyed them. At least, we thought they had destroyed them. It turns out Fur might have them."

Her eyes narrowed. "Fur has them?"

"From what I can tell."

She turned and looked toward the north. "You know that all fire shapers serve along the border. I saw Fur once. It was years ago, and the lisincend seemed to simply test the border. But he killed one of our shapers who made the mistake of crossing." She turned back to him, hard determination in her eyes. "I will help the draasin."

"And the others? Will they help?"

She smiled. "We have not yet freed the Doma shapers."

Tan laughed softly. Amia stirred next to him.

"What of you?" Cianna asked.

"Theondar asked me to find allies. The draasin are safe for now, but they need healing. If Incendin is powerful enough to do this, we need more help than even Roine realizes."

A shadow passed over Cianna's face and made her look drawn, tense. "Before you summoned, we were tracking a shaper. I thought it a Doma shaper, but that could not be. Not with what we saw where the draasin was injured."

"What happened?"

"That's just it. We lost them. It was a wind shaper. They took to the air, moving east over the sea."

"Zephra?" Tan asked, but that seemed unlikely. Were Zephra involved, she would have aided the kingdoms' shapers. And Zephra was to go to Doma, not across the sea.

"Not Zephra. She has a summoning rune were she to need to find us. This was different."

Tan stared out over the water. Roine might be right that they needed help, but Incendin continued with whatever made the fires burn brighter on the fortress. If it involved the creation of additional lisincend, they would truly be challenged, especially now that he saw what their shapers were capable of doing. They needed more than help, and they needed to stop the lisincend for good. They could use the draasin for help for part of that, but only after Asboel recovered and even then, he would be distracted by the desire to find the hatchlings. They needed additional allies.

"Where do you think they went?"

Cianna shook her head. "I don't know. There's not much across the sea. Zulas. Xsa Isles." She shrugged. "I'm no sailor, so I can't help."

Tan thought of the maps he'd seen. Could they find help they needed there? *Can you take me, Honl?*

The wind elemental seemed to consider the answer for a moment, flittering around Tan and Amia. *It will be dangerous.*

From what Tan had learned, Honl thought everything was dangerous. *We will only be gone a day or two, then we'll return to help fire.*

That seemed to appease the elemental. *I will help.*

Tan leaned back, staring at the waves splashing against the shore. This close to Doma, he wished he could find Elle. Likely she was well, living in one of the seaside villages, communing with the udilm. Were there more time, he'd find her and visit, but that was a luxury he didn't have.

A deep braying from the north startled him. It had been months since he'd heard the calls of the Incendin hounds. They weren't close, just far enough that he didn't think they needed to worry, but it meant they couldn't simply sit and wait. They would have to move soon.

The sense of Asboel was distant. How long before he recovered fully? How long before the draasin attacked the lisincend again?

If nothing else, after seeing what Incendin had done to the draasin, Tan knew Asboel needed more help than he realized. And he would be there for him.

CHAPTER 17

Another Attack

THE SHAPING OF WIND AUGMENTED by the wind elemental lifted them and carried them over the sea, moving through hot and dry air. Honl lifted them higher and higher to where the air was cooler and moved easily, a brisk current that pulled them along. Tan held tightly to Amia as they flew, feeling less secure than any of the times he'd ever flown with Asboel, though Honl gave no sign of dropping them.

Asboel was a distant sense in the back of his mind. From what Tan could tell, he nestled next to heat and flame. An image of Sashari filtered through their connection and he knew the draasin were still recovering.

Amia pressed against him, face buried in his arm. Her long, golden hair whipped around her, flipped by the wind so that it lashed against his face and arms.

"Do you think we'll find anything?" she asked.

"Cianna said they followed a shaper. If there are shapers, maybe we can find help."

"And if there is no help?"

Tan hesitated before answering. "As soon as Asboel recovers, I need to return to him. He intends to attack Incendin. I will be there when he does."

She squeezed him and said nothing.

Do you know where others like me can be found?

Honl swirled around him, a translucent tracing in the air. *There are no others like you, Tan.*

Any other time, he might have smiled. *Shapers. Do you know of other shapers?*

Let us return to your home. There are shapers there.

We need help. One of my people saw someone going this way.

It is dangerous.

Can you find them?

Honl waited a moment before answering. *I can find them, but it is not safe. You need caution.*

Tan wondered if Honl was always so careful.

They moved faster and further to the east. Water was still nothing but a blur beneath them, crests of white waves breaking the sheet of blue, when they began their descent. The ground showed flashes of green, but mostly it was rocky and desolate. It partly reminded Tan of Incendin, but there was none of the same warmth to the air, nothing that would make him feel Incendin's danger. In the distance, mountains rose, peaked with patches of snow. The air held the scent of pines and earth, but little else. As they landed, Tan reached out with his earth senses but found nothing that would explain to him where they were.

"This is where the shaper went?" Amia asked.

"This is where Honl brought us," Tan said. "Though I'm not really sure where we are, either."

"I think this is Par," Amia said, pointing toward the mountain. "You can see that peak from the sea. It marks these lands. But I don't think they have shapers."

Tan remembered it from the maps. If they were right, Par was a massive land, separated by the sea from Incendin and the kingdoms.

Honl fluttered someplace nearby, close enough that Tan could sense him, but more like a vague presence. Tan pushed out further with earth sensing, straining for answers. *Are you certain this is the place, Honl?*

As he asked, a shaping of fire lifted to the air from their right.

"Tan?" Amia asked.

He twisted to see fire spouting above the ground. The shaping was controlled, tight and strong, nothing like any shaping he'd ever experienced. It reminded him of nothing of what he'd found from Incendin shapers. This was powerful in a different way. There was a vague familiarity to it that Tan couldn't quite understand.

Another shaping lifted to the air from their right.

"What do you think that is?" Amia asked.

Tan focused on the shaping, trying to understand what he sensed. "It's not a shaping I've ever seen before," he started, "but I don't—"

He cut off when he felt another shaping building. This time, it was behind him. Not fire, but of earth. The ground rumbled, rolling toward them until it rippled around his feet. Tan stomped on the ground, sending out a request to golud.

The elemental didn't answer. As Ferran had taught him, he stretched out with his senses, connecting to the earth, and had begun a shaping when Amia distracted him.

"Tan!"

He tried turning, but the shaping of earth took hold of his feet, pulling him into the ground. Tan shaped fire, softening the ground as he'd once done within the archives, and with a loud, rumbling crack, he managed to free himself.

He turned to Amia and prepared a shaping of wind, but it didn't come. The shaping that had surrounded his feet had also grabbed her, trapping her between two massive chunks of rock.

"Release your shaping or I'll crush her."

Tan spun to see a man studying them. Nearly Tan's height and as muscular as his father had once been, the man wore black leather and had a closely shaven head. A long scar ran along the side of his face, and he was missing an ear. The earth shaping radiated from him.

Amia?

I can't...

She screamed as the shaping shifted. "As I said, release your shaping or I will crush her. I will not have her trying her shaping on me. It will not work." He spoke with a strange inflection and anger rang in his voice.

We will have to move carefully. If there are shapers of this much power here, we might be able to use them. Honl, Tan continued, *stay away for now. But watch us carefully.*

The wind elemental was somewhere far from them, but passed on a sense of assent.

Tan released his connection to the wind. Amia let out a relieved gasp. He resisted the urge to check on her, thankful that he could sense her through the bond. "Who are you?"

The man snorted. "I do not think you're in any position to be asking questions."

Another shaper appeared, this time on a gust of wind. Had he been the shaper Cianna had seen? There was something about the wind that felt off. Tan couldn't quite place what it was.

A new concern settled through him. Had he been wrong about the shapers they found in Incendin? Had they not been from Incendin?

"You found them. He will be pleased."

The earth shaper glared at the wind shaper. "I did not capture them to please him."

"No? Then you do it for yourself? You really are an odd one, Tolman."

Tolman sent a ripple of earth toward the wind shaper, who quickly lifted to the air. "Enough. Bind them in wind. We'll figure out what to do with them when we reach the city."

"You think this is all of them?"

Tolman looked at Tan and a dangerous expression played over his face. "If not, we will soon learn how many there are. If Incendin thinks they can attack us in our homeland, they will find that they will fail."

They were floated forward on the wind shaper's shaping. Their hands were bound in lashings of wind. Tan was impressed with how the wind shaper managed to do it, using invisible wraps of air to hold them snugly. He couldn't escape without a significant wind shaping.

The shapers thought them from Incendin. How would he convince them that they were kingdoms shapers? The control they displayed with their shaping was incredible. If he and Amia could convince them, they would be powerful allies.

Amia remained silent. Concern drifted through the bond, but she said nothing.

As they traveled, Tan felt a strange sense from the wind. The shaper used an elemental. Not ara. From what he could tell, ara was not in these lands. But it was a familiar and angry sense, like what he heard when he'd called to ilaz.

Any thought he had that Honl might help them was dashed when he realized that the shaper spoke to the elemental. How else would he manage such control?

Using the lessons his mother had taught, Tan listened for the wind. If he could hear what the wind shaper said—what he did with his shaping—he might be able to keep them safe. There was the buzzing, like a hive of bees swarming, but no distant voice. Without suddenly developing a mastery of the elemental, he could learn nothing.

"You are foolish to come here, fire shaper," Tolman said as they traveled. The wind shaper drifted them just above the ground, holding them over the tops of the bushes, threatening to drag them through the barbs their feet dangled over. "Have we not warned your kind before?"

Tan looked over. They thought him only a fire shaper. If nothing else, he could use that for now. "What kind do you think I am?"

Tolman turned to him and a dark smile played at the corners of his mouth. "You think I should believe you're not with the others?"

"We're not from Incendin. We came looking for help against Incendin."

The wind shaper glanced at Tolman. "The others said the same thing. They think we've not suffered attacks before? Now that Incendin is weakened, they think to attack here?"

Incendin was weakened? Did they know of the draasin attack on the lisincend already?

"We will learn what we need. If he lies, he suffers the same as the others."

The wind shaper chuckled. "Look at him. He is too soft to survive the test."

"What tests?" Tan asked. "Listen, we're only here for help—"

A wind shaping wrapped tightly around Amia, squeezing her. She writhed and kicked but couldn't do anything against it.

Tan studied the shapers, noting the intensity on their faces. Drawing through spirit deep within him, he shaped it through the bond to Amia. As he did, he understood her silence. She'd sensed them, using her ability. They would not be swayed, regardless of what Tan might say. Amia had sensed suffering, much like the kingdoms had experienced.

But couldn't that shared suffering create a connection?

The shaping squeezed more tightly on Amia, and she began to fade. With a surge of anger, Tan pulled on a shaping of fire. He no longer knew if he drew it from Asboel or the lesser elementals like saa, or how much came from within himself. He made the shaping into a tight ball of energy and flipped it at the wind shaper as they all floated overtop a barren area of rock. They had moved away from the patches of greenery and were now surrounded by nothing but sheer rock. If not for the crisp bite to the air, they could be in Incendin.

The wind shaper pushed against the fire shaping with a shaping of wind, releasing his attack on Amia as he did. With control that would have impressed Zephra, he wrapped the shaping of fire in wind and held it, slowly drawing the flames away from it.

He glared at Tan. "Try that again and I'll suffocate you."

"You may try," Tan said evenly. Would they react better to a show of strength? He held the wind shaper's eyes, unwilling to look away. "You might find I'm even less soft than you think."

Tolman let out a grunt of laughter. "Let it go, Wes. Let *him* decide what to do with these two."

They reached a peak in the rock. Tan gasped at the sight before them.

Far below were flowering trees, the golds and reds and blues filling the valley with color. Nestled in the midst of the trees was a massive city. The trees formed the beginning of what eventually became a stone wall around the city. Buildings rose above the wall, some climbing several stories high. At the center of the town was a tower made of slick black stone that reminded Tan of the Fire Fortress.

Wes lifted them with a gust of a wind shaping, carrying them with ease. He barely seemed to notice that he carried three of them on a shaping. Tan would have struggled with such a shaping. Zephra might even have struggled.

Tolman did something with a shaping of earth, somehow suspending himself as he went so that he flew alongside them. Tan could feel his shaping but couldn't see what it was that he did. None of the earth shapers in the kingdoms had ever managed to move like that. He strained with earth sensing to understand, but felt nothing that would explain it.

They soared above the forest. In the distance, water glistened off white caps. It would be beautiful if not for the fact of their capture.

Then they started down. The tower at the center of the city looked more like a series of spires splitting the sky. An occasional plume of fire lifted from the tops. Other shapings of the other elements followed, as if demonstrating the tower's strength. A high wall of smooth black stone rose up out of the ground. Tolman and Wes led them to a gate in the middle of the wall and Tolman sent a shaping at it. It swung open slowly.

Wes pushed them forward. The buzzing from ilaz droned on, but there was some variability to it, some changing to the intensity that told him that if he focused hard enough, he might begin to understand. It was there, if only he knew how to reach it.

The distant sense from Asboel remained there. The farther they came in Par, the less and less certain he felt that he'd be able to reach the draasin. Amia remained silent next to him. She was scared, but the anger inside her kept her silent as well.

The other side of the massive wall surprised him. Thousands of people walked the streets, most dressed in bright splashes of color attempting to compete with the color on the other side of the wall, nothing like the dark brown and black leather the shapers wore, as if the shapers set themselves apart. The animals were equally strange. There were thick-furred creatures that looked like horses with massive sides that pulled carts and wagons through the streets. Other creatures like squat lizards slithered along, some with riders seated atop them.

The smells were different, too. The air was warm and humid and carried with it the stink of dust and dung, but also that of exotic foods and spices, things Tan had never smelled before. He sensed at least a passing familiarity from Amia.

With all those differences, some things were the same. The rows of buildings looked like any other building in Ethea, though most were made reddish brown rock. Tan's earth senses picked up a large source of water nearby. More of the flowering trees grew all around them. Were he to reach with earth sensing, he might discover other things here that he had no explanation for, but he kept his sensing drawn tight around him.

The black tower loomed over everything.

It was like a presence, a physical sense that infused everything, as if determined to draw attention to itself. The flames spouting from the spires radiated heat and light. The other shapings came from the other spires.

If he could convince these people to help, they could be powerful allies. Then he could return and help Asboel, keep him safe before he attempted to attack the lisincend again.

They didn't make their way toward the fortress.

Tolman and Wes veered off down a side street made of hard packed rock. There were fewer people down this street, though those who did make their way along glanced only briefly at the shapers before hurrying on. They made a point of not looking at Tan and Amia.

The street let out onto another, this one secluded from the others. The faces of the buildings were different here. Like the others, they were made of thick stone, with doors of stout wood. Tan had seen little metal throughout the city to this point, almost as if it had been intentionally left off. None of the buildings had windows. Flat roofs arched over the edge of the buildings, leaving the street in shadows. This was a hidden place, he realized, kept apart from the rest of the city.

Wes stopped near a door along the middle of the street. He released the shaping of wind holding them above the ground and Tan dropped with a sudden jarring crash. He resisted the instinct to catch himself with a shaping of wind. Even were he able to suddenly shape wind, doing so would reveal the extent of his abilities and he wanted to hide anything other than fire for as long as possible, until he understood what danger they might be in.

Amia stood and dusted her hands on her legs, fixing Wes with an expression that softened. "I'm sorry for your loss."

Wes looked back at her with confusion for a moment before narrowing his eyes. "Do not try to shape me."

Amia relaxed her arms and opened her palms. "Not a shaping, but I sense your sorrow. You have suffered too much. But know that we are not the reason for your loss. We are not of Incendin."

A shaping of wind struck her across the face, knocking her back. "Do not presume to know me, Aeta. You think I don't know how you were responsible for what happened?"

He spat the last with a vehemence that surprised Tan. Even among the lisincend, there hadn't been hatred for the Aeta. How badly had they misjudged this?

Tan flung a shaping of fire at Wes, twisting it around him in a tight spiral. The wind shaper pushed against it, threatening to draw away the air the fire needed to burn, but Tan fueled it with saa, drawing the elemental. In these lands, it came willingly, granting him even more strength than in Ethea.

The shaping dropped when Tolman kicked Tan in the back, knocking him forward. "Enough." He looked at Wes and shook his head. "You're a fool. You've bonded how long? Five months? And you think yourself the equal to a fire shaper?"

Wes wiped a bead of sweat off his brow. "I am with most," he said.

"You will not touch her again," Tan whispered. He didn't bother keeping the heat out of his voice. "Or you will learn how hot fire burns."

Wes met his eyes for a moment before turning away.

Tolman laughed softly. "Oh, not soft at all, I think. You might actually have some use to us, boy."

The door opened. A wide, squat woman with thick jowls and beady eyes stared out at them. She studied Tan and Amia, then her eyes narrowed as she noted the tension between Tan and Wes. "What is this?" she snapped.

"Shapers. Incendin," Tolman said.

"We'll need more bonded to hold them. Dangerous otherwise."

Tolman nodded. "I'll stay. This one lets his emotions get him."

"Can you blame him?" the woman asked.

Tolman snorted. "Yes. As would he."

The woman tapped the door with a thick hand. "True enough. True enough. What are they?"

Tolman pushed Amia forward, though more gently than Wes would have. "Aeta. Probably nothing of use with her."

The woman's face pinched in disgust. "Of course. And him?"

"Fire. Powerful already. Nearly killed Wes. I'm surprised he hasn't transformed already. Might be why he's with her."

The woman snorted. "Maybe we can use them both."

"I didn't come to be used. I came to find help," Tan said in a rush. He needed to get them to understand why they were here. Delay only put the kingdoms at increased risk. "We're not from Incendin—"

"We'll see," the woman said, cutting him off. "We've got ways of knowing."

She took his hand in a firm grip. A wave of cold flowed over him. It took him a moment to recognize that she shaped water. And powerfully.

"Come on in." She stripped his pack. "You think he'll need the wraps?" she asked Tolman.

"For now."

"And the sword?"

Tolman shrugged. "I'll take it from him. Less danger to you that way."

Tan stiffened as his warrior sword was torn from his waist. He hadn't worn it long, but losing it felt like failure.

They shuffled him to the back of the room. Lanterns shaped from stone glowed with a steady orange light. Not flames, but not the same as shapers lanterns. Tan studied one, trying to understand what fueled them, but the woman pushed him along and through the building. Smells assaulted him, that of burnt bread and roasted meat and sweat. She shoved him down a hall lined with doors. Like outside, these were made of wood.

Everything else seemed shaped. Even the hinges were shaped, twisted from stone to form reinforced hooks the doors could swing on. The woman stopped him before one of the doors and pulled it open. She shoved Amia inside before closing it and twisting the handle. The woman moved further down the hall and stopped at another door and pulled it open.

"You'll have water and food."

Tan hesitated. They had to play this right. He might be able to shape all the elements, but there were powerful shapers here. Possibly as powerful as those within Ethea. He might not manage to escape if they couldn't convince them to help.

"We only came for help. We're not from Incendin."

"No? Fire shaper like you come from somewhere *other* than Incendin?" The woman laughed and shoved him inside, locking the door behind him.

CHAPTER 18

Captivity

THE CELL HAD A SINGLE BENCH and a ceramic pot. There was nothing else within it. No lantern, nothing to give any light. Tan pulled on a shaping of fire and set it glowing in his palm. Fire came easily. Saa swirled around the fire, dancing within it.

Tan wished he could speak to saa the way he spoke to the draasin. Maybe the lesser elemental would be able to help him here. Honl had departed, the elemental apparently nervous to help when other wind elementals were present.

Tan considered the cell. The walls were solid stone. He ran his hand along the sides, realizing that they were shaped into place. From what he could tell, most of the building was shaped into existence. That meant earth shapers of serious power, enough that they could create an entire building. The wall around the city seemed like obsidian, as did the tower. That meant fire shapers of equal strength. And he'd seen a wind shaper of considerable power. The woman shaped water and Tan wouldn't put it past her to have comparable strength.

What did it mean that so much shaping power was here?

Tan sat on the bench. It wasn't long enough for him to lay on, as if not really meant for a place to sleep. That left only the floor of the cell, but that was dusty and had a hint of dampness to it.

Amia.

He reached through the bond to her. Sharing the connection like this had uses other than knowing her emotions.

I'm here.

Are you hurt?

He sensed a dismissal of pain. *I'm angry.*

You said this was Par, but did you know there were shapers here?

Amia had a troubled sense. *No. There are some shapers in Doma and Chenir. Incendin has fire shapers. But few other shapers were ever found outside the kingdoms. I'm not sure the People knew why.*

Tan began pacing in the small room. He couldn't remain confined here for long. Asboel needed him, especially if Tan couldn't find help here.

We'll find help and then I'll get you away as soon as I can.

I'm not sure there will be help here. If not, are you sure that you can get us free?

If he had Asboel, he'd feel quite certain. Without the draasin, he was less so. Honl had not returned to him, but then, Tan didn't really know what to expect from the wind elemental.

I will keep you safe.

The bond between them let her know how uncertain he was that he could.

The door opened and soft orange light spilled in. The woman filled the doorway, blocking him from bolting, and the pressure Tan felt told him that she likely held a shaping ready. She frowned as she saw him standing, pacing from one end of the small cell to the other.

She cocked her head and considered him. "If not Incendin, where would you claim is home?"

It was a start. If he could get her to believe that he wasn't from Incendin, maybe he could get the others to believe as well. Then he could get the help they needed. "The kingdoms. Do you know the kingdoms?"

Her eyes widened slightly. "Dangerous. Nearly as bad as Incendin."

"Why would you say that?"

In answer, the woman grabbed his arm and pulled him from the cell. He didn't resist.

"Where are you taking me?"

"He asks to see you. You should be pleased. Is that not what you want? A chance to destroy him like all the others?"

Tan could do nothing but shake his head. "Who is he?"

The woman snorted, dragging him down the hall. "You will see."

As he passed Amia's cell, he sent her a warning. *Wait. I will know soon if this will work.*

Be safe, she replied.

Tan took a deep breath and let the woman lead him away. They stepped into a different part of the building, where the steady lanterns glowed within stone. She let go of him. The bindings still held, trapping his arms in place. He thought he could sever them, but doing so would only admit to them that he could shape more than wind. Tan wasn't ready for such an admission quite yet, not until he understood what was happening here.

She walked ahead of him, trusting that he'd follow, unmindful of the fact that she put her back to him. For all she knew, he would shape fire and destroy her.

Honl?

Tan sent the thought out on a breath of wind as they stepped outside the building, trying to send it silently. He didn't know what others sensed when he communicated with the elementals. Elle had felt him speaking, but then, Elle had also managed to learn to speak to the elementals as well.

Finally, the wind elemental drifted closer, still not visible, but the sense of him grew closer.

Careful here, Tan. There are places in this city where I cannot go.

Why?

Other wind is preferred.

The woman glanced over her shoulder at him and frowned. She paused at a street corner to let one of the strange lizard creatures pass. It moved slowly, carrying a young couple with long, colorful robes. Tan realized that the dress had levels of distinction. Some robes were more heavily embroidered than others. A few people wore scarves around their necks, some with them twisted tightly around their mouths. Other than Honl, not much wind blew through here.

The woman stared at Tan. "You will not shape me."

Tan looked from her to where Honl had been, but the elemental was gone. "I wasn't."

"Hmm." She shook a flabby arm at him menacingly. "Do not think because I haven't added to your bindings that you are free to try something reckless around me. As a fire shaper, you may not know that my water shaping lets me know when you're shaping. Think twice before you attack."

Tan hadn't known that about water shaping. It explained why Elle was able to sense him shaping, though other shapers could not. "Where are you leading me?"

"You keep asking the same questions. Is everyone from the kingdoms so stupid?"

Tan grunted. The comment reminded him of what Cianna used to say to him. What would she say if she knew he'd been captured while trying to find help? She probably would think him as stupid as she'd always accused him of being.

The woman laughed. "Now you won't even talk?"

Tan twisted so that he could see the buildings around him better. The street was narrow here, and much like the one where they held him, the flat roofs stretched over the road, as if hiding what passed beneath.

"What's your name?" he asked.

Her tiny eyes narrowed to little more than slits. "Garza."

"Why are you holding me?"

Garza tipped her head back and laughed. Her massive belly shook with it.

"What?"

"When attacked as often as we have been, we learn to protect ourselves." Garza's wide face scrunched up. "Otherwise, we lose those we care about. Like Wes."

She stopped before a tall, black doorway that blocked them from going any further down the street. The roofs covering the road prevented him from seeing anything else, but the door resembled the color of the tower he'd seen on the way into the city.

"What happened with Wes?" Was that the loss Amia had sensed?

She touched the door with a shaping of water that let it slide open. "Don't pretend concern when you come to destroy us, fire shaper. You will see that the Utu Tonah is not so easy to destroy." She pressed the tips of her fingers together and looked toward the sky, inhaling deeply.

"You've got it all wrong. I'm not here to destroy anyone," Tan said.

Garza laughed again. "Because you cannot. You will see."

She started through the door, leaving Tan to follow.

Garza pushed the door closed. On this side, a wide room opened before him. There was a low ceiling and lanterns stationed along posts worked all the way around, giving a soft glow and leading to the wide, obsidian stair at the end of the room. Decorative sculptures were carved or shaped into the posts, making them appear as massive sculptures, reminding Tan of the draasin. He paused at one, studying it for a moment, before moving on. Other doors opened into this room as well. As far as Tan could tell, the room held nothing but doors, as if other areas of the city all converged here, where they could lead into the tower. Everything around him appeared shaped. Had he not been trapped as he was, he might have taken the time to ask how.

Garza started up the stairs, pausing to look back at Tan. He took the first step, moving with uncertainty. His hands, bound in front of him, made climbing the stairs more difficult, and the steps had a slickness to them. He stared at Garza's back with each step.

The stairs ended at a wide landing. Tan glanced down the hall, uncertain what he'd see. A few orange lanterns hung on the walls here, casting their light against black walls of slick obsidian. The walls were otherwise bare. The floor was a simple white marble tile.

A few people moved in the distant shadows. Tan couldn't tell anything about them.

Garza turned and headed up the next flight of stairs. Again, she didn't bother to ensure that he followed.

Tan wished for more elemental connection, anything that would make him feel more confident. With Asboel recovering in Nara, he was left with Honl, but the wind elemental had none of the confident strength of Asboel. What other elementals could he reach? Saa had so far responded, but were there others?

Tan couldn't help but think he was walking into certain death.

Garza glanced at him and laughed again. “Do not fear, fire shaper. You are blessed. You will get to see the Utu Tonah before your end.”

Chapter 19

The Utu Tonah

THE STAIRS LET OUT ONTO a wide-open floor. Bright sunlight streamed through an opening in the ceiling and glittered off the bright white tile floor. Tan shielded his eyes at the sudden change. Next to him, Garza laughed again.

She led him toward a massive dais at the end of the room. A huge chair of gold rested at the top, surrounded by shapers. Most spoke softly and kept their heads bowed as they spoke to the man sitting in the chair. Tan could *feel* the power they shaped, though he didn't have any idea why that should be.

"Who is this?" Tan asked as they approached.

"Quiet," Garza hissed. "This is the Utu Tonah." She said it almost reverentially.

Tan prepared a shaping, drawing fire and wrapping it around his connection to saa. The shaping came easily, drawn from him, almost in a flood. He had to push back the power he pulled, uncertain why it would come so easily. Was saa stronger in this land?

A soft murmuring came from the shapers around the dais. A massive man rose out of the gold chair, emerging head and shoulders above the other shapers. He wore a simple green sash over one shoulder. His head was shaved bald and a scar wrapped around from one side to the other, much like it did with Tolman. Power radiated from him.

"What have you brought me, Garza?" the man said. His voice boomed, carrying the weight of a wind shaping. There was something else to his accented inflection that Tan couldn't quite place.

"They found this one along the border. Claims he searches for help."

"Help?"

Garza nodded. "It is what he claims."

"And what is he?"

"Fire. Strongly, too. Nearly took Wes. He claims that he's not from Incendin, but with fire burning so strongly, I think that unlikely. More likely is that he came here to transform."

The man laughed, his whole body shaking though it never reached his eyes. "Wes has not bonded long. He will gain strength in time, but he is foolish to press until he masters his bond."

"Only if he's not stupid enough to make a challenge until then. Considering what happened to Deysa, it is unlikely."

The man nodded. With a shaping of wind, he floated across the distance to Tan. A wind shaper. The power coming from him was enormous, enough for Tan to feel. He'd never been around a shaper with such power.

"Why have you come? Your people are weakened. You should be there, helping protect the waste."

A shaping built. With as much power as he felt around him, Tan didn't know if there might be spirit shapers around. If they were this skilled with shaping, why wouldn't they have spirit shaping? They understood the Aeta and what Amia could do. Could anyone here shape him with spirit?

Tan reached deep into himself, to where he'd learned he could draw spirit from, and wrapped a shaping around his mind, protecting it. As a shaper himself, he didn't know if it was needed but didn't want to take an unnecessary risk, not until he knew what these people were capable of doing.

Would they recognize a spirit shaping? If they did, the man's face didn't change.

"I'm not from Incendin. I'm from the kingdoms. Incendin attacks our borders and we need allies in the fight against them. Your people clearly know the danger Incendin poses. Work with us. Help us. Together we can stop Incendin. "

The Utu Tonah considered Tan for a moment, the shaping around him building. "He is from the kingdoms?"

The large woman shrugged. "So he claims, but he shapes fire too strongly to be anything but Incendin."

"And you're sure it's only fire?" he asked.

She shrugged. "What else would it be?"

"There are those in the kingdoms who shape all the elements without a bond. They call themselves warriors." The Utu Tonah turned on Tan, darkness crossing his face. "Is it only fire? Or is it more? Is that why you were sent?"

Amia—

Pain shot through his head.

Tan felt no sense of spirit shaping, nothing that would tell him there was a reason he couldn't reach her. He'd been able to connect with her before, but that hadn't been in this place. He hadn't been standing before the Utu Tonah.

The man turned to Tan, leaning close. He smelled of sweat and exotic flowers, nothing that Tan had ever smelled before. His breath stunk of hot smoke. There was strength—earthen strength—in him. He had a fluid way of moving such that power practically flowed from him.

Not just wind, he realized. This man was a warrior shaper.

"Who are you?" Tan asked.

The man's face drew in a wide smile. "You think to question me now? If truly from the kingdoms, your people have always been fools." With a flick of his hand, the shaping holding Tan's wrists released. "Fortunate that Incendin is now weakened and we can finally move forward. There is much power to be claimed in the kingdoms."

Tan rubbed along his wrists, running his fingers where the bands of air had held him. Ridges were left in his skin. Tan breathed slowly, trying to focus on his breathing as his mother had instructed, readying a wind shaping to add to fire if needed. A part of him doubted there would be anything he could do to stop this man if he attacked.

"If you control all the elements, you would have released yourself by now. A shame it is only fire. It has been many years since I last met a worthy challenge, but even he did not last long."

Who could this man have met? Lacertin would have been away from the kingdoms long enough, but it seemed to Tan that he would have mentioned something. Roine? As Theondar, he'd traveled for the kingdoms, but even then, Tan didn't think he wandered much beyond the confines of Doma and Chenir.

A mixture of fire and air swirled around Tan, leaving the skin on his arms dry and tight. The control this man managed was incredible. "For one of fire to reach these lands, you would have a bond pair. Tell me," he said, twisting toward Tan, "where is your bond creature?"

Tan shook his head, afraid to share anything with the Utu Tonah. Asboel was injured, left in Incendin with only Cianna to protect him. "I have no bond creature," Tan said.

The man snorted. Smoke hissed from his nose, almost like steam. "Hmm. You think you will find a bond pair in Par-shon?" he asked.

"I don't know what you mean."

The man twisted, swirling on a shaping of wind mixed with earth. With his shaping ability, Tan wondered if he would be able to escape even were he to have elemental help. Smoke spiraled in the Utu Tonah's hand and created a wisp of a shape. It hung suspended in his hand, looking something like a snake, then twisted, turning into a figure like the lizard he'd seen in the street, before changing again into what he imaged saa would seem. Then it changed, shifting and elongating, stretching so that it had a tail and spikes jutting from its back. Wings sprouted from the sides. A draasin.

The man knew of the draasin.

"Fire. A bond pair. Do not pretend you don't know what I mean."

Tan couldn't take his eyes off the shape in the man's hand.

"You've seen it," the man said.

Tan considered denying that he'd seen the elemental, but what would that accomplish? He would remain prisoner. Even were he to escape from the Utu Tonah, there were others who could recapture him. From what Tan had seen of these lands, there were many skilled shapers.

Help would not be coming from Par-shon. Tan felt suddenly certain of it.

"I've seen it," Tan said carefully.

The man's mouth twisted. "Draasin. They have been gone for too long. Others should have taken their place, but they did not. Why, I wonder, is that? Have you learned the answer to that mystery in the kingdoms? You claim no bond pair, but I wonder if that isn't why you've come here. You think to find one in Par-shon? We may not know fire quite as well as the others, but it still bonds. And now draasin. I will have it soon enough. Bonded have already been sent to claim it."

Sudden understanding rocked Tan. The attack on Asboel had not come from Doma shapers working for Incendin. The attack on Asboel had been too skilled for that.

That had been Par-shon shapers.

And he realized what the Utu Tonah intended. He would bond to one of the draasin. Before nearly losing Asboel, Tan wouldn't have thought such a thing possible. A forced bond. But now? After what he'd seen, there was no denying that the shapers of this land had remembered much of the shapings that had been forgotten by the kingdoms. At least the Utu Tonah didn't seem to know what had happened to his shapers yet. When he did, how would he react?

But what did he mean about Incendin being weakened? Could the draasin attack on the lisincend actually have given Par-shon the opening they needed?

"You think it safe to bond to a draasin?" Tan asked, trying to buy time until he better understood what was happening. "Saa or inferin would be better."

The man paused and turned to him. Fire suddenly swirled around him, called by a shaping Tan had not felt.

"You think I have not already bonded to them?" He laughed as he said it. Fire suddenly died, quenched by elemental or shaped power. Tan could no longer tell with this man. "It is interesting that you arrive seeking help at the same time I learn of the draasin. I did not know those in the kingdoms bonded the elementals any longer, though I would like to know how you came to Par-shon." He waited and Tan remained silent, afraid to answer. A dark smile pulled at the man's mouth. "Know this, fire shaper. You will not have it."

Tan swallowed. This man controlled too much power. If he managed to force one of the draasin to bond to him, there was little that Tan would be able to do to stop him. And then what?

"What will you do with the bond?"

The man laughed. "The same as with every bond. I grow stronger."

"And the bond pair?" Tan's bond to Asboel would keep him safe, but what of Sashari? What of Enya? The youngest had been through too much already, from the twisting of Amia's shaping forcing her to attack Ethea to kingdoms' shapers hunting her. Now for this man to want to forcibly bond her or Sashari? There might not be any coming back from such a thing.

"The bond pair serves as I demand. That is the way of the bond." He waved a hand at Garza. "I am through with him. He claims no bond, but we will know soon. Test him. If he fails, you may destroy the other."

"She is—"

The man waved his hand again. "It matters not. Go."

Garza bowed and grabbed him by the wrist and led him away from the room and the man. Tan felt the shaped power long after he left the man's presence. It trailed after him, almost as if the Utu Tonah shaped it after him. When they reached the stairs leading down, Tan risked a glance over his shoulder to see what the man was doing, but the others in the room had surrounded him again.

They reached the first landing and Garza dragged him away from the stairs.

"Where are you taking me?"

She shook her head. "No questions from you. You will be tested as he demanded."

"And what happens after the test?"

She looked over at him. Thick jowls shook with every movement of her head. "Either you pass or you do not."

"What happens if I pass?"

"Utu Tonah will have deemed you worthy."

"Worthy of what?"

They reached the end of a hall. A massive black door made of some strange metal blocked their access. Garza created a shaping of water—Tan felt it pulling on him as she did and this time, he thought that he could actually detect the way she shaped—and opened the door.

"Worthy of what?" Tan repeated when she didn't answer.

Light spilled out from the other side of the door, glimmering from dozens of runes carved into the marble along the walls. Tan stared, his mind struggling to understand what he saw but failing.

"If you told the truth, it will not matter," Garza said.

"How many are tested?" Tan demanded.

"All are tested."

Tan stared at the runes, wondering if he could make any sense of them. There was one that looked like it might be for fire. As he watched it, the rune seemed to swirl, drawing in a tight spiral. He blinked and the image disappeared. Another rune looked as if it might be wind, though the shape was nothing like those the First Mother had taught him. It didn't create the same effect as the other one. There was no swirling to it, nothing that drew his eye the way the first had. Tan pulled his attention away from them.

"How many pass this test?" Tan asked.

Garza looked at him as if it were a stupid question. "From Par-shon?"

Tan shook his head.

"Not from Par-shon? None for years." She pushed him in front of her, out into the middle of the floor. She tapped her thick arms with the flat of her palm and eyed Tan with a hint of sadness. "You will stay here."

"And then what?"

Garza started back toward the door, leaving Tan alone in the center of the room. She paused when she reached the door and looked back at him.

"Garza? What is the test?"

Without another word, she stepped from the room and closed the door with a shaping, sealing him inside.

Chapter 20

Testing Room

As Tan stepped into the room, surveying the walls around him, the runes began glowing brighter. Elemental power pressed out from them. He instinctively pushed back, using a shaping of fire and grasping for wind and water to strengthen his resistance. The runes shone with brighter light.

Tan closed his eyes, focusing on what he could remember from what the First Mother had taught him of runes. The image of them along the walls, the floor, even the ceiling of his new cell burned in his mind. With his eyes closed, he could *feel* the power generated by them. It was both the same and different from the runes worked on the warrior's sword.

The shape of the marks found here was different enough that he couldn't be certain what they represented. Elemental power, that much he knew, but more than that? What was the purpose of the test?

The shapings pressed out, growing stronger as power built in the runes. If he let them go much longer, he would be overpowered. He feared that. Could his elemental connections help?

Asboel.

Pain shot through his mind and Tan relaxed, letting go. Maybe if he tried a connection closer to him. Not Honl. The wind elemental seemed too afraid to help.

Amia.

As before, he met resistance, and pain blossomed in his head. Tan withdrew the connection, then reached for spirit. With a shaping, he pressed into it, using the shaping to reach for Amia. There was pain, but it was different. Tan slipped along the shaped connection to Amia, finding that with spirit, he could reach her.

Amia, he said again.

Tan. Where are you?

No time. Do you recognize any of these shapes?

He sent an image of the runes worked around the walls, mixed with a sense of urgency.

Amia took a moment to answer. *They are familiar, like what are used on the doors in the lower level of the archive. Have you found help?*

Not help. Please be careful with these shapers. Use what you must to protect yourself.

I can't…

Please, he begged, knowing what he asked of her. She might be forced to shape spirit to survive, but if she didn't, what would the Parshon shapers do to her?

Power surged against him, forcing him to release the shaping. He could not keep the connection to her if he were to die during this test.

Tan opened his eyes and focused on the runes. He might not recognize them completely, but he could sense the power coming from them in waves. There was a familiarity to the pulsing sense from the rune in front of him. He could almost see the way it pulsed, gradually intensifying before receding. The shape of the rune reminded him of what was used in the kingdoms, only for the nymid. This was water.

Tan released a request to the rune as if speaking to the nymid. It flowed from him. He mixed water into it, letting the shaping flow into it. Nothing happened at first, but then he felt a surge, as if water responded. There was a distant voice in his mind, nothing like the nymid or udilm, nothing that he could even understand, but it was there.

The rune went dark. Power still pressed on him, barely changed. Had he even done anything?

Tan turned to another of the runes. This was the one that had reminded him of fire. Of all the elements, fire should come easiest to him. He could reach for the draasin. He had used saa in shapings of fire. The rune should not present a challenge to him.

As he focused, he sensed the heat pressing from it. There was the almost imperceptible hissing sound mixed in. Tan crafted a shaping of fire and pressed it into the rune. As he did, he spoke to fire, using what he knew of the draasin, what he knew of saa, to communicate his intent.

It began swirling. Colors flashed. Then heat billowed out, a cloud of steam much like when Asboel snorted at him. Tan didn't flinch as the steam struck him. Pain burned across his skin, but he pressed a shaping through himself, using fire to heal.

The rune went dark.

Others still glowed. Nearly a dozen remained. The power in the room shifted, less pronounced than before. At least he didn't think he'd die instantly. At least there was the possibility that he might escape with his life, if only he could manage to figure out how to shut down the remaining runes.

Water and fire. Earth and wind remained, but why so many runes?

He scanned the wall, looking for a rune that marked earth. There, near the bottom of the wall behind him, he saw it. This looked much like the mark for golud, though it was different. Tan shaped earth and sent a rumbling connection through the shaping. Unlike before, nothing happened. He tried again, pulling on a shaping of earth as he tried speaking to golud. Again, it didn't work.

Could he be wrong? Maybe he needed to speak to a different elemental, but he'd never spoken to any other than golud. That didn't mean there weren't other earth elementals; he only had to figure out how to reach them.

The ground beneath him began to shake. Wind whistled through the room, swirling in a tight spiral. It pulled the air from his lungs and knocked him to his knees.

He pulled on a shaping of earth again, pressing it toward the rune, mixing another attempt at speaking to an earth elemental. Wind pressed on him, heavy and angry. A buzzing sound whispered through his ears, almost joyfully as ilaz drew away his remaining breath. Tan realized he should have tried wind before earth, but now he had no time to do it.

His vision faded and colors swirled across the corners of his eyes. Runes flickered behind his eyelids, a dying taunt.

Except… one stuck out. It was like the rune on the door he'd never opened in the archives. Similar to what the archivists used to mark spirit, but different. Would it work?

Tan reached deep within him and pulled on a shaping of spirit and sent it into that rune. Nothing happened. With all his remaining strength, Tan pressed into it, using a flood of spirit that he summoned. As he did, he mixed the other elements into the shaping. Like when he held the warrior's sword, a blinding light shot through the room, bright enough to see through closed lids. The power bounced off the rune and slammed into Tan.

It seemed as if time stopped.

Tan tried taking a breath, but his chest wouldn't move. He tried lifting his head, but it didn't work. His arms and legs refused to answer. Only his mind worked.

There was a sense of great power all around him. Tan peeled away, pulling himself toward that power. It seemed as if he separated from his body and hovered like a spirit in the air.

What was this?

He looked down. His body lay atop the marble, pressed by a shaping of wind coming through the rune. Ilaz circled in the air, a physical presence, almost inky. There was a distinct malevolence from the elemental. With a thought, Tan dismissed ilaz and it receded, blowing off into a corner. With the elemental lifted, his chest rose again, filling with warm air. Ashi.

The wind elementals conflicted in this place. Tan thought Honl afraid to follow him here, but maybe that had not been the case. He had gone *inside* of Tan, hiding within him, within each breath. The elemental swirled around the room, moving protectively around Tan.

You must be strong, he said to Honl.

Then even the elemental movement ceased. Time stopped altogether with Tan suspended above himself. He drifted up, the room no longer opposing him, and passed through walls, moving up and through the ceiling to the Utu Tonah, sitting upon his dais. Like with the lower floor, nothing moved. The shapers surrounding him stood in awkward positions, frozen with whatever it was that Tan had done. And perhaps he had done nothing. Maybe this was death, and he was granted one last image before fading.

Tan stared at the Utu Tonah. His bald head and thick scar around his face twisted grotesquely, frozen in place. Oddly, his eyes seemed to move, flickering past the shapers around him, as if seeing Tan. Runes appeared around him, glowing with soft light. It took Tan a moment to realize what it was that he saw. The runes held the bond to him. His body practically glowed with them. How many elementals had he bonded? How many remained for him to bond with?

With the connections to the elementals, the man would be even more powerful than Tan suspected. If he managed to bond one of the draasin, his power would increase that much more.

Now that he saw the runes on the Utu Tonah, Tan realized that the other shapers around him each had one glowing on them as well. Did *everyone* have an elemental bond? Was that how they shaped in Par-shon?

Tan thought of Amia and was drawn quickly through wall, rapidly reaching her cell. Three shapers stood outside, each with a glowing rune pressed into them. One was the wind shaper, Wes. Connected to spirit as he was, Tan sensed darkness from them and knew Amia was in danger.

Passing through the wall, he found her sitting atop her small bench. She clutched her hands together near her forehead. Her eyes were unfocused. Thankfully, she shaped.

She would need to understand that the three shapers outside her cell intended her harm. Could he grant her that knowledge in his insubstantial form? Tan pulled through spirit and the shaped connection to Amia, sending her all that he could about what he saw. Mixed with it, he shared what he learned of the Utu Tonah, how he bonded elementals. There was nothing more that Tan could share. He moved on.

What of the draasin?

The sense of the elemental was there, distant in the corner of his mind. Tan pulled on the sense and felt Asboel. Through the connection, he felt Asboel healing, the slow recovery. The other draasin rested around him.

They must bond, Tan sent to Asboel. *There is one here who will force it otherwise.*

It was a warning sent in case he didn't survive. He didn't know if Asboel even understood.

The shaping began to fail. Tan floated through the obsidian walls, pulled back into his body. Back in the room, only a single rune glowed in the middle of the floor, this pulsing in time with his heart. The specter that was Tan floated back into his body, pulled back into his flesh. As it did, he felt again.

He took a gasping breath. Honl swirled into his lungs, warm and welcoming, drawn in so that he could protect Tan.

Time lurched forward. The shaping failed completely.

Pain shot through Tan's chest. It took a moment to remember how the elemental ilaz had pressed on him, how the earth elemental had rumbled beneath him. Neither harassed him now. Only the single rune in the center of the floor glowed.

Then it too flickered out.

Tan was left in darkness and silence. He struggled to breathe. Fatigue overwhelmed him from the effort of shaping spirit. What kind of shaping was that? What did it mean that he had bound spirit to the other elements? He had thought spirit *came* from the binding of the others.

Fear for Amia filled him. The shapers had been near her cell. He did not doubt that much had been real, but now he was too weakened to do anything to help.

Maybe there was something he could do. He let out a breath, releasing Honl. *Help her,* he breathed. The elemental hesitated, then swirled away, disappearing through the crack beneath the door.

The pain jolting through him made his arms and legs stiff and sore. Tan shuffled across the floor, moving toward the door. His head throbbed from the effort of his shaping.

The door hissed open.

Garza looked inside. Her beady eyes widened when she saw him. She grunted and stepped into the room. With a quick shaping of water, she lifted him and dragged him out, letting the door seal shut after him.

"Garza." His voice came out in a grunt.

She shushed him with a wave of her hand. "You live. Utu Tonah is pleased." She looked at him with something that might have been compassion. "It might have been better for you had you not."

CHAPTER 21

A Place of Separation

THE MASSIVE WATER SHAPER DRAGGED Tan through the obsidian building, pulling him down the hall and toward the stairs. She lifted him on waves of water shaping. After what Tan had seen while in the room, he wondered if she was bonded to one of the elementals and if that was how she shaped. Did she shape anything on her own? Did anyone in these lands? Had he any strength remaining, he would attempt a spirit shaping to see, but he couldn't manage anything in his condition.

"Few survive the test," she said softly. "Usually, that is for the best."

"Can you shape anything on your own?" Tan asked. His strength began to return, but it seeped into him slowly. When he felt the pull of fire, he drew the strength of saa toward him, readying a shaping if needed. He stared at the walls, realizing that runes were marked along them. Garza didn't give him the chance to determine their purpose.

"Quiet," she said.

"I saw his bonds," Tan said.

Garza hesitated and turned to Tan, holding him in the air with a shaping he could only just begin to fathom. The forced connection to the elementals made them powerful and gave her abilities the kingdoms' shapers would not be able to replicate. "Then you saw how powerful the Utu Tonah is. That was the gift he gave to you."

She continued onward, drawing Tan along with her. Down the stairs, she turned toward one of the doors. He couldn't be certain, but it seemed a different door than she'd used when entering the building the first time. She paused long enough to form a shaping and push the door open.

Sunlight blinded him. Tan raised his hand to his eyes to block the sudden brightness. Garza pulled him forward, not concerned by the change. Smells assaulted his nose. There was the stink of sweat mixed with the coppery salt of blood. Beneath it all was the undercurrent of rot.

As Tan's eyes adjusted, he saw that he was in what looked to be a wide, open courtyard. High walls of black obsidian surrounded him on all sides, arching overhead. Runes etched into the walls nearly twenty feet over his head glowed softly, reminding him of the testing room. Pressure radiated from them. The runes were shaped differently than any that he'd seen before.

He was not alone in the courtyard. Others dressed in rags and tattered clothes glanced at him as he entered. Two were men with long, graying beards. One of the men was thin and frail, his back stooped and leaving him looking as if he might topple over. The other man turned toward Tan with a wild look to his eyes. A woman, her ragged hair snarled and jagged, stared at him through hollowed eyes. She wore little more than wraps of cloth around her chest and abdomen.

Garza released him. "You will stay here until he decides what he will do with you next."

Tan considered the others. How long had they been here? "What of my friend?"

Garza's eyes flickered. "She is Aeta."

Tan waited, thinking there had to be something more, but Garza said nothing as she turned back to the door, quickly disappearing behind it, leaving him shut in this strange place.

Amia.

Pain arced through his head as he tried reaching for her. Tan crumpled to the ground, grabbing at his head.

It had been the same in the testing room, the same where the Utu Tonah had been as well. Something about the obsidian or the runes kept him from connecting to her. It also blocked him from reaching Asboel and Honl.

Given what he'd seen with the runes, he feared the reason: the Utu Tonah sought to separate him from his bonds. At least in the testing room, he had managed to reach through spirit to call Amia.

Could he do the same now?

Tan stretched deep within himself to draw upon spirit. He dipped into it and formed a shaping, wrapping himself in it. He pulled this shaping toward the connection he shared with Amia and tried pushing through it. Pain again raced through his mind, blocking him.

Tan released the shaping. He dragged himself to his knees and looked around. Panting breaths seemed to help with the pain, at least enough to push it deeper down inside him. He couldn't reach Amia.

Another, then. Could he reach the wind elemental?

Honl, he called. This time, the pain was not as severe. Tan wasn't forced to his knees, though he wobbled from the effort of sending the communication.

There came no response.

What of Asboel? He would be farthest from here, the hardest to reach, but could their connection make it possible?

Tan focused on the thought of the draasin. Even that sent streamers of pain through his mind, like hot knives stabbed deep into his eyes. He wiped tears away.

His elemental connections would fail him here.

That didn't mean he was powerless. He could still shape, couldn't he?

He focused on his breathing. The air flowing in and out of his lungs felt different than it did in Ethea, though there was familiarity to it as well. What had he seen in the testing room? The wind elementals battling? Ashi might not be the dominant wind elemental here, and he was certain it wasn't ara. That left wyln or ilaz. Tan focused on the calling of the wind. It didn't buzz to him, not as his experience with ilaz had shown him.

Wyln, he whispered softly to the wind.

Pain tried piercing his mind, but Tan breathed through it. The elemental was close here. It was in him, breathing through him.

The wind elemental didn't respond. Perhaps Tan was wrong. Elementals were not found everywhere, only in places of convergence, though from what he'd seen of Par-shon, the elementals were frequent here. Maybe this *was* a place of convergence.

How had it worked before? He stared at the runes glowing on the walls around him. They had to be important.

Tan tried again, this time focusing on the form of the wind, holding in mind an image of the rune he'd seen in the testing room as he did. *Wyln.*

A soft murmuring came to him, faint and distant, but there. The elemental *was* here. Tan breathed it in, trying and failing to call its power.

What of saa? Fire had always answered him before. Would it now?

Tan tried it and saa flooded into him with only a hint of the pain he'd felt before. Tan focused on an image of the rune for fire used in the testing room, and even that faded. Warmth surged through him and with it came a sense of strength.

Saa. Tan hissed as he spoke this, trying to reach the elemental. In Ethea, saa was a weak elemental, but it was found everywhere. Here, saa seemed different, stronger. Could he speak to saa as he did to the draasin?

Fire swirled within him. There was strength but no sense of substance.

Tan shifted on his feet, looking around the courtyard. He needed to be free of this place, needed to find Amia and make certain she was safe. If Honl failed, what would happen with her?

Please help the Daughter, Tan hissed.

He didn't know if it worked. The sense of heat and fire remained buried within him, unchanging. If only he could speak to saa the same way he spoke to the draasin.

Tan tried again, wrapping himself in another shaping of spirit. After everything he'd been through, he had little strength remaining. *Find safety,* he sent to Amia.

Pain stabbed through him and he sunk to his knees, his vision going black as he did.

Movement caught his eye and he rolled over. How long had he been out? One of the men—the healthier-looking man—shuffled toward him, crouching as he made his way. He tugged on his beard, pulling on strands of hair and twirling them. Sunlight had shifted in the sky and now reflected in the man's eyes, giving him a strange light.

"You're a shaper, not one of the bonded," the man said. His voice was gravely and soft, as if accustomed to screaming.

Tan attempted to ready a shaping of fire, uncertain what to expect. He mixed in a shaping of wind, unconsciously combining them. Pain pulsed in his head as he did; it receded when he mixed another shaping of spirit. "Who are you?"

The man smiled, showing a row of jagged and broken teeth. "Who am I, he asks? Nobody. Not in these lands."

There was a familiar accent to his voice. "In what lands were you somebody?" Tan asked, sitting up. He wiped dirt off his hands, smearing them across his legs. If he could find his sword, he might be able to manage a strong enough shaping to reach freedom.

And then what? How many bonded shapers were in the tower? He'd seen dozens around the Utu Tonah, too many for him to face on his own, even were he not prevented from shaping.

The man cast his eyes at the walls nervously before shifting his attention back to Tan. "Somebody. Nobody. It matters little where he is concerned."

Tan glanced at the other two in the courtyard with him. Neither met his eyes. The woman stared at her hands, picking at the skin around her fingers. Dried blood caked along the nails. The other man looked blankly around the courtyard, seemingly oblivious to everything else around him.

"Why are you here?" the man asked.

Tan turned back to him. The man had come close enough for Tan to smell the sickly stink on him. It was the rot he'd smelled when he first came into the courtyard. He shuffled away, holding his shaping at the ready.

The man smiled at him again. "You can't shape here. He has made certain of that."

Tan wasn't so sure he was right. Wasn't that what he'd been doing? Saa still filled him and Tan held a shaping ready.

"Why am I here?" Tan asked.

The man hesitated in his approach. "You have something he wants. We all do."

"And what is that?"

The man tilted his head back and cackled. "He asks what. He doesn't know? Can't he feel the separation? No no no. He must not know."

Separation? Tan's heart fluttered. Was that the reason the Utu Tonah sent him here? For his bonds? Tan thought the Utu Tonah hadn't known of his connections, but what if *that* had been the purpose of the testing room? Had Tan shown him his connection to Honl? Asboel?

Would he be able to separate them from Tan?

Once, Tan would have thought it impossible, but then he'd seen what had happened in Incendin. The shapers there had nearly severed the connection he shared with Asboel. But he felt no pain as he did then.

Tan considered the man again. The accent to his words, the fluid way he walked.

"You're from Doma, aren't you?" he asked. The man stood taller for a moment and Tan knew he was right. "He took your connection to the udilm."

The man's face twisted in anger. He crouched low but looked as if he readied to strike. He twisted the long strands of his beard around in his fingers. "Protect the shoreline. Keep Incendin back. That was my task. That was *my* task!" He glanced at the rune Tan suspected indicated water on the wall overhead, apparently preventing him from shaping.

"What happened?" Tan asked.

He thought of Elle, of the new connection she had made to the udilm. She had wanted nothing more than to speak to the elementals and he had helped her reach them. But if shapers from Par-shon were to take her, what would she be able to do to keep them from separating her from that connection? Elle could barely shape.

"Pain. Water stolen from me, the bond stripped. Most die, but not I!" He danced in place, the madness in his eyes making his steps light.

Tan looked over at the others. Were they able to speak to elementals as well? But the Utu Tonah had so many bonds. Others had them as well. Where were the rest?

"Not all survive the taking of the bond," the man said, as if anticipating the question. "It is painful. Most can't tolerate it for long." He tipped his head back and laughed again. "But I survive! He keeps me here, taunting me with life." He touched his beard, twisting the strands into long braids.

A renewed fear came. There was another bond that he would have revealed in the testing room, one that he didn't think possible to sever, but what if the Utu Tonah could?

Tan looked back to the door. They knew she was Aeta, but did they know she could shape?

Amia needed him now more than before.

He focused on saa and created a shaping of fire. It bubbled before fizzling out, drifting away harmlessly. The sense of saa filled him, but he couldn't use it. Tan tried wind, but the same thing happened.

The man tipped his head and flashed his jagged teeth. "No shaping. You will understand."

Tan stared at the door. How long did he have? How long did Amia have before they tried to separate him from her? And what would they do to her when they did?

CHAPTER 22

Working with Water

TAN DIDN'T MOVE FOR HOURS. Shadows began to creep over the courtyard, leaving it in long shadows. So far, the only person to come had thrown open a hidden hatch to toss food into the courtyard. The others had scrambled over to it, greedily snatching whatever scraps they could find. Tan hadn't moved.

Each time he attempted a shaping, the same thing happened. Worse, pain began in the back of his head, at first slowly, but now building to the point where it couldn't be ignored. The Utu Tonah tried to take his bonds.

Not just his elemental bonds would be severed, but the connection he shared with Amia.

His breathing became erratic and he did not fight it. Not this time. Anger simmered in him. Tan felt it as a hot, physical thing. Maybe his mother had been right. Maybe fire *had* changed something about him, leaving him more like the lisincend. But if it would help him keep Amia safe from Par-shon, he would use that anger and let it fill him.

He stared at the runes. Through the rage, they seemed to shimmer and writhe, almost as if alive. They were the reason he was cut off from Amia. It was because of them that he couldn't reach Honl and Asboel. It was because of them that Amia would suffer.

Tan reached within himself and found the well of spirit. This time, he plunged into it, wrapping himself in the sense of it. He pulled each of the elements to him, and rather than binding them together, he used them to increase what he could draw of spirit. Pain flashed through his mind briefly but then was gone, burned away by the spirit shaping.

The runes taunted him.

With a burst of shaping, he sent spirit mixed with each of the elements at the runes. They pushed against his shaping, as if made to hold him back. Tan focused, drawing on saa and wyln and reaching toward the earth and the water in the air all around him. Powered by spirit, the elementals answered, almost as if drawn to him, like saa drawn to fire. With the shaping, he pushed *through* the runes.

There came a loud *crack* and the runes stopped glowing.

Tan released his shaping. Weakness flooded him, but the elementals refilled him, granting him their strength. He turned toward the door. *Amia!*

The sending went out like a booming shout. He expected pain, but there was none. Only silence. Had the bond already been lost?

The anger surged through him anew. Tan pulled on spirit, drawing on the power of the elementals, filling himself much as he had once filled the artifact. He pressed this shaping through him, through Amia, forging the bond between them and solidifying it. No one would sever his connection to her.

She sighed. He felt or heard it, no longer certain of which.

Be ready. I am coming.

Tan shifted his focus to Honl. He had asked the wind elemental to help but didn't know if he had answered. Maybe he had been unable, severed from his connection to Tan. The sense of him was fading. There was no pain, not as there had been with Asboel when the shapers tried to separate the bond.

As he had with Amia, he sent a surge of spirit through the connection. It was thready, weak, but Tan pulled from stores deep inside of him, augmenting them with power lent by the elementals of this place. Part of him wondered why they would help, but the bond the Utu Tonah forced upon them was not of their choosing. He suspected the elementals suffered with what was done to them.

The connection to Honl strengthened, then surged in his mind. *Help Amia*, Tan said.

The wind elemental gusted away, suddenly freed.

Tan focused a shaping on the obsidian walls around him, meaning to create a way to freedom. In spite of the strength coursing through him, the shaping failed. The only way to freedom would be through the doors.

And now the Utu Tonah would know that Tan was not confined as expected.

The Doman man stood watching Tan with wide eyes. "How did you…" He tipped his head. "A warrior? Could it be? None for decades, and none with such power. No no no. Not like that. Not with spirit." He spoke mostly to himself, twisting around as he did, practically dancing.

The man knew of warriors and somehow knew that Tan could shape spirit. What else might he know? Could he help Tan find Amia? Could he help him get free from Par-shon?

"Can you shape?" Tan asked.

The man closed his eyes. A sickly smile crossed his face. Then he nodded. "Water returns. Not as strong as before the separation, but it is there."

"Good. We're getting out of here."

The man looked at the walls and waved a crooked hand. "Out? Out? Where do you think we can go? These walls confine. There is no out."

Tan tipped his head toward the doors. "We go out the way we came in."

"And face the Utu Tonah? You might be a warrior, but you're a fool."

"I'm a fool," Tan agreed. "But no longer a trapped fool."

Tan started toward the door. As he did, it opened a crack and then smashed open with a shaping of wind. Wes floated in on a gust of wind. He spied Tan and turned to him, an angry expression on his face. The last Tan had seen of him had been when separated from his body during the testing. Wes had been going toward Amia then.

"He is displeased with what you've done here."

A spiral of wind caught Tan. Tan pushed out with a shaping of fire, mixing it with water and the wind grew heavier, lowering him to the ground. Tan drew on saa, forming a ball of fire, a shaping he copied from Cianna, and flipped it at Wes.

His eyes grew wide as Tan pushed it with increasing speed augmented by a wind shaping. Wes lifted to the air, flying above the fireball that crashed harmlessly into the door in an explosion of sparks.

"Not just fire," Wes whispered.

Tan breathed in, unable to tell if it was ashi or wyln. Both responded to him. Tan pulled on the power lent by the elementals, mixing it with his own shaping, and lifted to the air to hover before Wes. "Not just fire," he agreed. "And for me, it's not stolen."

With a silent request, he called to both ashi and wyln, using what he'd learned of speaking to them to ask for their help. He might have only spoken directly to Honl, but the others of the elementals were there, drawn to him by his shaping.

Had he only been a shaper—had he been unable to reach the elementals—he would not have been able to free himself. Wes might even have been strong enough to stop him. But with their help, the elementals swirled around Wes, separating him from his wind connection.

His wind shaping faltered and Tan attacked, wrapping him in swirls of fire that pulled him down to the ground. With a tap beside the man's now-prone shoulder, he sent a shaping through the earth. It separated, pulling Wes inside, wrapping him with bonds that he couldn't escape.

Wes glared at him. "He is more powerful than you. He will soon have the bond he desires, and there will be none who can stop him. Then we will destroy Incendin and keep them from ever attacking again."

That meant the draasin, Tan was certain.

"We want the same thing!" Tan shouted.

Wes didn't have the chance to answer.

A powerful water shaping surged from the Doman man and poured into Wes's mouth, flooding him. Wes's eyes went wide as he struggled to breathe and failed. He flopped on the ground, confined by the shaping of earth.

A buzzing drifted past him, swirling through the air, before disappearing.

Tan looked away from Wes. "Why? There was nothing he could do to us!"

The man stared proudly at Wes, eyes glaring at the once-bonded shaper. "*Now* there is nothing he could do." He looked over at Tan. "You think you would have reformed him? You think he would have willingly abandoned his bond? Even if it were possible. Better to let the Great Mother decide his fate."

Tan turned away from him in disgust.

Flames crackled along the edge of the door from his shaping. Others would be coming. He needed to hurry. He glanced over his shoulder at the three who had been trapped with him. Only the Doman seemed to have returned in any meaningful way.

"Come on," Tan said. "Grab the others."

"There's nothing left of them. They should stay."

Tan thought of how he'd nearly lost his bond to Asboel. To Honl. To Amia. How would he have felt? Would he have survived as long as they had?

How had his mother survived the loss of her bond before?

"No," he decided. "They come."

The Doman took another look at Wes before touching both the woman and the other man on the shoulder. They looked at him with blank expressions but followed him through the doorway.

Lanterns glowed with orange light. Inside this building, Tan's sense of the elementals faded, suppressed by runes placed along the walls. Was that how the Utu Tonah maintained his power? Others might not be able to shape, but with enough bonds, even the suppression wouldn't matter.

Tan found the stairs and hurried down. Amia would be this way, but first, he had to wait near the bottom. They moved slowly, the halting way they walked telling Tan that they were unaccustomed to much activity.

Power surged somewhere overhead. Was it the Utu Tonah or one of the others? There were too many bound shapers for him to take on by himself. Once he reached Amia and knew that she was safe, he could figure out what they needed to do next. He would have Honl bring her to safety, even if it meant that he remained behind.

The woman stumbled and slid past him on the stairs.

Tan lifted her back to her feet. She was light and smelled of stale urine. When she looked at him, there was barely a flash of humanity in her eyes. With more time, he would see what he could learn about her, determine if there was anything he could do to help bring her back. He'd try with the other man as well. The Doman had recovered quickly enough.

"Warrior!"

Tan spun. The Doman was lifted in the air on a shaping of combined fire and air. He writhed, kicking at the air, trying and failing to shape. Whatever protections had been placed around the building by the Utu Tonah prevented the Doman from shaping.

A pair of bonded shapers stood on the top of the steps, looking down at them. Power flowed around them. How many bonds did they have?

Here in this place, Tan wasn't sure he would be able to do anything to help, either. He reached for fire and saa, the easiest of the elementals for Tan to reach in this place. Power flowed through him, the fire elemental adding to what Tan could draw. He tried a shaping but like it had in the courtyard, it faltered. He pressed out with even more, drawing from spirit. This solidified his connection to fire.

Tan drew the flames away from the Doman, pulling them toward himself, but not *into* himself. He'd made that mistake before, learned what happened when he attempted to draw elemental power into himself. Fire practically begged for him to draw it in, but Tan ignored it and diverted it so that it crashed in a barrage of sparks and sputtering flames along the walls.

With a quick shot of spirit mixed with fire and air, Tan knocked the shaper to the ground against the nearest rune, shattering it. The man remained unmoving.

The wind shaper was powerful. More powerful than Wes. Drawing spirit as he did, he could almost see the runes of power glowing through his shirt, as if tattooed on his chest and forming the bond with the elementals. There were two, one for wind and one for...

Earth surged beneath him, throwing him off his feet.

Tan landed atop the woman and rolled to the side, afraid that he had crushed her. She blinked and stared up at him with an unchanged glazed expression.

The steps heaved in another earth shaping. This one was even more focused, drawing more power than the last. Wind mixed with it.

The runes worked along the walls were designed to keep him from shaping, but spirit allowed him to override them. Could he do the same to the bond marks on the shaper?

With a shaping of spirit and wind, Tan sent a flicker of power at the rune for wind on the shaper. As it struck the rune, an explosion of air shot came from it, knocking him back. The shaper staggered. Tan didn't wait for him to attempt another shaping. Wrapping earth and spirit, he sent this toward the other rune. The ground shook and split, knocking the man off his feet.

The Doman started toward the fallen Par-shon, a shaping already building, the shattered rune freeing him to shape.

"No!" Tan shouted. He pointed at the fallen shaper. "Can't you see?"

"See? I've seen far more than you what they will do for power," the Doman said.

"The bonds are broken. Without them, he can't shape anything."

The Doman looked at Tan with a haunted expression. "You don't know what it's like, warrior. You haven't seen what they've done..."

Before Tan could react, the Doman sent a shaping of water at the man, drowning him as quickly as he had Wes. The man kicked once and then fell still.

Tan turned away, sickened, and knelt next to the woman, making a point of ignoring the Doman shaper. "Are you okay?"

She blinked, nothing more.

Tan glanced back at the Doman. He helped the other man to his feet and slipped an arm around his waist, helping him down the reminder of the stairs. At the bottom, the man looked at Tan, defiance in his eyes.

"Where now, warrior?"

Tan focused on the connection to Amia. She was out there, not far from him. He pointed and started toward the door he indicated. How many more shapers would he have to face before they managed to escape? Once he reached Amia, he would have to get them to safety, if such a thing was possible here. And then?

They needed to get away. This land was dangerous for shapers. Had Roine known? Had his mother? More than any of the other shapers, Zephra would be in danger.

Zephra...

Honl called her name in the back of his mind.

What is it about Zephra?

Ara is here. She *is here.*

At the door, Tan froze, unable to move. His mother was here? Why would she have come here? What would drive her to this place?

The same thing that had driven him. Help with Incendin. What had she found when she went to Doma?

Amia. Is she safe?

For now.

And Zephra?

Honl didn't answer. Tan thought he might have disappeared, leaving him alone again.

Honl? What of Zephra?

Ara will be taken from her.

Chapter 23

A Shaper's Death

THE DOMAN STARED DEFIANTLY at Tan, as if waiting to be chastised for what he'd done. Now that Tan knew his mother was here, he didn't know what else to do. Was there anything that he *could* do? He had wanted to get Amia to safety, but now that wouldn't be enough.

He shaped the door open and hurried out. Once out in the open, power flooded through him, no longer limited by the runes in the walls. He sensed where Amia hid and ran to her, weaving through the streets. The few out and about gave him a wide berth. Tan doubted he would have long before the Utu Tonah sent shapers with real power after him.

He pushed the woman he'd brought from the holding area along with him. She didn't resist, but her steps were stiff and slower than Tan would have liked. He pulled on Honl and lifted her on a shaping of wind, scooting her down the street. He looked over and realized the Doman used water shaping to help the other addled man they'd rescued from the courtyard.

"What are you looking for?" the Doman asked.

Tan barely paused to look over at him. "A friend."

"Another shaper?" Tan nodded. "They're probably gone, then."

"She's not gone," Tan said. He sensed her, the bond between them vibrant and strong in his mind. How much longer before she *wasn't* safe?

"Are you certain? He prefers to test all shapers. Those with any connection to the elementals are culled, separated. Those who can only shape are killed."

That must have been why most failed the testing. What did it do? And how had he known what Tan could do, unless the Utu Tonah was somehow connected to the runes used in the testing.

"I'm certain," Tan said.

They turned a corner that led down a street darkened by the flat roofs stretching over it. He paused at the door he sensed Amia behind and shaped it open. The other side was dark, but his sense of her blazed brightly inside.

"Amia?" He stormed in, readying a shaping of fire and wind were they needed. Spirit lingered just out of reach, but Tan wouldn't have to strain to add it if that's what it took to keep her safe.

She stepped out of the shadows and looked past him to the others. "Tan? What is this?"

"There's no time to fully explain. Are you safe?"

"I am now. There was violent wind and… that was you, wasn't it?"

"It was the elemental. I sent him for you."

She stepped up to him, pitching her voice so that only he could hear. "How did you know I was in danger?"

"I'm sorry I couldn't do more than I did."

She bit her lip. "I was forced to shape. I sensed what they intended for me. What they wanted for you."

He knew how much that had cost her. After everything she'd been through, the one thing she didn't want to do was use her shaping against others. And now she'd been forced to do it. He could feel her struggle with her actions, the way they tore at her. Tan wrapped his arms around her and pulled her in a tight embrace.

As she relaxed, he turned to the Doman. "What's your name?"

The man eyed him a moment before answering. "I am Vel. Velthan."

He tipped his head toward Amia, who met his eyes. "Can you take Vel and these two? You won't have to shape anyone again. The wind elemental will keep you safe and take you from here." Tan glanced around the darkened room. "Where's the sword?" He thought of what he'd managed with it when facing the shapers the last time. As much as he hated it, he might need it again.

Amia shook her head, her eyes tightening. Anxiety surged through their bond. "They took your sword away. And you're coming with us," she said. "I've sensed what you've been through, Tan. There are too many shapers here."

"They're not shapers. They force bonds between elementals. That's how they get their power." He leaned into her ear, sweeping loose blond hair away as he brushed her cheek with his lips. "Zephra is here," he whispered.

Behind him, Vel gasped. Tan turned back, half-expecting another attack.

Vel stared at him. "Zephra lives?"

"How do you know of her?" Tan asked. Vel's eyes were clearer than they'd been seen since they left the courtyard. Madness still danced in them, but not as it once had.

"I'm from Doma. All know of Zephra."

Someday, Tan would have to learn more about his mother. It seemed more and more he learned, the less he really knew.

"She's here?" Vel asked.

"She shouldn't be, but she's here."

Vel looked toward the street. A shaping of water built from him, almost as if he tried to reach for Zephra. "You will try to help her?"

"I have to," Tan said.

Vel studied Tan a moment, sweeping his eyes over him. Then he nodded. "I will come."

Tan opened his mouth to object, but another shaper might be useful. "If wind will take you away from here, can you watch these two? See if you can help them?" he asked Amia

Amia glanced at the other two shapers. Neither had spoken. Neither had really even moved since they reached Amia. Her shaping built with a pop and then eased. "I… I don't know that I can keep them safe." Not without shaping, she didn't have to say.

"You did what you had to," Tan said.

"Did I? Wouldn't the First Mother have said the same?"

Tan held her in his arms for a long moment, stroking her hair. If something happened to him, he wanted this last moment with her. Even more than facing Incendin, he feared the Par-shon shapers. They were powerful in a way even the lisincend couldn't match. "Then watch over them. Keep them as safe as you can for me."

Amia took a shuddering breath. "There might be little I can do."

"I have to—" Tan started.

Amia silenced him with a kiss. "I know what you have to do. There isn't anyone else able to do it."

Tan hesitated, looking at her and feeling the knot form in his throat. Putting her at risk was his fault. "I shouldn't have brought you here. Had I not come, you would've been safe."

"You're only doing what Theondar asked."

"But he wanted allies. Instead, we've found a new threat. I've exposed the kingdoms to a new threat." And because of the draasin—because of his connection to the draasin—Incendin had been weakened, giving Par-shon the opportunity to attack.

"Had you not come, we would never have known what we face." She turned to the door. "The wind elemental has done well so far. Without him, the others may have ignored my shaping and claimed me. He helped hide me."

Tan wondered if Honl was still with him. He couldn't see the elemental but felt his presence in his mind. If he didn't ask Honl to attack, would the elemental help? *Honl. Can you do this?*

The wind elemental swirled around him, fluttering at his clothes. *You wish them to reach safety?*

There was a sense of eagerness as he spoke of safety. The wind elemental was so different than the draasin. Where Asboel wanted nothing more than to attack, Honl sought to avoid conflict. Would he be able to count on Honl if needed?

I wish them away from the city. I will join you when I can.

They will be safe, Tan.

Tan hugged Amia one more time, wishing there was the time to tell her his feelings, for her to understand everything that she meant to him. Every moment of delay was a moment someone else he cared about suffered.

I feel the same, Amia sent.

Tan smiled and opened the door, pulling the woman and the other man along with him. Amia touched his cheek and then wind lifted her and the two into the air. They streaked up and away from the city. Tan watched until they were little more than specks in the sky.

"You're certain they will be safe?" Vel asked.

Tan tore his eyes away and turned toward the obsidian tower. Would they have to go there to reach his mother? "As safe as they can be."

"You're bound to a wind elemental? Like Zephra?"

Tan shook his head, surprised that Vel would know about the elemental. Tan didn't think Roine had even known. "Not like Zephra. She's bound to ara."

Vel turned toward the sky. "That was not ara?"

"Ashi."

Vel tensed. "But you are from the kingdoms, no?"

"I am. Why do you ask?"

"Why would you be bound to an Incendin wind elemental?"

Incendin? Could that be true? If so, why would Honl not have told him?

It made a certain sort of sense. The elemental was drawn to warm air, drawn to Asboel, but was there something more to it that Tan didn't know? Could that be where his fear came from?

"Because I'm also bound to fire," Tan answered.

He pulled on saa, letting the elemental fill him. Here in Par-shon, it was easy to use saa. There was something about this place that allowed the connection to strengthen, much like there was a reason Tan had bonded to Asboel when he had. Could it be the reason he spoke so easily to the nymid in the lake near the place of convergence?

What if that were the key to reaching the elementals? All he needed was to find where they were strongest. He suspect ilaz was the strongest wind elemental here, but Honl still had some strength. And what of the draasin? Tan couldn't imagine Asboel being weak anywhere.

"You are formidable, warrior, but the Utu Tonah has bonded dozens of elementals. You cannot hope to defeat him by yourself."

"But I'm not by myself," Tan told him. Vel tipped his head, waiting. "You'll be with me."

Vel smiled, again showing his ragged row of teeth. One hand twisted absently at his beard, twirling it between gnarled fingers. "For Zephra?" he asked.

Tan nodded. "Then away from here, back to the kingdoms."

Now that Honl was gone, he wasn't certain that he'd be able to get them away easily, but that didn't mean he wouldn't try.

They made their way around the outside of the obsidian fortress. The shape and color were so much like what he saw from a distance of the Fire Fortress. The entire place seemed designed to repel power.

How long had Par-shon and Incendin battled? As long as Incendin and the kingdoms? Longer? The threat of Incendin would explain why Par-shon sought power, but not why they wielded it as they did. Had the kingdoms ever known about Par-shon? If they had, how had the kingdoms been spared from attack?

Maybe he had it backward. Had the threat of Par-shon been why Incendin chased power?

"What does it do?" Tan asked, nodding toward the fortress.

"You've felt what it does," Vel said. "He uses power to maintain power. There are none with the strength to oppose him who can enter. It's why he has remained in control so long."

"They steal the bonds from those they capture?"

"Some bonds are stolen. Others they force. Not many bonded any longer. The elementals choose safety."

"They elementals choose this?"

"Not the bond," Vel said. "They avoid shapers. Bonding shapers places them at risk. When I bonded Ul... the udilm," he said, catching himself as Tan often did when speaking of Asboel, "she knew the risk."

Maybe that was the reason the kingdoms had not faced the threat from Par-shon. There were no longer any bonded shapers. "Why bond at all, then?"

"There are benefits to the elemental. Surely your elementals have shared that with you."

Tan continued to stare up at the tower. "I've not bonded the wind for long. And the draasin does not share anything."

Vel nearly tripped and grabbed Tan's arm. "You have bonded to one of the draasin?"

Tan nodded.

"But they have been gone from this world for centuries."

"Not any longer," he answered, thankful he hadn't asked Asboel to bring him to Par-shon. What would have happened had the draasin carried him across the water? The bonded shapers had nearly broken their bond while in Incendin. Had Asboel come here, there would have been nothing Tan could have done. "They're free."

"You managed to find one young enough to bond?"

"Not young. Old enough to bond," he said. Tan didn't know quite how old Enya was, but her youth made it unlikely that she would bond. Even Asboel resisted the bond, claiming the Great Mother wanted it, though he didn't seem to know the reason why she would. "I think age grants the draasin a certain wisdom."

"That is not—" Vel cut himself off and looked up at the obsidian fortress. "Does he know?"

"I don't know. He tested me. When I lived, I think he intended to steal those bonded to me. He knows of the draasin. It's the prize he seeks."

Vel's eyes widened. "If he gains a bond to one of the draasin, he will have greater elemental power for each. Dangerous. So very dangerous. Then only Incendin opposes him. They have held Par-shon back for centuries, but with strength like that..."

Vel twisted along the street, grabbing at his head and pulling at his beard. His eyes twitched as he flickered his gaze around the street, widening each time he glanced up at the fortress.

"What do you mean only Incendin opposes him?" Tan asked.

The Doman stopped and turned to Tan. "You don't know?" He shook his head and madness flashed through his eyes. "Of course he doesn't know. None understood. That was Incendin's fault. They are too arrogant. Had they only asked for help, maybe all would be different. Arrogant and foolish. Now they can't request help. They have to force it."

"What are you saying about Incendin and Par-shon?"

"Why do you think they have embraced fire as they have? They could not learn to bind elementals, not as the Utu Tonah did, but they can master fire, force it in ways even the elementals will not go."

"Twisted Fire," Tan said.

The madness cleared and Vel looked at Tan with a pained expression. "Twisted, yes. That is what the udilm claim. I thought that as well. Always agreed with udilm. But they did not see what I have seen. They have not experienced severing the connection. Only she did." Vel tugged on his beard, his eyes drifting up toward the top of the fortress. "Now, perhaps I understand. Twisted, yes. But needed."

Tan couldn't believe what Vel claimed. Could Incendin—could the lisincend—actually have been created in an attempt to keep Incendin *safe*? Tan had assumed they wanted power, that they wanted to destroy the kingdoms, but what if all of that had been wrong?

It would explain why they had taken shapers from Doma and why those shapers had never truly attacked the kingdoms, even now that the barrier had fallen. They were taken not to attack the kingdoms, but to keep Incendin safe.

Was that what the twisted lisincend had meant when he claimed that freeing the lisincend placed the kingdoms in greater danger? Was that why Tan had failed when he tried to restore him?

What did it mean that Asboel and the draasin had attacked the lisincend? Could they have inadvertently weakened Incendin to the point where Par-shon could attack?

Even if true, it didn't make what Incendin had done any better, but there was a certain sort of sick sense to it. What would the kingdoms have done to keep themselves safe?

Tan knew the answer. The ancient warriors had provided it. They would trap elementals in a place of convergence. They would force them to power an artifact that could draw more power than any shaper was meant to control. That was what the kingdoms' shapers had done. Wasn't that just as twisted as what Incendin had done?

"Where is Zephra?" Vel asked, dancing around the outside of the tower. "Come out, come out!" he called in a sing-song voice.

"Quiet," Tan hissed.

But the Doman was right. They needed to find his mother. That might even be the easiest part. Rescuing her would be the real challenge, especially if the Utu Tonah had taken her. There was one way he could find her, only he wasn't certain it would work: the summoning rune coin.

Tan pulled it from his pocket and held it in his hand, flipping it between his fingers. With Zephra, wind would summon, but he needed something more than wind, especially if he needed to penetrate the barriers of the fortress. Tan mixed spirit with a shaping of wind drawn through Honl and shaped it into the coin.

The rune on the coin glowed softly. Tan focused on it, wondering if it would let him trace her location, fearing that she might be in the fortress. If his mother was there, he might not have enough shaping strength to reach her. Even with Vel, the two of them wouldn't be enough to keep them safe when dealing with the Utu Tonah.

The rune on the coin pulled on him, but away from the fortress, leading him away from the city in the opposite direction from Amia's route.

There was a risk that the coin had been dropped. That by following the rune, he wouldn't find anything and would instead lose time that he might need. But Tan had no other way of knowing where to look.

Vel stood on his toes and peered into Tan's hand. His face flattened and he tugged at his beard again. "That is Zephra's mark," he said.

Tan studied the water shaper for a moment. "How do you know Zephra?"

Vel smiled, flashing his yellowed teeth. "Does anyone really know Zephra?" he asked.

Tan cocked his head, trying and failing to think of an answer.

Leaving the city presented a different type of challenge. Without Honl, Tan wasn't sure he had enough strength to take to the air. There was one way he might be able to do it, but he hadn't watched Roine travel enough to know if he could. The warrior had warned of the dangers to him if done wrong, but there was no other choice.

Fire and wind. Water to stabilize. Earth for strength.

Tan shaped the first two easily. Water came more slowly, but he found the stability needed to hold the shaping. Then earth. He grabbed Vel and pulled the shaping to him as Roine had instructed.

All the practice working with the other elementals gave him the necessary strength. At the last moment, Tan pulled a mix of spirit into it. Blinding white light struck and they were lifted into the air.

For the first time, he truly felt like a cloud warrior.

Tan didn't know what he had expected. Pain. Fire. Something. Not this.

They were standing in the open near the base of the fortress when the bolt of lightning struck, then he was soaring in the sky. There was no wind, barely a sense of movement. He focused on the rune, letting it draw him. And then they were there, landing with a split of lightning, just as bright as the first.

Tan had been brought to a wooded area, the trees newly singed by the lightning Tan had traveled on. His earth senses told him that a stream ran nearby and the air smelled of mold and dirt mixed with the bitter taste he'd smelled when Roine had traveled by storm before.

Vel eased away from him, stumbling toward a tree and clinging to it for support as he took in their surroundings. He built a shaping, as if he expected an attack to come at any moment.

"Where is she?" Vel whispered.

Tan stretched out with his earth sensing. The rune had brought him here. That meant his mother was here—or at least the summoning coin was. "I don't know."

The coin pulled on him and he turned, following it.

Tan didn't really need the coin to guide him. Touching base with his earth sensing allowed him to practically feel the person lying on the ground.

A moan drifted through the trees.

Tan ran toward the sound, instinctively avoiding loose branches strewn across the ground and roots that tried tangling his feet. The earth was soft and spongy, but the faster Tan ran, the more it seemed to firm up beneath him.

He saw her lying near the base of a tree. Wind swirled around her, but weak and thready.

"Mother?" he called.

Behind him, Vel sucked in a breath. "Zephra is your mother?"

Tan ignored him. Her face was a mass of bruises. Her dark hair was wild, dead and dried grasses tangled within it. She looked up at him weakly when he lifted her.

"Tannen? You shouldn't be here! This place is dangerous for those bonded."

"What happened?" he asked.

Vel pushed Tan aside and ran his hands over Zephra. A water shaping built, strong and confident. As it did, his mother breathed in deeply before trembling and falling back to the ground. Her eyes fluttered open and then closed, losing focus as she did. Wind whispered up in a weak shaping, spinning around Vel before fading again.

"Vel?" she whispered.

"Shh, Zephra, easy."

"But you're gone—"

"Not gone."

Tan looked over at Vel. "Seems you haven't shared how well you know her." He laid his mother back on the ground near the tree, propping her up so she could look at him. "What happened with ara?"

She shook, her body convulsing for a moment. Vel smoothed her hair.

"Can you heal this?" Tan asked.

He looked over at Tan. The hollow expression that had been in his eyes when Tan first met him returned. "There is no healing this. It comes from losing the bond."

Zephra convulsed again, this time stronger. Her legs kicked wildly, flailing out from her.

"Will it pass?"

Vel didn't answer. Tan should have known that he would not.

"Vel? Will this pass?"

He looked over at Tan. "When the Great Mother calls her home."

CHAPTER 24

The Healing of Spirit

TAN HELD HIS MOTHER, cradling her against him. He'd already lost her once, but since getting her back, their relationship had not been the same. Tan's growing affection for Amia was part of it, but not entirely. He missed the carefree way his mother had been before Father died, the way she had seemed content. Would he ever sense that from her again?

"There's nothing that can be done for her?" Tan refused to believe that; there had to be a shaping that could help.

Vel crouched next to Zephra. The wild look to his face had softened and he seemed the sanest he'd been since Tan had met him. "I've seen this before. It happens with most. First the shaking, then it stops."

"What stops?"

Vel shook his head. "Everything. Breathing. Heart. That's when the Great Mother calls them back. It's peace." He looked at Zephra with wide, sorrowful eyes. "For someone as bound to an elemental as Zephra, it's not a surprise that she should suffer when separated from ara."

Tan held his mother, unable to believe there was nothing he could do. She had survived it once before; why not now?

But this time was different. From what she'd said, the last time had been because her elemental died. This time, the bond was stolen from her.

"You have to know a shaping that will heal," he said to Vel. "You're a water shaper once bound to udilm!"

"Water can't heal spirit," Vel snapped.

Water might not be able to heal spirit, but maybe spirit could. Was there anything he might be able to do?

He took his mother's hands. They were already growing cold. She trembled, the convulsions coming more frequently now.

I will need strength. Zephra needs me to have strength.

He sent the request to all the elementals he could: Asboel and Honl, to the earth and water that he couldn't reach well here, and on to the lesser elementals that he didn't expect to respond, saa and wyln.

Strength flooded into him and Tan pulled on it, drawing it toward him as he focused a shaping while pulling on spirit. He filled himself with power, drew all that he could of spirit, weaving into it the shaped power that he'd summoned. It was immense, more than he'd ever attempted before.

This time, he would have no connection to follow. Unlike with Amia and the elementals, where he could track along the connection they shared, what he did now would have to come entirely from him. He didn't have the skill or experience, but Zephra didn't have time for him to gain what he needed. He *had* done something like this before except ara had guided his shaping that time.

Tan pushed the spirit shaping onto his mother. Her back arched and she sucked in a breath, but nothing more.

There was a barrier, as if she blocked him. With a surge, Tan pressed through it, using the draw of spirit to guide him. Water shaping washed from him, and he used that to probe her injury. Earth and wind mixed in, even a touch of fire. All helped him understand her injuries. Then, like a distant gust of wind, he sensed what was wrong.

The connection to ara felt like a jagged shard in her mind. Tan pressed through it, pushing along the connection like he had so often done with the connections he shared with Amia and the elementals, and came to the severed end.

Could he heal this? Could spirit let him seal it off?

Doing so would separate her completely from ara. Would his mother want to live like that? *Could* she live like that?

Maybe there was another way. Might he be able to reestablish the connection? Ara may not respond to him the same way it did to Zephra, but Tan could reach the elemental, even severed as this was.

With a spirit enhanced shaping, he sent out a request to ara. Then he waited.

Nothing came.

There had to be more to it. How did he know which of the elementals to call?

The same way he reached Asboel and now Honl. He needed the elemental's name.

Asboel responded differently than Enya. Honl was different than other ashi elementals. If he ever learned enough of the nymid, he might bond there as well. Maybe one day, he would understand the earth elementals enough to bond. The name was the key.

"I need his name," he said to his mother.

Her eyes fluttered. Her mouth opened. No words came out.

But he heard it anyway.

The name drifted to him, faint and playful, conjuring up an image of a face to match: *Aric.*

The name went out on a spirit-strengthened wind shaping. This one had force and direction and floated through the jagged separation, at first unanchored, simply waving in the wind. Then it was drawn, as if summoned, pulled toward something.

Tan readied a shaping of spirit and wind. If he were right, he would need both to fix the connection. Then he met resistance.

Wind fought him, a mixture of ashi and wyln and ilaz. Even ara, Aric now bound to the Utu Tonah or another, fought against Tan. Had Tan been healing anyone else, he might not have been strong enough. He might have given up, receded for a different fight. But this was Zephra. This was his mother.

Zephra had lost the wind once. He would not be the reason she lost it again.

Calling on spirit, Tan shaped through the elementals strengthening him and pressed out with even more spirit than before.

Aric.

The wind elemental hesitated. As it did, Tan sensed what he needed to do. A shaping of added wind and, surprisingly, water. This pierced through the wind elemental.

Something changed. The elemental floated free for a moment, and then Tan shaped it again, drawing it toward the broken connection.

Aric gusted toward her willingly. Tan used spirit and air and bound them together, sealing the broken connection. Wind suddenly swirled around his mother in an agitated storm.

You healed her.

This from ara. Not simply ara, but Aric. Tan could tell.

She is Zephra.

Aric sighed and the wind around Zephra eased.

What will happen to her? Tan asked.

The bond is restored.

Will she live?

Aric danced around her, floating first above her, then, on a captured breath, through her. *She will live.*

Tan settled to his knees, relaxing next to his mother. His head pounded with the effort of what he had done, but not as it once would have. The elementals had gifted him with increased stamina. Tan still hadn't discovered what the elementals received from the shared connection, but he trusted that one day, he would. Right now, he needed to rest. They weren't done in this land yet.

He rested. Vel leaned against a nearby tree, saying nothing. Both of his hands gripped his long beard. His eyes flickered around the trees, watching for imagined—or maybe not so imagined—threats.

After a while, his mother began to stir. She sat up on her own. She looked from Tan over to Vel, staring at him for long moments, before turning her focus back to Tan.

"How was this possible?" she asked.

"Mother," Tan sighed, relieved to have her back. "How are you?"

"Better than I should be."

"What happened?"

The bruises that had been on her face were gone, fading during one of the healing episodes, though Tan wasn't certain it if was his doing or Vel's.

"I came to Par. I shouldn't have."

"Did you know what was here?"

She let out a shaky breath. "Nothing. Only that Incendin was known to attack the island. We've never known why." She closed her eyes, and Tan wondered if she needed the rest or if she spoke to her elemental. "You weren't the only one Theondar sent searching for allies. There have been stories, but we've never really understood. None from the kingdoms have made the journey. Only warriors or…" She trailed off and shrugged. "Others able to shape with their elementals. We've been too busy fighting Incendin."

Tan glanced at Vel. He seemed oblivious to their conversation, his eyes unfocused and staring straight ahead. Tan had expected him to ask for help restoring his elemental, but he had not. At least, not yet. In time. Maybe by then, Tan would have enough strength to do what he asked.

"He says Incendin provides protection from Par-shon," Tan said, motioning to Vel.

His mother twisted and stared at the water shaper. For long moments, she said nothing. "You were dead," she whispered.

The Doman blinked. The hollow eyes looked over to Zephra, meeting hers. "Not dead. Stolen."

"We thought the sea…" She dragged herself to her knees and crawled to him, touching his hair and his face. "I couldn't believe it when I saw you. I thought it a vision from the Great Mother as I died."

Vel laughed. "A vision. Look at this," he said, tugging on his beard. There was still an edge of madness to the sound. "And this is your son?"

Zephra nodded. "This is Tan."

Tan shifted to watch them, feeling vaguely uncomfortable. "Who is Vel?"

His mother looked over to him. "A man I knew once, long before meeting your father. When I went to the university to train, he remained in Doma. There weren't many with his gifts. I was stationed along the barrier when I heard he'd been lost to the sea."

"And Father?"

His mother closed her eyes. "Grethan knew of Vel, but Grethan… He was a wonderful man. Strong. He kept me grounded."

Tan swallowed as thoughts of his father rolled through him.

"Where did you find him?" Zephra asked.

Tan shook his head. "There is a place in the city. Walls of black obsidian. Runes marked upon the walls. It is a place of separation."

Her eyes widened. "How is it you didn't lose your connection to the draasin?"

"Not only the draasin," Tan said. "I have bonded a wind elemental. And Amia." She gave no reaction. "I could feel what they did, how they used the runes to separate me from them. They would steal the natural bond, transfer it to one of their shapers."

She shuddered. "How did you not suffer that same fate?"

"Spirit."

She frowned. "But you shape spirit differently. That's what she said."

"You were speaking to the First Mother."

"I had to know. Most of the ancients shaped much like you. They could bind the elements together, twist them, and form a semblance of spirit. It was not true spirit, but served much the same. Somehow, the understanding of that shaping was lost over time, not the ability. The ability to shape spirit—to *truly* shape spirit—has always been rare. The First Mother thought that was all you would be capable of doing."

"She thought I came at spirit shaping too late," Tan said.

"That's what she told you?"

"Because she was unwilling to see that I'd already formed a connection with spirit. That was why Amia's bond has been so solid. We are shaped together, spirit to spirit. It was because of her I learned to reach for spirit."

His mother let out a frustrated sigh, her eyes drifting to stare at the sky. "I've been a fool," she said softly. "I feared that she shaped you, that were unwilling to protect yourself around her. Instead, you have shaped each other." She sat staring for long moments at the clouds before turning and taking his hands. "Can you forgive your mother?"

"If you will give Amia a chance. That's all I ask."

"Where is she now?"

"Somewhere safe. Away from here."

Tension eased from Zephra. "Spirit. And did you mix it with the elements?"

Tan nodded. "How did you know?"

"The ancients. There are some works that reference what happens when mixing spirit with all of the elements. It creates a powerful shaping, something unlike any other."

"He destroyed the runes," Vel said.

His mother studied Tan. "When the runes were destroyed, what happened?"

"I could reach through the connections I'd formed. Like I did with you, I used spirit to heal the connection, to bind us back together."

"Had he not been here, Zephra, you would have died," Vel said.

She sat quietly, watching both Tan and Vel, but finally got to her feet, wiping her hands down her legs as she caught her balance. She took a moment to spin a finger through her hair, fixing the black hair into a tight bun atop her head. Strength had returned to her eyes. Tan understood now where it came from: ara filled her.

"You haven't said what you found when you came," Tan said.

"No."

There was something to the way she said it that gave him pause. "Why?"

"I wasn't certain I should tell you before."

Tan frowned. "And now?"

His mother smiled tightly. "I should not have doubted you. That was my mistake. I have made many, but that might have been the greatest." She touched his heart and his forehead with the tips of two fingers. "You are what the kingdoms has needed for generations. Perhaps centuries. You have struggled to find someone to teach you, to help guide you in your shaping, but the answer is that there simply is not anyone able to show you what you need. For one like you, there might never have been another able to provide much more than guidance. You are a warrior, Tannen. A true warrior." Pride filled her voice. "As to why I'm here, I followed a trail. I wasn't certain what I would find, if anything. When they caught me, I don't think I was the target. There are other elementals of ara captured. I can sense them."

"What did you find?"

"A Par-shon shaper near the kingdoms. I didn't think he'd realized I saw him. Now, I know I was mistaken. I didn't know what he wanted or why he was there."

"Where?" Tan asked, already suspecting he knew the answer.

"Nara."

Nara. When Tan closed his eyes and focused, he could sense Asboel in Nara. The draasin was there, healing, slowly recovering from the attack only days before. The shaper had likely intended to draw the draasin away.

Had it really only been days? It seemed like forever. And the draasin hatchlings were still missing, taken by Incendin. Strange that Incendin might be the safest place for them right now.

"He knows of the draasin. The shapers attacked him once before. They must have learned where he is." Asboel had been lucky to escape with his life the first time when he'd faced four shapers. What if the Utu Tonah sent more? A dozen? What if the Utu Tonah went himself?

Vel shook his head. "How many draasin survive?" Vel looked from Zephra to Tan. "You've already told me that only a very old draasin can bond."

"He is safe." The connection to Asboel remained strong. He was safe. Distant, but safe.

"But what of the very young?"

Tan hesitated. Wasn't it Fur after the hatchlings? Wasn't that what Honl had shown him? But if Incendin didn't bond to elementals—if they didn't know how—what if Incendin didn't actually want the hatchlings, but only wanted to keep Par-shon from bonding them?

Asboel! He pushed out with a shaping of spirit, shouting to the draasin. *The hatchlings are in danger!*

The connection to Asboel came slowly, as if clawing its way back to the surface of his mind, as if his sending woke the draasin. That was the only reason Tan could think that Asboel hadn't known of the danger he'd been in while in Par-shon.

Maelen. Twisted Fire has the hatchlings. They will suffer for what they have done.

Twisted Fire, Tan agreed, *but not as you know it.*

He sent an image of what he'd learned, of the runes and the stolen bonds and what he'd nearly lost. Asboel didn't respond at first.

You think they seek the hatchlings?

Tan didn't know, not with certainty. And he feared what would happen if Asboel came.

We must hunt together or we will both fail, Tan told Asboel.

Frustration surged through the bond with Asboel. *I will wait for your return.*

Tan turned to his mother. "How did you escape?"

"I was never captured."

"But the bond. They separated you from your elemental."

Zephra looked toward the city barely visible in the distance through the trees. "I followed one of the shapers here. That was what Theondar asked. But it was a trap. There were others."

"You managed to fight them off?"

She closed her eyes and sighed. "Not me. That was his sacrifice."

The translucent face of Aric fluttered around his mother, and Tan understood what had happened, how Zephra had managed to get free. The wind elemental had sacrificed for her, willingly separating so that she could be free.

"I shaped myself here. Several of their shapers were lost in the attack, but there was one who lived. Fire shaper. Powerful. I've never seen anything like it."

The anger that had surged when he had learned what happened to Amia returned. "He will know. They will know they failed." He thought of Nara, of the draasin there, and of the Utu Tonah, determined to bond the draasin. How powerful would he be if he managed to bond to one of the draasin? What danger would that pose for the kingdoms? "They know of the draasin, and I know where they will go next."

CHAPTER 25

Return to the Kingdoms

THE WIND SHAPING CARRIED them quickly across Par-shon. Zephra allowed Tan to guide it, drawing on his connection to Amia to draw them in the right direction. From what he could tell, she was safe for now. Considering the bonded shapers found in Par-shon, Tan didn't know how much longer that would be the case.

Questions plagued him as they made their way toward Amia. How long did they have before the Utu Tonah reached Incendin? How weakened were the Incendin defenses? Would the kingdoms manage to hold back Par-shon?

That they needed to rely on the strength of Incendin as a defense terrified Tan.

Aric and Zephra lowered them to the ground in a swirl of dust and air. The land was rocky and desolate here, nothing like further inland, where the city was found. Amia came out from behind a pile of rock when Tan landed.

"You found her?" she asked.

Tan motioned toward his mother. "She was injured, but we found her."

Amia performed a shaping that built with a sharp pop. She turned to Tan. "And you healed her." She frowned, tilting her head. "But you didn't heal only her. I sense what you did. There was spirit—"

Zephra stepped in between them. "If you're done shaping me?" she snapped. She glanced at Tan and her tone softened. "Amia, I have not treated you as you deserve. I can tell what you mean to Tannen. When this is over, I would like to make right the way I've treated you."

Amia glanced at Tan. "I would like that, Zephra."

His mother nodded. "Now. We need to return and warn the kingdoms. Theondar will need to understand the threat Par-shon poses. We've focused so long on Incendin that we haven't considered the possibility that there might be other power that could threaten us."

"You return," Tan said. "I need to help the draasin."

His mother opened her mouth as if she would argue, but she studied him a moment, nodding slowly. "You think you can reach the draasin in time?"

"I have to. The Par-shon shapers bound to elementals can work together. This allows them to separate the shaper from spirit, from the bond. They nearly managed this once with the draasin."

"I've witnessed this," his mother said.

Amia pulled on his hand. "Will there be anything I can help with in this?" she asked.

Tan knew many ways her spirit shaping might help, but all that came to mind was images of what might happen to her when confronted by a dozen shapers. When they had freed Asboel from the shaping, she had helped him know where to find the shapers. That could be invaluable. But going with him now put her at risk of needing to shape those from Par-shon, and she was determined to avoid that. He would do what he could to protect her from needing to go.

"There is always something you can do to help," he said.

Amia motioned to the two they had rescued. The woman had a little more life in her eyes. The man still stared blankly. "I've done what I could with them so far, but I didn't want to push too hard, not if there might have been a need for me to help you." She paused and caught her breath. "Since learning of the First Mother and what she did with the Great Mother's blessing, I've wondered if there was any way to use spirit to help the people. Once, I would have thought it an easy answer. These people are lost. I can sense that much about them."

"Roine said the Aeta were making their way to the kingdoms," Tan reminded her. "They will be safe."

Amia touched her neck, where the band of silver marking her as Daughter of the Aeta had once been. "I keep trying to refuse my place, but this is why the Great Mother gave me my gift. I can help these two as much as I can. Maybe lead the others. I don't know if I can, but I need to try." She looked to Zephra, strength coming to her eyes. "I will go to Theondar and warn him. You are the fighter, Zephra. Tan will need you."

His mother smiled and shook her head. "You're more a fighter than you realize, Amia. But I will fight with Tannen."

Vel stepped forward. All of the madness had faded from his eyes. He tugged at his beard, but with less force as he twisted the ends together. "You'll help them?" he asked Amia. When she nodded, relief washed over him.

"How will you get her to Ethea?" Zephra asked.

Honl.

The wind elemental swirled around him. *What you ask is difficult for me here.*

Then let me help. Tan shaped fire, drawing from the strength of saa in these lands, and added more warmth to it. Honl grew stronger, swirling with more force and intensity. *Take them to Ethea. See them safe. And then I will need your help. The draasin will need your help.*

To the elemental, Tan pushed an image of the broken university and the stone circle where shapers had landed over the centuries.

And you? Honl asked.

I will save Fire.

He hugged Amia tightly. "Tell Theondar that we will need him. Not the leader of the kingdoms, but the warrior. If they send more than a few shapers, we will need all the help we can gather."

"Come back to me," she said.

He smiled and pulled her in another tight embrace, afraid to say anything more, then closed his eyes and sent the confirmation to Honl. The wind elemental lifted Amia and the others in a powerful gust and they soared toward Ethea.

Zephra took a deep breath as Amia faded from view. "Bringing both of you with me," she told Tan and Vel, "will take most of my strength. When we arrive, it will take time for me to recover."

"I'll take Vel," Tan said.

"Without the elemental to help?"

Tan gripped Vel's arm and started his shaping. Each time, it became easier. "It's as you said, Mother. I'm a warrior."

He pulled on the necessary shapings of wind and fire, mixing water for stability and earth for strength. Through this, he added spirit as he had before. Then he drew it toward him, focusing on the distant sense of Asboel.

Lightning flashed from the sky, erupting near his feet and lifting them into the air.

Like before, the shaping took them quickly, with no sense of movement, only great power. Then he stood on the edge of the bleak Incendin waste.

Incendin was a hot, angry place, but some plants managed to grow. Shoots of small, stubby brown plants with thick, rubbery-looking fingers grew out of cracks in the rock. Tan sensed a darkness within them, enough that he knew to stay clear. Even if he hadn't been able to sense their malevolence, the sharp barbs, like needles or tiny spears, that poked out of them would have been a warning. Short scrub brushes, twisted and scalded-looking, were scattered about, almost as if they were the last survivors of the heat coming from the Fire Fortress. He sensed no other life around. For that, he knew to be thankful. Incendin hounds lived in these lands. Beyond that, he didn't know what else could survive.

The Fire Fortress burned with a bright light. Streaks of black worked within the red turrets and towers that he couldn't imagine holding life. Nothing about the Fire Fortress looked like it could support life.

Only, that wasn't quite right. The flames flickering around the Fire Fortress danced with an angry life of their own, and less than when Tan had seen it last, too. The flames shifted and moved, pulled on the hot Incendin wind, but they looked weakened. Could the Fire Fortress be part of the reason that Par-shon had never attacked the kingdoms?

Tan released Vel's arm as Zephra caught up to them. She hovered over the Incendin waste, unwilling to even touch down.

Tan pulled the summoning coin from his pocket and held it in his palm. He nodded to his mother. "There are others who can help. Theondar sent shapers."

Zephra pulled her summoning coin from her pocket and shaped it. "It will be better if we both summon them."

Tan performed a similar shaping but mixed spirit to add a sense of urgency, uncertain if it would work. Would the kingdoms' shapers even be able to reach them in time?

The sense of Asboel bloomed within him, suddenly hot and bright and everywhere.

Asboel!

Maelen. I will hunt with you.

Not hunt. The hatchlings are in danger. There are those who would seek to force a bond.

Asboel roared in his mind. *Not in danger. They live!*

Tan looked toward the Fire Fortress. Asboel had somehow managed to reach the fortress, had found the hatchlings. What did that mean for the defenses Incendin provided against Par-shon?

How did you reach them?

Twisted Fire. They were foolish enough to bring them toward your kingdoms.

Tan stared at the Fire Fortress. Why would Incendin have brought the hatchlings away from the Fire Fortress and return them to the kingdoms? After everything Incendin had done to destroy the hatchlings, now they would return them?

He could think of only one reason. Incendin *wanted* the kingdoms to have the hatchlings. They knew what Tan and the kingdoms' shapers would do to see them safe. It would shift Par-shon's focus to the kingdoms.

"Clever," he said.

"What is it?" Zephra asked.

"Incendin. They've returned the hatchlings to the draasin. The lisincend were weakened by the draasin attack," he said. "They must know that Par-shon seeks the draasin as they did. They saw what happened with the draasin already."

"But where are they?" Zephra asked.

"Nara."

"The kingdoms will suffer," she said softly. "If we thought Incendin dangerous, they are nothing compared to what I saw in Par."

"I don't think you saw the worst of it," Tan said. "When *he* comes, there's no one who can stop him."

Tan turned his focus to Asboel. *Are they safe?*

Sashari has brought them to safety.

Where?

Tan didn't expect anything different than the image Asboel sent to him. It was of Nara, the place where they had been before. Heat swirled around it, protected by the shaping made by the great fire elemental.

But Tan knew that wasn't safe. Par-shon knew of the draasin den, knew where to find them. And now they knew how to reach the hatchlings. They would have been safer in Incendin than they were in Nara.

We must get there. Now.

A massive shadow swirled over them and Asboel landed in a heavy beating of wings and hot wind. Vel gasped and took a dozen steps back and away from the draasin. Tan ignored him, focusing on Asboel.

The draasin lowered his head and fixed Tan with his golden eyes. *You have been right about much, Maelen, but trust the draasin to keep the hatchlings safe.*

I have shown you that there are others—dangerous others—who seek the hatchlings.

Twisted Fire. Let them come. They have provided little challenge to me.

Not Twisted Fire. The others who captured you.

I was weakened keeping Enya from withdrawing fire. I am not so weak any longer.

They have bound elementals.

As have you.

They steal *the bonds. That was what they were attempting when they subdued you. There are dozens like that. There is one among them who has bonded* every *elemental except the draasin.*

Asboel roared.

You understand why they cannot have the hatchlings?

It is not the first time the bonded have come for the draasin. Come, Maelen. You will hunt with me now. Sashari will not allow the others near.

I have seen them. She may not be able to stop them.

Asboel snorted. Steam and spurts of flame came from his nose, leaving Tan unharmed.

When it abated, Tan looked to his mother. "I will go with him. Follow carefully. The other draasin might not take kindly to your presence."

He climbed atop Asboel's back. The warm spikes welcomed him, a comforting fit. Tan had ridden this way many times now, and each time felt right. This time, he wondered if he might be able to travel faster on a shaping than what Asboel could do, but he would let the draasin lead him. This was a fight they needed to do together.

They took to the air on the draasin's massive wings.

Asboel streaked toward Nara, moving more quickly than Tan had ever flown with him. All around the draasin's wings, Tan was aware of the connection to the wind elemental, ashi helping push Asboel along. There was a connection between the two elementals. Was it the same way with others?

But why wouldn't it be? Deep within Ethea, golud and the nymid mingled. Tan didn't know if they supported each other, but the connection seemed little different than what he saw from ashi helping the draasin.

What will happen if all of the elementals are bound? Tan asked.

Power.

He already has power.

Asboel twisted to look at him. *You have seen how elemental power is different in places.*

Tan nodded. The wind and fire elementals were different in Parshon than in the kingdoms. Probably the other elementals as well, though Tan hadn't the time to fully investigate.

You asked once about greater and lesser power. To the Mother, there is a different distinction. There is older and younger. The draasin are among the oldest, but the others have strength. Over time, the younger can become the older.

That's why the nymid have gained strength?

Nymid have always had strength. They lacked connection.

What kind of connection?

Asboel dipped his head, already starting to dive toward the ground. *The kind we share.*

Asboel landed solidly on the ground, sharp talons gripping for purchase in the hard Nara rock. He tipped his head back and twisted his head, sniffing. His tail switched from side to side, revealing more of his agitation than anything through the bond between them.

What is it?

Something is amiss.

Sashari? The hatchlings?

Asboel twisted, his golden eyes practically glowing. *They are here. They are protected. Sashari will keep them safe.*

What of Enya?

Asboel faded briefly from the bond between them. Tan suspected he reached for Enya through the fire bond, that shared connection that allowed the draasin to communicate.

She remains with the others.

Then what?

The answer came in a sudden surge of shaping power exploding from above.

CHAPTER 26

Elemental Anger

THE POWER THAT ERUPTED around them contained wind and earth and water and fire: all the elements working together. They had even more strength than Tan had seen yet, or thought to anticipate. They worked in concert, the attack building rapidly.

Asboel absorbed as much fire as he could, pulling it from the fire shaper. He roared as he did, anger and rage fueling a horrible sound.

Saa! Asboel shouted at the other fire elemental. *You dare attack the draasin!*

Saa is not in control, Tan said. *It's as I told you. The elementals were forcibly bound. Free the shaper and you free saa.*

Asboel lifted into the air. Fire spouted from his mouth as he created a ring of fire around Tan, Vel, and Zephra.

The shaping that built around them hesitated. Tan took that moment to take to the air on a bolt of lightning. He hovered above the ground, searching for the shapers. Amia would have been helpful here. She might have been able to give them enough of a warning to avoid the attack.

Tan saw nothing below him.

With growing fear, he looked *up*. In Par, he'd noticed that even the earth shapers had managed flight, somehow pulling that ability from the earth elemental. Could they manage the same in Nara?

Above him were shapers. They circled, and Tan counted thirteen—more than Tan and Asboel could face alone. Probably more than they could face when Zephra arrived.

Tan drew through spirit, searching for the rune bonding the attackers to the elementals. His heart sunk. Each shaper had at least two marks. Even were he to separate them from one, they would have another bond to draw power from, strength that rivaled what the best kingdoms' shaper could attempt.

Asboel lashed out. Fire spiraled from his mouth, but there were fire shapers among those attacking. They pulled the fire off, sending it harmlessly back to the ground.

Honl!

Tan sent an urgent call to the wind elemental. Would he have already reached Ethea with Amia? Could he reach Tan in time?

Hot wind swirled around him. Tan released his shaping and let the wind elemental hold him aloft. It was not Honl—not at first—but ashi.

Asboel roared through the shapers. He snapped at one—a thick, balding man with close-shorn hair—and ripped him from the sky. The shaper dropped in a heap, falling lifeless to the ground. Tan thought he should feel remorse but didn't. Instead, he was thankful Amia's shaping no longer held the draasin.

Asboel lunged toward another shaper, but they had seen what happened and created a buffer using wind thickened with water.

It prevented the draasin from getting too close. He bounced off it, snapping with a frustrated snarl.

They attacked him with steady violence. Shapings of earth and water lashed at him. The strength of the shapings was more than Tan could fathom, more than he could summon. Two shapers came at him. Without ashi helping, he would have been overpowered. As it was, he managed to avoid the shapings but wasn't able to do anything else.

He had to help Asboel. If Tan could get through the barrier, he could reach the shapers, but there wasn't anything he could do while trying not to be shaped himself.

Tan readied a shaping, forming it over himself. As he did, he recognized Honl. The wind elemental had returned and swirled around him, ready to be called on. Would he be strong enough? Would he risk himself to help Asboel? *Help Fire, Honl. Please.*

The wind elemental hesitated, then raced toward Asboel as Tan shaped himself into the air. He pulled on elemental power. Not Honl or Asboel, but on ashi and saa, drawing strength from the elementals around him.

With Honl's help, Asboel pierced the barrier. Another shaper fell.

The Par-shon shapers shifted their focus entirely to the draasin.

Tan pulled on a shaping of spirit, mixing it with air and water, and struck the runes on the woman shaping those two elements near him. When she fell from the sky, her short brown hair caught fire. She screamed as she fell.

He should feel sympathy or remorse, or *something*, but all he felt was pleased that she was no longer a threat.

A tall, muscular man waved his hand and three shapers split off from the others, turning to face Tan now he'd revealed himself. He studied his new opponents and blanched: most of the others had two runes binding them to the elementals. These three had four.

Tan pulled on the sense of spirit within him, drawing the shaping as strongly as he could. Spirit would weaken him the quickest, but it was the one elemental they couldn't shape.

He drew on each of the elements, pulling fire, earth, wind, and air together, binding them. To this, he added spirit. As before, the elementals of this land were drawn to the shaping, granting him power, and he added this to his shaping. Had he the warrior's sword, he might be able to aim. Instead, he focused on pushing the shaping away from him in a burst.

Blinding white light arced out from him.

Tan tried to focus it on the shapers. He struck two, and they disappeared in a flash of white light. It missed the other shaper, the muscular man hovering on a cloud shaped from air and water.

The effort of the shaping drained Tan and he fell.

Honl! Asboel!

Tan didn't have the strength to force the sending. The ground rushed up toward him.

A burst of air caught him. Tan twisted his head and saw his mother's tight face.

"You can't shape like that without focus," she warned.

She set him to the ground and then bounced back into the air, sending an attack of wind spiraling around a pair of shapers. Zephra was a skilled wind shaper and bound to ara, but she faced shapers with bonds of their own. They broke free of her attack and turned wind against her.

Fire spiraled toward her, mixing with water in a rush of hot steam. From somewhere hidden, Vel sent a shaping of cooling water, keeping her from harm.

Tan stood on the ground watching, too weak from his shaping to do anything.

They were outnumbered and did not have the same strength the Par-shon shapers could summon. There were simply too many. They would fail.

Asboel. Send Sashari away.

The draasin roared. *There is no other place for her to go, Maelen.*

Great anger and sadness flooded into Tan through the draasin. If this was going to be the end for him, he would go fighting for his friends.

He focused on his breathing. To this, he drew strength from the air and earth. The other elementals would help. Saa might not answer him, but he could summon. The land was too dry for water elementals, but he could try.

Help me. I must free the bonded elementals.

He sent the request wide, to all the elementals that might be near enough to respond.

Slowly, too slowly, strength returned to him. He pulled on it, drawing it from elementals he had no name for but who answered his summons nonetheless. It rose within him, giving him enough strength to shape himself into the air again.

His mother glanced over at him. The expression on her face told him that she knew what would come, but she resolved to fight. Asboel still attacked, but more slowly than before, his thick sides dripping with blood from attacks Tan had not seen. Honl aided him, but even the wind elemental was injured. Tan hadn't realized how easily the elementals could be harmed. Would Tan lose his bond as his mother had once lost hers? Would it matter if none of them survived?

He readied another shaping, pulling spirit to mix with the elements, knowing even as he did it that it wouldn't be enough.

The air crackled with sudden power. Lightning struck.

Tan blinked weakly and looked over. Lightning?

Streaks of fire and wind and earth crushed two of the nearest shapers. Theondar jumped, flickering from lightning bolt to lightning bolt, a warrior's sword held out from him, guiding his shaping. Even with Theondar, the shapers were too many.

"Your sword, Theondar!" Zephra yelled over the raging sounds of the battle.

He glanced over at her, pausing in the shaping of earth and sending rock flying to the sky. "The sword? What of it?"

"We need a true warrior." Roine frowned and Zephra motioned toward Tan. "Give it to Tan!"

Without questioning, he tossed the sword.

It tumbled toward Tan. One of the Par shapers sent a gust of wind to push it away, but Zephra intervened, shooting the sword back to Tan on a powerful shaping guided by ara. Tan caught it and turned to face the other shapers.

With a deep breath, he drew in the strength of the elementals. This time, he even borrowed from Honl and Asboel. It might weaken them as he did, but he needed everything he could draw. He focused this strength, binding the elements as he drew upon spirit, and shaped through the sword.

White light spouted from it.

Tan aimed at the shapers. The nearest fell in a flash of light. He shifted to the next, and he fell. One after another, Tan shaped with spirit bound to spirit, a shaping he did not even fully understand other than to recognize how powerful it was.

The attack turned. Asboel took out a pair of shapers. Theondar stopped another. A blast of fire from the ground—Cianna, Tan realized—stunned one long enough for Zephra to wrap him in air. Tan took care of him from there with a focused shaping through the sword.

It left only the muscular man leading them.

He shaped with delicate skill, pulling on each of the elements. He bound them together, mimicking what Tan had done.

Tan held his breath, afraid that the other man might have the ability to shape spirit. If he did, he would be more formidable than any of the other shapers.

An explosion radiated from the shaper. Hot air and flames buffeted Tan, throwing him back. Honl helped hold him in place, keeping him from tumbling under the strength of the shaping. Chunks of rock and dust shot toward him and Tan raised his arms in front of his face to block the debris from striking him.

Then the explosion began to fade, leaving him hovering on a wind shaping assisted by Honl. He looked over to see his mother holding her hand to her face. Blood streamed through her fingers, but she was otherwise unharmed.

Asboel crashed to the ground and wrapped his tail around him. He slunk toward a pile of rocks. From where Tan was, he saw Sashari as she crawled out of the same pile of rocks. There was a distant sense through the fire bond Asboel had shared with him that told him the hatchlings were there. Tan would meet them later. For now, it was enough that they were safe.

All of this to protect the hatchlings and still they weren't completely safe. Now that the Utu Tonah knew of them, others would return. Tan might be better equipped to face him, but they had lost too much already.

Theondar landed on a shaping of earth and air and turned to Tan. Pain pulled at his eyes. "I followed the summons when I realized both you and Zephra sent for help. What was this? Not Incendin shapers. They were almost like warriors."

Tan sighed, looking at the fallen Par-shon bonded, wishing there had been a different way to save them. "They're from Par-shon. They bond the elementals. Some are forced; others, they steal."

Roine glanced over to where Asboel had disappeared. "I should not have sent you."

Tan shook his head, lowered to the ground by Honl. The wind elemental circled around him with warmth, supporting him. "This wasn't your fault. I'm a warrior, Roine. As are you."

Roine opened his mouth and then clamped it shut, nodding to himself. "So you are."

"When I learned of the hatchlings, with what had been happening at the Fire Fortress, I thought Incendin to blame." Tan sighed, looking across Nara, letting the heat wash over him. Out there was the Fire Fortress, Incendin shapers that had somehow managed to fend off an attack from Par-shon for decades, maybe longer. Now what would happen? Now that Incendin had been weakened—that the lisincend no longer ruled—would Par-shon attack Incendin?

"I don't think it was Incendin at all. I think Par-shon attacked. That was what we saw. But Incendin had the hatchlings. Something about them helped Incendin push back the attack. And then the draasin attacked, destroying the lisincend. It weakened Incendin." It was hard to believe that he had come to view the weakening of Incendin as a dangerous thing, but for how long had Incendin stood between Par-shon and the kingdoms? Now that Incendin could no longer provide that buffer, what would happen?

Tan studied the rocks Asboel had disappeared behind. Would the draasin allow him to protect them? With the power the shapers of Par-shon controlled, the draasin would be in danger unless they allowed shapers to help. And if they continued to seek revenge for what happened with the hatchlings, Incendin would be further weakened.

But where could he take them? Where would they be able to hide from another attack?

He could think of only one place. "You need to know about Parshon, Roine. As the ruler of the kingdoms now, there is much you will need to know. We will have to prepare. Others will come. If the Utu Tonah comes, we might not be strong enough."

"What are you saying?" Roine asked.

Tan looked over at his mother, at Cianna, even over to Vel. Would they be ready for what he suspected would come? Now that the Utu Tonah knew of the draasin, only the kingdoms stood between him and the power he sought. Too many shapers had died battling Incendin for them to be ready.

Tan sighed, feeling along his bonds. To Asboel, injured and curled up in his den. To Honl, swirling around him, hiding around Tan. To Amia, safely in Ethea.

After all that he'd been through, all he wanted was peace. A chance for he and Amia to be together. Time for him to understand the bond he shared with Asboel and with Honl. Instead, they faced the possibility of a worse attack than Incendin. But it was the reason the Mother had given him his gifts. Tan was certain of that now. And how long had he wondered why he was able to not only shape all the elements, but speak to the elementals?

And he began to understand what had driven Incendin to seek power, even what might have driven the ancient scholars to seek the power of the artifact. As much as he might want to avoid using it, would he have any choice were he to save those he cared about?

"War is coming, Roine. And I don't think the kingdoms are ready."

Epilogue

TAN MOVED THROUGH THE TUNNELS beneath the palace, waiting for Asboel. The draasin claimed to know a different way to reach the tunnels, a way that didn't require going through the archives, but wanted to keep the secret from Tan.

Amia stood next to him, clutching a cloak around her. She held a shapers lantern out for light. "Does Roine know what you're doing?"

Tan shook his head. No one would know what he did here. They couldn't; otherwise, the draasin would not be safe. After what he'd learned once he returned and managed to open the massive doors that had been closed for centuries—how the lower level of the archives had once been used to trap the draasin—he wasn't sure he wanted anyone to know. "Until they're old enough to defend themselves, we have to protect them from Par-shon."

"Why did you think of here?"

Tan touched the door behind him. A massive rune was marked on the door, one that resembled what he'd found in Par-shon. Now he understood what it was, if not why it would be here. "They've been here before. I've never specifically asked Asboel before, but this door," he said, patting the thick wood, "and this rune make sense now."

He felt Asboel approach. The draasin moved more slowly than usual. How much was from the still-healing injuries sustained during the attack with the Par shapers, and how much was from the fact that Asboel guided the hatchlings along with him? Maybe it was a combination of both.

Bright eyes appeared out of the shadows and peered at Tan. *Maelen. I am unconvinced of your plan.*

Where else would you go? Tan asked. *If you remain in Nara, they will find you. In Incendin, you run the risk of Twisted Fire. The Daughter and I are the only ones who will know you are here.*

Tan peered behind Asboel and saw Sashari. She remained silent, nothing but steam hissing from her nostrils. She eyed him carefully. Her long, barbed tail was tense and wrapped protectively around the two small hatchlings Tan couldn't clearly see.

And Enya? he asked.

She remains untrusting of your kind. More so now than ever before.

We have given her no reason to think otherwise.

Not you, Maelen. Only Twisted Fire.

He wasn't ready to share with Asboel that Incendin was not the real danger. The draasin was so focused on what Incendin had done to him and the hatchlings, but Tan would need him to understand what else they faced. Incendin remained dangerous, but after what he'd seen in Par-shon, he viewed them differently. All this time, they'd thought Incendin wanted power for the sake of power. Now Tan had to convince the others that there had been another reason. When he tried healing the lisincend, he'd felt resistance, that he'd wanted only the power the transformation had given him. Now he understood why.

But that could come later, once they determined and better understood the risk. For now, they needed to secure the hatchlings so they had a chance to grow without fearing a bond forced upon them.

We will use your den for now, Asboel said.

Tan turned to the rune and was forced to stand on his toes to trace his fingers around it. It marked fire, but it was more than that. A powerful mark, one that could have been used in the trapping and binding of the draasin. Perhaps that was why it had been here originally, but that didn't mean it had to remain used like that.

He pulled on fire, drawing on the power of Asboel as he pulled through the bond. He mixed it with spirit, suspecting it might be the only way to power the rune. It began glowing softly.

Tan pressed on the rune and the massive door swung open, wide enough for the draasin to enter. He stepped aside, letting Asboel lean his head inside.

A spurt of flame erupted from the draasin's nose, lighting the den, then Asboel withdrew his head.

Sashari and the hatchlings moved inside. Asboel stood outside, guarding the door.

You can join them, Tan suggested.

Not until I know if it is safe.

Asboel, Tan started, looking up to his bond pair, *these were made for your kind.*

They were.

Have you ever been here?

Not I.

No, the ancients had managed to trap Asboel and the other draasin somewhere else, to use them to power the protections of the artifact.

Others of your kind?

They never managed to force the draasin to bond.

That didn't mean they hadn't tried. Why had Asboel allowed the bond to him? Had it only been because Tan could help with Enya? *I'm sorry.*

Didn't you once show me that you can't change what has happened? You are not like them. You are Maelen.

Tan wished that would be enough. *There is another. He's more dangerous than any we've faced before. He will come again. Now that he knows of you, he will come.*

Without the shapers the kingdoms once had, they would not be prepared for what was to come, and Tan wasn't certain Roine or the others would agree with what he already knew would be necessary: to survive the Par-shon attack, they would have to learn from Incendin.

That was for another day. Today, the draasin were safe and secure in their new den. Amia was safe. His mother was restored. Eventually, Tan would attempt to heal Vel, though he didn't know if he was too far gone to do much for.

And then? Then the preparations would have to begin in full before Par attacked, to hunt or become the hunted.

Asboel lowered his head and met Tan's eyes. *Maelen,* the great fire elemental began, *you will never hunt alone.*

DK HOLMBERG currently lives in rural Minnesota where the winter cold and the summer mosquitoes keep him inside and writing.

To see other books and read more, please go to www.dkholmberg.com

Follow me on twitter: @dkholmberg

Word-of-mouth is crucial for any author to succeed and how books are discovered. If you enjoyed the book, please consider leaving a review online at your favorite bookseller or Goodreads, even if it's only a line or two; it would make all the difference and would be very much appreciated.

Others Available by DK Holmberg

The Cloud Warrior Saga

Chased by Fire
Bound by Fire
Changed by Fire
Fortress of Fire
Forged in Fire
Serpent of Fire
Servant of Fire

The Painter Mage

Shifted Agony
Arcane Mark
Painter for Hire

The Lost Garden

Keeper of the Forest
The Desolate Bond
Keeper of Light

Assassin's Sight:

The Painted Girl
The Forgotten

Made in the USA
Monee, IL
31 July 2022